SHOWING MERCY

SHOWING MERCY

KIM PRITEKEL

SAPPHIRE BOOKS

SALINAS, CALIFORNIA

person, please purchase an additional copy for each recipient. If you're reading this book and did not purchase it, or it was not purchased for your use only, then please return to your favorite ebook retailer and purchase your own copy. Thank you for respecting the hard work of this author.

This and other Sapphire Books titles can be found at

www.sapphirebooks.com

Kim's other books

Standalones
1049 Club
After Shadow
Blinded
Connection
Damaged
Shadow Box
She Who Would be King
Swann Song
The Gift
The Plan
Wild
Zero Ward

Dance with Me Series
Curtain Call
Encore Performance

The Traveler Series
The Traveler - The Hunted
The Traveler - The Hunter

The Wynter Series
Finding Faith
Taking Liberty
Justice Won
Keeping Hope

Dedication

For all those who made it happen.

Chapter One

Pueblo, Colorado – 1941

It was a gloomy, cloudy day. She'd always remember that little detail, considering how many others would be lost to the trauma of the event. Mercy Faulkner stood next to her mother at the gravesite, still as a statue. They hadn't had the money to have a funeral in the church, so her mother took what the mill offered, which was a quick graveside service with a simple casket and headstone.

She glanced over at her mother, Wanda, who still seemed to be shellshocked, though the accident had happened nearly a week ago. Her father, Arthur, had worked at the CF&I steel mill since he was seventeen years old. Twenty years later, he lay in a box before them with a sprig of wildflowers on top.

Large brown eyes glanced up at the sky as the clouds began to gather and grow heavy as the sky began to rumble, deep in its belly. She glanced to her mother again, wondering if they should stay out as it seemed it would start raining. Wanda didn't move a muscle, other than to wipe at her eyes with a wadded-up kerchief—her father's—again.

Mercy's gaze swung to the priest, a kindly older man who'd agreed to perform the service even though the Faulkner family had never set foot in a church of any kind, let alone the large, beautiful Sacred Heart where Father O'Brien worked. His voice droned on and on, the sky seeming to agree as it rumbled again.

"In His holy name," the priest was saying, crossing himself in that crazy way that Mercy didn't understand. "We pray. Amen."

The couple dozen gathered muttered a response in kind, Mercy moving her lips but saying nothing. The crowd began to disburse, a few stopping to give their condolences to Mercy and her mother. She knew none of the men, who claimed they had worked with her father. Again, she remained silent.

At fifteen years old, Mercy felt like a child in that moment. She felt lost and confused and very scared. She'd shared a close bond with her father, her mother a more quiet, hard woman. She went about her daily duties with silent grit, not a whole lot of hugs and sympathy. So, in dealing with her father's death, she was on her own. Some moments she felt like the grief was so heavy and thick that it strangled the very breath from her body.

"Wanda, I'm so sorry."

Mercy's attention shifted to the male voice that was suddenly close to her. She glanced up to see James Popperton, who had grown up with her father, the two like brothers. He'd left Pueblo and moved to a mountain town about three hours away called Wynter years before. She hadn't seen him since she was a little girl.

"Thank you, James," Wanda said. "I appreciate that."

He nodded, hat in hand. "Listen, I need to talk to you."

Wanda nodded. "All right. We can head back to the house. I can make some coffee."

Mercy smiled dutifully when the man with dark brown hair gave her a kind smile as he donned his hat and pulled up the collar of his jacket as the first raindrops began to fall. The trio followed the line of mourners out of Mountain View Cemetery. They marched to their car, her father's 1927 Ford Model T. Her father had promised to teach her how to drive it this year.

In silence, she and her mother drove to the small house they lived in, not far from the mill. The small two-bedroom was on a street populated entirely by other mill workers. It was overall a tight-knit community, as much as her mother would allow it for the Faulkner family.

Her father had been a fun, outgoing man who loved to chitchat and laugh and fish. Her mother, on the other hand, was more sullen and all about the work. If there was no work to be done, she'd create it. She honestly had no idea how her parents had ended up together. Yes, she'd heard the phrase "opposites attract," but she was pretty sure that whoever had coined it hadn't met Arthur Faulkner and Wanda Sachs.

She remembered her father yelling at her mother on some mornings, "Stop being such a goddamn Puritan!" She hadn't understood what he'd meant by that until she was a little older and would hear his angry and frustrating mutterings. What she'd gathered from all of that was that her mother had given him exactly one chance to be a father. When he'd succeeded early in their marriage, that was it, and her duty was done.

Obviously, Mercy knew nothing about this subject, but the fact that not one boy had even turned her head or left her remotely curious aligned her a bit more to her mother's view.

The house was a small square structure with white siding and dark brown trim. No garage, only a front curb to park at. The neighbors' houses on either side were only a couple feet away.

Mr. Popperton's car pulled up behind their Ford. With a gentlemanly, after-you wave of Popperton's hand, the three headed up the walk to the front door, which Wanda opened to allow entry. The inside was like the outside: simple, tidy, and unremarkable. The only real splash of color was the blanket her mother had crocheted that was folded on the back of the couch.

"If you'll take a seat, James," Wanda said, leading their little train of three into the kitchen. "I'll make coffee. Mercy, take Mr. Popperton's coat and hat."

"Yes, ma'am," she murmured, doing as asked. She took the items to the coat tree by the door and hung them up before returning to the kitchen to retrieve two coffee cups, one for her mother and one for their guest, as well as the sugar bowl and little bottle of milk, delivered that morning from the milk man.

Finally, coffee gurgling to life from her percolator, then poured and served, the three sat down. Mercy was curious what the man seated to her left would have to say, though her stomach roiled a bit. She knew life was about to change but wasn't sure just how much.

"So," he said, looking from one to the other. "Again, I'm so sorry, ladies. I'm devastated to have lost Art. Can't even imagine how you two must feel."

Mercy wanted to beg him to give her a hug, cry in his arms, and tell him that she was devastated, shattered inside and that part of her had died along with her daddy. But, seeing the iron curtain that was her mother's expression, she did none of these things. She simply stayed quiet, as she so often did.

"I got your letter, Wanda, and spoke to my brother-in-law, Henry, and he spoke to his business partner and father-in-law, Justice. Now, as I explained to you, they own quite a few of the businesses together in Wynter, and they're willing to give you a job and a place to live, you and Mercy." He gave them a sad smile. "Place to start over." He looked at Mercy. "You'll go to school with my son Samuel, Mercy. He's right around your age, though I know you two haven't seen each other in several years."

She nodded and gave him a weak smile of acknowledgment. While it wasn't the magic wand she'd been hoping for, a fresh start might at least be the beginning of healing.

☙ ❧ ☙ ❧

Only allowed to pack the two suitcases that were kept beneath her bed, Mercy had to make important choices. Everything else would be left behind, donated, or discarded. Everything she'd known would vanish. The home she was literally born in, her school, classmates, neighbors, the very streets she saw every single day.

Sitting on her bed, she held the last gift her father had given to her, which was for her fifteenth birthday, three months before. He'd come to her bedroom just before bed, where she already reclined reading. He'd sat on the edge of her bed, hand behind his back.

"Don't tell your mother," he said quietly. "She'd be cross at us both." He gave her the quirky little smile that seemed to be reserved only for his little angel, as he so often referred to her. He brought his hand out to reveal a small box in his palm. It wasn't wrapped, but he held it out to her. "I wanted to get you something special," he explained as she took the box.

Mercy pulled the box lid off to reveal a silver necklace with a tiny angel pendant. Brown eyes widened as she took it in. "Oh, Daddy," she whispered.

"Now," he said, gently taking the box from her and removing the gift. "Your mother would be angry if she knew I'd spent the money on something so 'extravagant.'" They both smiled at the dramatic way he said it, no matter how true it was. He urged her to turn her back to him so he could put the necklace on her. "But, you're my little angel and always will be."

She gathered her long, auburn hair to one side so he could fasten the silver chain. "Thank you so much, Daddy." She turned to face him again when the necklace was in place and secured.

He smiled and leaned over, leaving a kiss on her forehead. "Happy birthday," he said softly. "My little angel."

A tear trailed down Mercy's cheek as she stared down at the necklace in her hands, the silver chain spilling over her fingers like her father's own blood. She gasped when she heard her mother yell to her to hurry up from the other room. She glanced that way and quickly placed the necklace back into the protective pouch she kept it in, too afraid her mother would see it if she wore it.

She stuffed the pouch inside the unzipped back

of her teddy bear, the one and only her mother allowed her, knowing she'd never have to get rid of it. "I love you, Daddy," she whispered, then stuffed the teddy bear in her knapsack. It was time to go.

It had been a very long drive and a very cold one. It was September, and in Pueblo that meant mild temperatures still for another month. But as they headed into the mountains to their new home in Wynter, the change in altitude and climate was sharp. By the time they hit the town proper, it was later afternoon and Mercy's face was cold, her lips numb.

Finally, after miles and miles of nothing, the road curved around to reveal farmland patching the earth to the right, farmhouses, silos, and other such structures playing companion. A white church appeared, steeple held high to God. Houses began to fill in the space as the road straightened out, then buildings of commerce.

Cars came and went, people populating the wooden sidewalk, clearly a relic of the town's storied past from the turn of the century. The former mining town now turned lumber and textiles, or so Mercy had read. Her eyes were wide as she looked from one side of the street to the other. She was curious about this new place, this new home. Finally, the Ford pulled up in front of one of the buildings. It was a two-story brick building, the bricks whitewashed. There was a wooden sign that read *Wynter Hotel*, though painted letters, long faded, on the second floor read *Wynter Saloon*.

"Wow," she whispered. She couldn't help but

wonder what all that building had seen over the years. "Is that where we'll be living?" she asked.

"No," Wanda said, turning off the ignition of the car. "That's where I'll be working. That," she said, pointing to the building next to it. "Is where we'll be living."

Mercy nodded. It was also a two-story brick building, though red brick and not as large as the hotel. She was delighted to see the business on the lower level was a soda shop.

The teen's attention was garnered by the approaching figure. "Good evenin', ladies!" A man, who looked to be in his late forties with brown hair streaked with gray at the temples and extremely kind blue eyes, stood at Wanda's window, which she quickly rolled down. He gave them both a winning smile. "Sorry to startle you. So happy you got here safely. I'm Henry Wynter, and me and my boys are here to help you ladies get moved in."

Mercy glanced to her mother then back to the man. She gave him a shy smile before she climbed out of the car, following her mother's lead. Henry was there with two of his three sons, Billy and Ned, explaining that Leo was off in the Navy, stationed at Pearl Harbor.

"Can you believe that?" he'd said, excitement in his voice. "Wynter boy all the way in Hawaii!"

"Wonder if he'll ever come back after all the time spent at the beach," Ned, the second-oldest Wynter boy, said as he carried up three boxes to the new apartment.

Mercy only halfway listened to their conversation as she helped as best she could, though she was largely asked to step aside and relax. Henry had explained that she and her mother had already had such a long day with the drive, and that their suffering was over for the evening. Though she certainly appreciated the sentiment, she felt lazy watching them come and go as they unloaded the Ford.

The apartment was reached from a narrow, steep set of stairs entered by a door just beside the door to enter the soda shop. At the top of the stairs was a hallway that led to the back window of the building, four doors on either side, all leading to the small apartments. Two of them were two-bedroom units, one of which she and her mother would be renting.

The place was pretty small, with a tiny living room and a kitchen that just barely fit the table for two already placed there in the furnished apartment. The two bedrooms weren't much larger than jail cells, but Mercy didn't care. She was just grateful to have her own. A dresser and twin-sized bed were about all that fit in there.

She was, however, thrilled that they had a bathroom of their own. She knew a lot of apartments, especially in old buildings like this, did not. It contained a sink, commode, and a small bathtub that was almost too small to take a proper bath in but roomy enough to stand in to take advantage of the showerhead that was poised overhead.

"This is the last box, Mrs. Faulkner," Billy Wynter said as he entered the apartment. He set his load on the floor next to the neat stack that had grown as the young men and their father had trotted up the stairs with Mercy and Wanda's belongings. The younger of the two brothers, he stood with hands on hips as he looked around.

Mercy had noticed the young man had a quiet

way about him. He looked to be a few years older than her though still of school age, as opposed to his older brother Ned, who had stated that he was twenty. Billy had dark brown hair and beautiful, bright, light blue eyes. He was very handsome. His smile was quick, dimples flashing each time.

"Thank you, young man," Wanda said, looking as tired as Mercy felt.

"Yes, ma'am. Um," he added, a hand coming up to rub the back of his neck. "My father asked me to tell you ladies that we'd like to have you over for a proper supper tonight. No real food in here yet, so…" He indicated the kitchen.

Mercy looked to her mother for a response, as she knew her own thoughts about this wouldn't matter. Wanda, who was already beginning to open boxes, glanced at the young man. She looked around the mess in the living room then over at Mercy, who stood awaiting the verdict in the archway that led to the small hallway where the bedrooms and bathroom were.

"Very well," she said. "We accept."

"Um," he said, glancing over at Mercy before back to Wanda. "If you want, you can catch a ride with my sister, Bethany, who works downstairs at the shop." He shrugged. "So you don't have to drive any more after such a long day."

"Your sister works?" Wanda asked, surprise in her voice. "And drives? Just how old is she?"

"Yes, ma'am," he said, pride evident in his tone. "Well, my parents and grandparents own these two businesses, you see," he explained, indicating the building they stood in and the hotel next door. "So, us kids help out. Always have. And, Bethany is my twin.

We just turned seventeen over the summer."

Wanda nodded. "I see. Well, yes. Once your sister is finished with her duties, we can ride with her."

"Alrighty," he said, all grins. "I'll tell her to come get you when it's time to go." He glanced at the watch on his wrist. "An hour or so."

"We'll be ready," Wanda assured.

He nodded then, sparing a glance to Mercy, and left the apartment. Mercy watched as her mother engaged the locks after the door had been closed behind Billy Wynter. She looked around, feeling a bit out of sorts as they had so much to do. Everything had changed so quickly and so completely irrevocably that she was left feeling shellshocked and as if she were living somebody else's life.

"Unpack your bedroom and then help me in here," Wanda barked, knocking Mercy out of her reverie.

Dutifully, the teen went to her bedroom. Glancing toward the window, it was then that she noticed that it was the fire escape for the second floor. Walking over to it, she unlatched the window and pulled the bottom half upward. Assured it would stay up, she rested her hands on the windowsill and leaned out the window.

The air was so fresh as she closed her eyes and inhaled. It was crisp and clean. So very different from living across from the mill. The tall smokestacks were constantly belching out the byproduct of the steel made within the CF&I complex of buildings. Not here, she marveled.

She noted just outside her window was a small metal platform with protective railing that had metal stairs attached to it, which seesawed their way down to the ground below. She didn't much care about the escape route down but certainly could see availing herself of the little outdoor space. Perhaps reading?

Hearing her mother's footsteps heading toward the small bedroom hallway, Mercy quickly shut the window and locked it. The last thing she wanted was for her little secret escape to be taken away.

Chapter Two

We must make a good impression," Wanda muttered, nearly yanking the hair out of Mercy's head with the quick, harsh brush strokes. The hour was nearly up and Wanda had insisted they stop unpacking and ready themselves for Bethany's arrival and supper with her family. "I want you to change dresses, too."

Her back to her mother as the long, auburn strands were brushed, Mercy rolled her eyes. She saw absolutely no need for any of this—particularly her mother brushing her hair as though she were five instead of fifteen.

"I think we should put some of those pretty bows in," Wanda was saying when there was a knock at the apartment door.

"I'll get it!" Overjoyed to get away from her mother as she was beginning to head into her infantilizing "my little girl" mode, Mercy shook her head, allowing her long hair to flow around her shoulders and down her back after the tight hold Wanda had had on it. She reached the door and unlocked it before pulling it open.

Out in the hall stood the absolute female version of Billy Wynter, which of course was usually what happened with twins. She stood a couple inches taller than Mercy, her dark brown hair swept up in a messy updo. But what absolutely froze Mercy to the spot were her eyes. They were the same color as Billy's, that beautiful robin's-egg blue, but there was a spark, something in these eyes that spoke of intelligence and no nonsense.

Mercy was already of the opinion that she herself was utterly plain, what with her long hair that her mother refused to let her cut, not quite brown but not quite red. Her eyes, which Mercy's father had told her were like the eyes of a doe—big, brown, and beautifully expressive —were to her just big and boring. They were nothing like the keen eyes staring back at her.

She was still in her work uniform, which to Mercy's surprise was the same as the boys wore. She wore the red-and-white-striped button-up shirt with a red bow tie. She did, however, wear a white skirt instead of the white trousers. She smelled of sweets and ice cream.

The young woman who stood there was something off the silver screen with creamy skin and a facial structure that begged for an artist's paint brush. Her lips were full and had a natural rosy tint to them. In a word, Bethany Wynter was beautiful. Mercy felt shy and unworthy of being in the presence of such a creature.

Looking down at her clasped hands, Mercy cleared her throat. "Um, hi."

"Hey," the young woman said. "You guys ready to go?"

Mercy spared a glance up into her eyes and nodded. "I think so." She turned away from her, only able to fully breathe once she did so. "Mother," she called out. "Bethany Wynter is here." She turned back to the young woman who still stood there, giving her a shy smile before again looking down at her hands.

"Are you okay?"

Again, Mercy glanced up at her when she heard the question. She nodded. "Yes."

"You look like you're about to throw up," Bethany said, crossing her arms over her striped shirt.

Probably because she felt like she was. But, Mercy shrugged shyly. "Long day."

"Hello," Wanda said, stepping up beside Mercy, her jacket already pulled on and Mercy's jacket held in her hand. "It's chilly out, dear."

Feeling like a child, Mercy kept her irritation inside, as always, as she was dressed like an infant. It was annoying when they were alone, but in front of this older girl, so beautiful and everything Mercy wished she could be, she was deeply ashamed. To her relief, Bethany turned away and made her way toward the stairs during the "dressing."

The two finally followed the older teen, reaching the top of the stairs as Bethany was about to hit the door at the bottom. "My goodness," Wanda muttered. "She's in a hurry, isn't she?"

Mercy didn't respond, still angry at her mother's behavior moments before. They hurried down the stairs to catch up, only to find Bethany waiting for them out on the sidewalk.

"I'm just over here," she said, nodding across the two-lane main street of the town and toward the old Chevy parked there in a small parking lot. "Mrs. Faulkner," she said, the trio making their way across the street after a Buick purred by. "You can park your Ford here. This lot is for those who live in the apartments or work in the two buildings." She indicated both sides of the street. "Can get pretty darn busy."

"Thank you," Wanda said, her strap heels clicking aggressively on the pavement as they made their way to the truck.

"Um," Bethany said, looking at the small cab and the two would-be passengers. "May be rather cozy, ladies."

"Mercy will ride in back," Wanda said, not even looking at her daughter before she walked over to the passenger door.

Mercy said nothing, but she briefly met the apologetic blue gaze of the young woman about to climb behind the wheel. She heaved herself up into the bed of the truck with its metal sides and wooden floor. She huddled up against the back of the cab as Bethany got the old truck rumbling to life. Soon enough, they were on their way.

By time they reached the narrow two-story house, surrounded by wooded land, not a house in sight for at least a mile in all directions, Mercy was frozen solid. She was curled up as much as could be while still sitting upright. She winced as she tried to stretch out her legs as the two doors squeaked open from the cab.

"Hey."

She glanced over, teeth chattering. Bethany stood at the side of the bed, her hands resting along the top of the side wall.

"Come on," Bethany said softly. "Let's get you warmed up."

Mercy nodded, crawling over to the side where Bethany gripped her with surprisingly strong arms to help her climb out of the truck. "Thanks," she barely managed, teeth chattering.

Feet firmly on the gravel driveway, Mercy met Bethany's gaze for a moment before looking away in subservience. She waited for her mother to join them, then followed along to the house. She was looking forward to getting inside. Her teeth continued to chatter and her fingers were numb.

No, it hadn't been an incredibly long drive, but the temperatures had dropped shockingly fast. It was more in the southern part of the state and was part of what was known as the brown belt. Pueblo was a far more temperate climate, with milder winters and hotter summers. This was unexpected.

When they entered the house, Mercy was taken aback by the shrill laughter that met her ears. Her eyes widened in surprise tinged with fear when she saw Ned and Billy gathered around a blonde in the kitchen, who seemed to be the source of the laughter.

"Don't you dare, William Henry!" she screeched.

"Don't worry, Mama!" Ned exclaimed, grabbing his younger brother and tackling him to the floor, the two brothers wrestling as giggles filled the air. "Gonna get it!"

"No!" Billy snorted, flopping over onto his back as he tried to fend off his brother. "No, not the pants!" He laugh-screamed as whatever Ned had stuffed down his trousers made contact.

The blonde was laughing, trying weakly to push Ned away from Billy but her own laughter, as well as the two boys', seemed to make it impossible.

"Can you all not act like wild animals?" Bethany chuckled, reaching a hand down to her twin. "We've got company."

Billy took the hand and got to his feet. He turned his back and seemed to reach into his trousers, tossing something hard into the sink. Ned slapped him on the back, grinning. "That's what happens when you try and slip ice down the back of Mama's dress."

The blonde cupped the cheeks of both boys, leaving a kiss on each before she smiled at the guests. She was lovely, Mercy thought. She looked to be a bit older than her mother, her blond hair cut into a stylish do. Her eyes were brown and her smile beautiful, just like her daughter's.

"Welcome. Sorry, but this one," she said, glaring playfully at Billy, "decided to get cute before you came." She stepped between the boys and took Wanda into a hug, Wanda stiff. "I'm Rachel, and I'm so sorry for your loss, honey," she said kindly. "Can't even imagine."

"Thank you," Wanda said, her voice flat.

Rachel gave her a kind smile before turning to Mercy. "Hey, sweetheart," she said softly, pulling the teen into a warm embrace. "So sorry about your daddy," she murmured into it.

Mercy nearly melted into the much-needed embrace, but knew she couldn't. The kind words, and warm tone that delivered them, were nearly her undoing. She felt a hand rub her back in motherly comfort before she was squeezed and released.

"Thank you," she managed. "Ma'am," she added, remembering her manners through the emotion she was pushing down. She gave the lovely older woman a brave smile when Rachel cupped her cheek before moving away.

"I'm the mother of these heathens," Rachel said, again lovingly cupping the cheeks of the boys before she walked over to Bethany and gave her a tight squeeze. "Welcome home from work, my sweet girl."

Mercy watched, never knowing a mother could be like that. It almost made her feel uncomfortable, the amount of physical affection the family displayed, right out in the open. Her father had been affectionate with her, hugs or little squeezes of the hand, but only during their private time when he said goodnight. In public, her mother glared and complained of Arthur "spoiling the girl."

"Welcome!"

Mercy was startled by the booming male voice, only to see Henry trotting down the stairs from the second floor. He was, as he'd been earlier that day, all smiles. He gave Wanda a respectful kiss to the fingers and Mercy a peck to the cheek.

"We're so happy to have you ladies to our home." He walked over to Rachel and gave her a kiss on the lips, the lovely blonde caressing his cheek with her fingers. "Missed you today, my love," he said.

Mercy took it all in, no idea what to think or say. And, the reactions—or lack thereof—by the Wynter children told her that this was normal behavior for the family. "Oooookay," she said to herself, settling in for an interesting dinner.

❦❦❦❦

Mercy could feel eyes on her. She glanced over to see Bethany looking at her before she returned her gaze back to the road. The headlamps of her truck sent twin spotlights to illuminate the dark streets before them.

"You look scared to death," Bethany noted.

Mercy cleared her throat, forcing herself to look over at the driver, one of two this time, as it was far too cold for Mercy to ride in the back of the truck now. Wanda had remained at the Wynter house to discuss her new position, which would start the next day with Henry, so Bethany had been asked to take Mercy home. After all, she had school the next morning.

Mercy honestly wasn't sure what to say to the observation, as it wasn't entirely incorrect. She felt so out of her depths, and the two hours spent at the Wynter house had sent her even deeper into just how lost she felt. A close-knit group, that was clear. And even so, they'd all gone above and beyond to make her and her mother feel welcome and even part of the family while they were there.

Was that normal?

Realizing that Bethany's words were still hanging in the air, she knew she needed to respond. "Um," she murmured. "A lot of different things." She knew it was lame, but not untrue.

Bethany nodded. "I can understand that." She slowed as she neared a stop sign, surprising Mercy when she made a quick left turn, when Mercy knew the correct way was straight ahead. "Let me show you something," Bethany said, seeming to sense Mercy's discomfort. She drove the Chevy a bit before slowing. "That's the school," she said, glancing over at her passenger as the truck stopped in front of the single-story brick building. "It's an easy walk from your place. Pay attention."

Mercy was initially confused, but as the truck got moving again, she realized that Bethany was driving the route slowly, easing to a stop at every corner, making sure Mercy saw the street sign illuminated by her headlamps before continuing on. Mercy mentally noted each one, as she knew there was no second tour.

Sure enough, it was an easy enough route, basically in a giant Z pattern. It was just knowing which two streets to turn on to create the diagonal bar of the letter. It wasn't long before they were in territory Mercy recognized. The Chevy pulled up in front of the soda shop, the engine idling as Bethany glanced over at her passenger.

"Tomorrow," she said. "Look for Pops."

Confused, Mercy met her gaze. "Who's that?"

"I think you know him," Bethany explained. "Samuel Popperton." She grinned. "He's grumpier than my great-grandad trying to take a piss. Pops has been his nickname since he was about eight years old. He's your age."

"Oh," Mercy said, relieved. "Yes, I know him. Well," she amended. "I know *of* him. Haven't seen him since we were little, so…"

Bethany nodded. "Well, he's our cousin, so it'll give you a little tie-in to kids here." The beautiful soda jerk indicated the town around them. "This isn't always an easy place for kids to try and fit in." She met Mercy's gaze. "Nobody likes Pops, so he'll be relieved to have a friend."

Not entirely sure how to feel about that, Mercy nodded. "Um, okay."

Bethany chuckled. "You'll be all right. Any real problems, just find me or Billy." She met and held Mercy's gaze. "Okay?"

Mercy took a deep breath and nodded. "Okay. Thank you."

Bethany nodded. "'Night."

"Goodnight."

Mercy climbed out of the truck then headed toward the building that was to be her new home. She glanced over her shoulder when she heard the truck rumble away, red taillights fading into the darkness. She pulled open the door that led up the narrow flight of stairs to the second floor.

She'd been shocked when she'd been given the key to the front door, let alone allowed to leave with the veritable stranger that was Bethany Wynter. But, here she was, standing in front of their door. She used the key she'd been given and unlocked the apartment door, letting herself in. As expected, it looked as it had a couple hours before.

It was dark, so she made her way over to a lamp, flicking on the light, which she'd leave on for her mother, as well as the unlocked door for her to enter, whenever she got home. She took the unobserved opportunity to look around. Her new home. She didn't really care that it was smaller than their house, as she didn't utilize much of the house other than her bedroom, anyway.

When she wasn't helping her mother clean, she'd stayed unseen, unheard, which she'd learned from a young age was the best way when her father wasn't around. Though small, the apartment was cute. She looked in the cabinets and the Frigidaire, all empty of food, of course. For a moment, just a fleeting moment, she allowed herself to dream.

What would it be like to have a place of her own someday? To choose where the furniture was placed, what she wore, and how her hair looked? She walked to the bathroom and snapped on the push switch for the light. She studied her gaze in the mirror above the basin, her face, her eyes, which easily showed how tired she was. It wasn't just physically tired, which she was, but emotionally exhausted.

She wanted to cry. She wanted a really good, throw-a-fit cry. Not an option, she settled for squeezing her eyes closed and taking a long, deep inhale before slowly releasing it. She needed sleep. Yes, new town, new home, new bed, new life. She had no choice but to embrace it. Maybe, just maybe, she'd be able to figure out who she was. After all, Mr. Popperton had said this was a new start.

So, she thought, washing her face and brushing her teeth before heading to bed. She'd start anew. Maybe she and her mother could find some happiness. Maybe *she* could find some happiness.

She was skeptical, but as she climbed beneath the covers after setting her alarm clock, she hoped for good dreams. Not dreams of her father dying and calling for her, as it had been for so many days. But, maybe dreams of what was to come.

Chapter Three

School was school, she supposed. Most looked similar, though this one was much smaller and different in that all grades were housed in the same building, known as Wynter Mountain K-12. She was told that there had been talks the last few years about creating a separate senior high as classes were getting a bit cramped.

But for the time being, she would start her sophomore year of high school with fellow students aged five through eighteen. Billy and Bethany were both slated to graduate. She'd followed the mental map Bethany had been so kind as to give her the night before and had made it to school with plenty of time to find her locker and struggle with the lock until it finally opened.

It was time for the midday break, and she was grateful for the lunch that Rachel Wynter had packed for her the night before, knowing there wouldn't be food in the apartment to make her one. It amazed her just how thoughtful and kind the Wynter family was. From what she understood, it had been Henry Wynter's father who had founded the town.

Rachel's parents, Justice and Thea, had been some of the earliest to populate the town. Their only child, Rachel, had been one of the first born in Wynter. As she carried her lunch pail to the cafeteria, Mercy thought about that. How incredible that must be, to be such an integral part of the town's core beginning.

"I'm supposed to join you."

Knocked completely out of her train of thought, she looked to her left to see a young man walking beside her. "Excuse me?"

He glanced at her, eyebrows drawn beneath the shadow of the short brim of his wool flat cap. "Did you misunderstand me?" He wore a pressed white shirt, buttoned to the top, and a buttoned vest over it, the grayish-brown of his vest matching that of his trousers. He looked quite tidy and neat.

"Well, no. But why are you supposed to join me?" she asked.

Again, he looked at her as though she were a simple-minded twit. "My cousins, who else?"

Getting irritated with his pompous tone, she stopped. "I don't know you," she said. The boy could stop or keep going—she didn't care. "I don't appreciate your assumption that I do," she added when he did stop.

He placed a hand on his hip, which he threw out a bit. "They didn't tell you I was joining you?"

"I have no idea who 'they' are," she said. "It would be incredibly helpful to your cause if you gave me some names." She glared at him. "Including yours."

He let out a dramatic sigh and held out his hand. "Samuel Popperton. Sam only, please."

She took his hand, noting the somewhat limp hold he had on hers as they shook hands. "Okay, Sam. Mercy. And, who are your cousins?"

"Leo, Ned, Bethany, Billy," he prattled off as they began to walk again, the hallway crowded as their fellow students slammed lockers, textbooks tossed in and lunches grabbed out. Their peers yelled to each other, ran, or shoved. Sam sidestepped a couple of arguing boys. "Ring a bell?"

Mercy nodded. "Yes. I think it was mentioned somewhere along the way in the blur that's been the last week."

He nodded, as though satisfied with her response. The cafeteria was a large room with long tables and bench seats set up in rows, a center aisle between them. There was a line of kids waiting to get a tray of hot food, scooped by men in aprons and paper caps.

"This way," Sam directed, heading off to the left. Mercy followed, noting kids she'd seen in her classes so far, some glancing her way, though most ignored them as they were already engaged in conversations or unpacking bagged lunches. Sam finally sat down at one end of the long table, nobody else sitting on the end he chose.

She sat down and unpacked her own pail. Her attention, however, was quickly taken over by her unexpected companion. She watched as he opened his lunch box. With very particular care, he removed every single item, from wrapped sandwich to crackers to washed and cut carrots sticks to an apple, placing them just so in a little semicircle on the table in front of him. Everything was placed a certain amount of space apart from its closest edible neighbor.

He glanced up at her from his task. "What?"

"Pops, you're just a crazy man."

Mercy gasped at the sudden male voice and group that had begun to surround them. The voice belonged to Billy Wynter, who had a few other boys his age with him as well as Bethany and another young woman who plopped down next to her as the group sat at the table with them.

"I've told you," Sam growled, glaring at Billy, who sat next to him. "Don't call me Pops."

Billy grinned with boyish charm. "Well, come on now, you're fourteen going on ninety, Pops." He winked over at Mercy as he snagged a carrot from Samuel's bag.

"William Wynter!" Sam exclaimed, slapping at his cousin's hand.

"Ow!" Billy laughed, dropping the carrot back into the bag.

Mercy felt incredibly shy and suddenly very suffocated as more kids, all looking to be upperclassmen, squeezed in at their table. Soon enough, a dozen of what seemed to be Billy and Bethany's friends had joined them.

"Okay, all," Billy said, knocking on the table as though starting a meeting. "Wanted to introduce you all to our new friend, Mercy Faulkner. She's a sophomore here and I want you all to look out for her. She just moved here from Pueblo."

She smiled shyly as she got an array of greetings: *Welcome! Hey, there. Nice to meet you. Got a fella?* She blushed deeply at the last comment, the boy who asked receiving a backhand to his arm from Bethany.

"She's been here a day, Richard," she muttered to him.

He shrugged and rubbed the back of his neck. "Sorry."

Mercy gave him a small smile, the young woman sitting next to Bethany catching her attention. She was looking at her, her blond hair stylish at her shoulders. She was lovely with green eyes, equally as lovely as Bethany. She had a pinched look on her face as she studied the younger newcomer, and it made Mercy nervous.

Mercy looked away and turned her attention to her lunch. She listened as the group of friends ate their own lunches as they talked, laughed, and gave each other guff about this, that, or the other thing. Clearly a close-knit group of kids. No doubt, she thought, they'd all grown up together.

She understood that Billy had been trying to be sweet, and it was admittedly sweet, but Mercy felt like a zoo animal. She could feel the looks at her, hear the muttered words between the boys about the "new girl." She hadn't been the new girl since her very first day at school, period. Like these kids, she'd gone to school with the same group of peers since kindergarten. She missed her friends, missed the familiar faces of those who weren't friends.

This was going to be hard.

❧❧❧❧

It was just shy of two miles to the school and then back to the building where the apartment was. Mercy quickly stowed her bookbag and changed out of her "good clothes" before heading over next door to help her mother at the hotel. It had been two weeks and the two had fallen into a routine that worked well enough.

Mercy got herself up and to school, her mother already at work, then back from school, changed, and on to help her mother. She was up until late helping with dinner cleanup then homework. She was tired pretty much all the time, but that's how her mother said it should be. It would keep her out of trouble.

Yes, since Mercy was the epitome of a troublemaker kid. Sure.

The hotel was a two-story structure with a basement that she'd heard housed a natural hot spring, but she'd never been. She'd never even seen such a thing. Was it like a giant bathtub? A hole in the stone floor of a cave? A swimming pool with warm water? She was intrigued, but not enough to seek it out.

The hotel had twelve rooms, very small, but they were often rented by the men who came and went from the lumber mill. Much like when the town had been all about mining—before the mines had dried up thirty years or so before—it drew in young men looking for a new start.

The single ones ended up at the Wynter Hotel, which had once upon a time been a boarding house and saloon. Now, not necessarily a boarding house anymore, it served a similar purpose. Many of the men who came into town stayed in a room, sometimes up to a month, she was told, until they could find a more permanent housing situation.

Down by the mines were tiny shacks that Billy had explained to her were for the married miners back in the early years. They weren't much bigger than the apartment she and her mother were sharing, so she couldn't even imagine an entire family in one. They were still inhabited today, some still by those who were miners in their youth. Now, they were bent-over old men dealing with black lung.

One such man, Dwayne, sat in the hotel's small restaurant on the main floor. The saloon had long ago become a basic eatery. The old man with his hunched shoulders and thinning silvery hair sat at his regular table near the back.

"Good evening, Mr. Dwayne," she said, giving him a smile as she refilled his coffee cup.

He looked up at her, one eye ghostly white from the cataract that covered it, the other brown one watery yet friendly. "Evenin', Mercy," he said in his deep, gravelly voice. "Thank you kindly."

"You're very welcome, sir," she said, finishing with the coffee. "Can I get you anything else?"

"Nope." He shook his head. "If'n it's okay, just gonna sit here for a bit before headin' on home."

"Of course, Mr. Dwayne. Take your time." She gave him a kind smile and took his empty dinner plate before moving on to the kitchen to leave them for Sam, who was the dishwasher and who also helped to clear tables as a busboy.

The kitchen was small, but the cooks got the job done. The food wasn't the best, but with very few other options, it was certainly doable. "I'm telling you," Sam said, accepting the dishes she set on the counter next to the double sink he was working from. He spared a glance at her from beneath the brim of his flat cap. "I'm going to open a café in this town that will blow your mind."

She'd heard it all from him before but admired his dedication to his dream. "I'm sure it will, Sam."

"You just see if I don't!" His words were passionate, his gaze boring into hers as if daring her to argue.

"Are you still wanting to put it in that empty lot just down the way across the street?" she asked, humoring him. She knew how much it meant to him, though wasn't sure why. If Samuel Popperton was anything, it was determined.

"You and your café, kid." George, the head cook,

chuckled. "What are you gonna call it?"

"*Sam's*," Sam said, as if it was so obvious.

"You should call it, *Pop's*," one of the other kitchen workers offered, making the group laugh.

"You laugh now," Sam exclaimed, pointing a finger at the other men, soap suds dripping off it. "But it'll happen and it'll be a huge success. Just you wait and see!"

Feeling bad for the young man, who was clearly getting upset by their jeering, she placed a hand on his arm. "I believe you, Sam," she said, suddenly feeling very much that she did. "I think you'll do it."

He met her gaze, the flush of anger on his cheeks beginning to fade. "You can come and work for me," he said.

She gave him a kind smile. "I'd be honored to."

Leaving him to his task, Mercy grabbed the order for a table that was ready, heading back out of the kitchen to deliver the food. When she did, she saw another table was filled with Billy and some of his friends, most of which had crowded the lunch table with him every day at school.

"Hey, guys," she said, stepping up to the table and handing out an armful of menus. She endured the stares, some stopping at her breasts before moving on as they opened the paper menus. One of the things she'd found most difficult to get used to as she'd developed over the past couple years was the stares, particularly at her chest.

"Okay, boys," Billy said, slapping his hand on the table as if bringing a meeting to order. "It's on me." He looked up at her and gave her a charming grin. "Burgers all around."

Surprised, she nodded and wrote down the order with the number ordered next to it. "That's very generous of you, Billy."

"Well," he responded. "It's a beautiful day outside and a Friday to boot."

She gave him a shy smile. "It certainly is."

"Drinks, fellas?" Billy asked brightly to his compatriots.

Mercy wrote down orders—Coke, malt, chocolate milkshake—but one of the boys had a different idea.

"You in a tall glass with ice."

She stared at him with wide eyes. "Um…"

"Apologize to the young lady," a firm voice said behind Mercy.

The boy's eyes widened as he looked at whomever had said it. "Uh, Mr. Kilkoyne, sir, I was just havin' some fu—"

"Now."

The boy swallowed and looked shyly up at Mercy. "Sorry," he muttered. "I was just teasin'."

Mercy wasn't sure what to say, so simply nodded then turned away from the table so she could get their drink orders taken care of. She turned to come face-to-face with the person she'd heard so much about and had very much looked forward to meeting—Justice Kilkoyne. The person who stood before her was not what she'd been expecting.

She knew Justice was in his late sixties, but the person standing before her had such a spry, youthful spirit and look that he looked more than a decade younger than he was. A full head of salt-and-pepper hair, cut short, though his bangs fell over his forehead. Dark eyes, nearly black, twinkled, and his smile was instant as their gazes met.

He wore a long-sleeved shirt with three buttons at the neckline. It was tucked into baggy trousers with suspenders. His hands were shoved into the pockets of the pants. What got her the most, however, was the fact that this person didn't quite look... She tried to clarify what she was thinking. She knew he was Billy's grandpa, but somehow, something was off. She absolutely could not put her finger on it.

"Nice to finally meet you, Mercy." Justice's voice was kind, the tone a bit soft.

"You, too, sir," she said instantly. "I've heard so much about you."

"As I have about you from my grandson," he said with a wide smile. "I hope you and your mama are okay? Have everything you need?"

"Oh, yes, sir! Thank you so much. We're very grateful."

His eyebrows fell. "None of that 'sir' business. You call me Justice or nothing at all."

"Yes, sir—" She cleared her throat. "Justice."

He placed a hand on her shoulder and squeezed lightly before his hand fell away. "Listen, my Angel and I want to have you two over for dinner, you hear?"

She nodded. "Yes. I'll let my mother know."

"Good deal." He turned and sent one final glare at the boy at the table then walked away, heading out of the building.

Mercy watched him go, unable to look away. There was something about him that she was so intrigued by. Shaking herself out of it, she turned to head to the kitchen to fill the drink orders for the boys at the table.

"Mercy," Billy exclaimed, hopping up from his seat and trotting after her.

She turned to him just before she reached the kitchen door, which was behind the long, intricately carved bar, which she'd been told was original to the building and used when it had been a saloon. "Yeah?"

"Hey, listen," he said. "First off, sorry about Tony. He was a real jerk. If Grandpa hadn't said anything, I would have."

She gave him a smile. "Thanks, Billy. I appreciate that."

"So, tomorrow me and some of the guys, Pops, Bethany, and Helen are gonna hit The Hole." He shrugged. "Have a campfire, cook some wieners..."

"What's The Hole?"

"Oh, it's a kinda of a creek, I guess. Not quite a river, but I guess more than a creek, thinking about it." He gave her an adorable grin. "Summertime we swim, wintertime we ice skate, but not quite warm or cold enough." He shrugged. "Just hang out, you know?"

She chewed on her bottom lip for a moment. She wanted to but wasn't sure if her mother would allow her to. "Well, I need to ask my mom. So, if you can give me the time and everything, I can ask."

"Okay," he said, all smiles. "I can do that."

Chapter Four

Mercy blew out a breath. She was so nervous as she stood just outside the door to the stairs that led to the second floor of their building. It was a pleasant day, though no doubt it would turn cold by nightfall. Autumn was certainly in the air, the leaves of the trees gorgeous in their rainbow of transition.

Wiping her sweating palms on the length of her wool coat, her nerves tripled when she saw Bethany's truck pull up to the curb. She gave her a little wave before walking up to the passenger-side door. "Hi."

"Hey there." Bethany gave her a welcoming smile. "Ready to have some fun?"

"I think so." Mercy got settled as Bethany got them moving. "Thanks for picking me up. So sorry to be a pain for you."

"Nonsense. Not a pain at all," Bethany assured. They drove in silence for a few moments before Bethany asked, "Did your mom give you guff about going today? I know you do a lot at the hotel to help."

"Um," Mercy hedged, remembering the horrible argument all too well. "It worked out," she said. "As long as I'm not alone with the boys, that is."

Bethany's eyebrows fell. "Why? Billy would never let anything happen to you. Or Pops, for that matter." She grinned. "He may be little, but he's a mean pup when he needs to be." Bethany met Mercy's gaze. "Got it, okay. Helen and I will be sure to keep you with us, then."

Mercy nodded, the pretty blonde coming to mind at the mention of her name, as well as the distinct feeling Mercy had that Helen wasn't fond of her for some reason. "Okay," she said, pushing the image away. "Thank you."

"So, what do you think, now that you've been here for a little bit?" Bethany asked, easily navigating the streets of their little town. It was just before eleven on a sleepy late Saturday morning.

"I like it okay, I suppose," Mercy said. "I really miss my father and my friends back home. But," she added with a shrug. "Wynter is a really nice little town. The people are nice."

"Again," Bethany said, sparing her a glance as she pulled the truck up to a stop sign. "I'm so sorry about your dad. I'm so close to mine, I can't even imagine."

"Yes," Mercy agreed. "It's been tough."

"How's your mom handling it?" Bethany asked, getting them going again and headed farther up into the foothills where trees were becoming more plentiful, surrounding them in gold, orange, and red.

"She doesn't really talk about it much," Mercy said, not entirely sure how to answer the question. She didn't feel that saying, *she's become meaner and I don't like being around her* was an appropriate response.

The truck drove down a dirt road that looked far more like a pathway cleared by decades and decades of traffic, until they reached a clearing. Other cars were already there, including Billy's old beat-up Buick. It absolutely amazed her that the Wynter kids had cars in a time when many families didn't even own one.

They climbed out of the truck and Mercy could hear voices as well as running water off to the right through the trees. She heard laughter and talking and could smell a campfire floating on the breeze.

"Hey, sis!" Billy called out. "You finally decide to show up?"

"Go suck an egg!" she yelled back.

Mercy was shocked by Bethany's gutsiness when it came to, well, just about anything. She was thoroughly amused, though tried to hide her smile. She met Bethany's amused gaze.

"Boys," the older girl muttered. They shared a moment of sisterhood understanding before making their way into the trees.

After a few minutes lost in the colorful wonderland, they emerged to the other side. A small, rocky shore butted up to a slow-moving body of water which, as Billy had said, was smaller than a river but larger than a stream. A small but hearty campfire was crackling, logs pulled up to encircle it for seating.

Most of the six or so there Mercy recognized. Sam was there, currently in what looked to be a fairly intense discussion with a boy Mercy knew to be named Elmer, and of course, Helen. She smiled when Mercy and Bethany broke through the trees, quickly scooting over on the log she sat upon, patting the newly made space in invitation.

Mercy glanced over at Bethany to see her grin appear as she walked over to the blonde. She'd watched the two over the weeks and had been a bit confused. They were friends, obviously, but the way Helen watched any and every other female that got anywhere near Bethany was so strange to Mercy.

What was she worried about? They seemed to be

really good friends and were always together, so surely it was a strong friendship.

"Hey. Glad you made it."

Mercy turned to see Billy grinning down at her. "Want a Coca-Cola?" He nodded toward the small glass bottles that had been placed in the water, no doubt to keep them cold.

"Oh, um, yes, please." She watched as he hurried over to the group of bottles and snatched one out, using a church key to remove the cap as he walked back over to her. "Thank you, Billy."

"Yeah, of course." His smile was winning, making an already handsome face downright swoon worthy.

One thing Mercy had noticed about the Wynter children, and certainly the twins, was that they all looked like they belonged on a Hollywood film set somewhere. And, when she'd met their parents, particularly their mother, who was absolutely stunning, she understood why. She certainly saw that the gene pool in the Wynter family was strong and impressive.

"Weiner?"

Mercy was torn from her thoughts when Sam was suddenly in front of her, a stick in one hand and a raw frankfurter in the other. She looked at the two before meeting his gaze. "Oh, yes. Thanks, Sam." She cradled her drink against her side with her arm before taking the items and carefully spearing the meat onto the thin, sharp stick.

"Got room over here, Mercy," Bethany said, patting a large rock placed not far from the log she shared with Helen.

Mercy took the seat and smiled at the two women before she braced her drink between her feet while placing the business end of her stick into the fire like the others, cooking her lunch.

"Scoot," Billy said, shooing his friend who was hogging up the whole log to Mercy's right. The friend, whom Mercy thought was named Jud, scooted over to make room.

Now pinned between the Wynter twins, Mercy turned back to her task.

"Where's Tyson?" Bethany asked, leaning forward on her log to see past Mercy to her brother.

"Sadly," he said pointedly. "He proved he couldn't be a gentleman." He nodded toward Mercy. "Told him he wasn't invited."

"Good for you," Bethany said, nodding in approval. She met Mercy's gaze and gave her a little wink. "He's a dope on a good day."

"Oh," Mercy said, sighing in relief. "Okay, good. I felt terrible for a moment there. He's your friend," she added, looking from Bethany to Billy and back. "He has more right to be here than I do."

"Why?" Billy said around the bite of hot dog he'd just taken. "You're our friend too, Mercy. My grandpa taught me to never, ever let a man treat a woman like property," he said. "Me and my brothers had that drilled into our heads since we were little boys." He nodded across the campfire at his cousin. "Pops, too."

"Huh?" Sam said, turning to look at Billy at the sound of his nickname.

Billy grinned and waved him off. "I'm just sorry Tyson acted like that, Mercy."

"It's okay," she said. "Sadly, I've come to expect that sort of thing."

"Well, not if you're with me, you shouldn't." He seemed angry, heavy eyebrows falling as he studied the stick and hot dog he held in the flames beside Mercy's. "A real man treats a lady like the angel that she is," he said with an emphasizing nod. "That's what my grandpa says, and I agree." He grinned over at her. "You know, until I was about eight years old, I thought my grandma's name was Angel. That's what he calls her. Imagine my shock when I found out that her actual name is Thea."

Mercy smiled, finding that sweet. "Sounds like something my father would have done if given the chance. Your grandparents been together a long time?"

Billy's smile widened. "Justice Kilkoyne has loved Thea Kilkoyne for just shy of fifty years now," he said. "Since he was all of seventeen years old."

"They adore each other," Bethany added. "Can only imagine a love like that. See, Billy and I got our grandma's eyes," she explained. "And, Grandpa is always saying that he can see forever in the skies of her eyes."

Billy chuckled, making Mercy swing her head from her left side to her right. "He sure does."

Mercy was charmed. She'd love to see a love like that. Her father had been such a romantic, and it had all been lost in such a mean-tempered woman like her mother. "I think that's so sweet. I only met your grandpa for a moment last night, but..." She shrugged, looking back to Bethany. "He seemed really kind, even besides standing up for me to your friend."

"If the Kilkoyne or Wynter family care about you," Bethany said, meeting Mercy's gaze. "There's nothing they won't do for you. Justice and Thea taught us that."

"And then our parents," Billy said, picking up

the story, Mercy's head whipping around back right again. "They've never been with anyone else. Basically been together since birth. Well, Mama's birth anyway," he amended. "Dad's two years older."

"Really?" Mercy asked, eyes wide.

"Yup. Grandma once told me that by the time they'd hit school age, her and grandpa knew it would take a crowbar to separate those two."

"Wow," Mercy murmured, looking back to her hot dog. She couldn't even imagine.

⁂

The afternoon had gone really well. Mercy had even joined into a conversation or two with the group. In a setting like this, more relaxed, away from the pressures of school and other peers, she found Bethany and Billy's friends to be amusing and actually pretty sweet to her. They'd laughed, and for the first time in a very long time, she just felt like a teenager. She was even able to forget about the bargain she'd made with her mother that finally got her permission to attend the gathering: she'd give up every single weekend for the rest of the month to work at the restaurant and hotel.

That sentence would begin the following day, Sunday. For now, she was going to allow herself to enjoy her Saturday. She shrugged into her jacket as the temperature began to fall, which felt especially cold as she was sitting so close to the water.

"Let me help you with that," Billy said, leaning over and holding the heavy wool jacket so she could slide her arms into the sleeves.

She gave him a sly smile. "Thanks."

"Ain't they done peeing yet?"

Mercy glanced over to Elmer, who was looking at Billy.

Billy glanced to the log, which Mercy realized had been vacant for some time now. "Oh, right." He began to stand up. "I'll go make sure they're okay."

"No," Mercy said, pushing to her feet. "Let me?" She shrugged. "I need to stretch my legs."

"Well, we can go together," Billy said. "Don't want you to get lost."

Together, the two headed into the trees. A perfect gentleman, Billy kept his hands in the pockets of his trousers as they walked. "So pretty this time of year, isn't it?" he asked conversationally.

"It really is," she agreed. "I mean, back in Pueblo we have trees, obviously, but nothing like this." She trailed her fingers over the rough bark of an aspen to emphasize her point.

"Do you miss it?" he asked. "Pueblo."

"I do. Well, my friends and stuff. The town," she added with a shrug. "It's much prettier here." She gave him a little smile.

"It definitely is," he said, giving her a pointed look, which made her blush. "So, you think you'd wanna go grab a malt with me sometime?"

Mercy felt her stomach flip, but she wasn't sure exactly which direction. Was it an excited flip or an anxious one? Perhaps a bit of both? "I don't know if my mother would allow that."

He nodded. "Well, we can make it a double date?" he asked, hope in his voice. "Maybe you and me, and my buddy Elmer and his girl?"

Okay, now she just wanted to vomit. "Um," she managed. "I can ask."

"Okay," he said, sounding relieved. "Okay, yeah."

Something caught Mercy's attention off to the left. As they continued to stroll, Billy prattling on quietly about whatever, her full focus was pulled to what she was seeing. The two women were far enough away that what made them stand out was the blond of Helen's hair. Helen was backed against the trunk of a tree and Bethany was leaning against her. They were…kissing.

She was stunned, but even so she couldn't look away. Helen's hand was buried in Bethany's hair, their bodies pressed together as the kiss was pretty intense. Mercy felt the tiniest spark that suddenly came alight in her belly. That tiny spark slowly grew to warm her from the inside, even as it confused her and made her feel deeply uncomfortable.

"What the hell?" Billy said, surprise in his voice. "Bethany!"

Mercy gasped, yanked out of her daze of watching the two. She blinked rapidly and forced herself to look away.

"What the hell are you doing?" he demanded.

Helen cried out, shoving Bethany away from her. "Oh my god!" She took off in the opposite direction of Mercy and Billy.

"Helen, wait!" Bethany took off after her and Billy began to chase them both.

"No!" Mercy exclaimed, grabbing his arm, nearly sending him flying back into her as she propelled him around. "No," she said again, no clue why and no clue where the confidence was coming from. "Leave them alone."

He stared down at her, blue eyes wide. "What?"

"They weren't hurting anyone," she said, pleading in her voice. Her grip released his arm only to lightly grab the front of his jacket. "They weren't hurting anyone," she said again.

He looked back in the direction his sister and the other woman had scurried, then back to Mercy. Running a hand through his hair, he sighed, and it sounded irritated. "Fine."

⚘⚘⚘⚘

Billy had dropped her off at home, as Bethany and Helen hadn't returned to the shore. Though they hadn't told the others what they'd seen, Billy's obvious change in mood had made things a bit uncomfortable, and soon things broke up.

Now, making her way up the narrow staircase to the second floor, Mercy wasn't sure what to think. Still stunned by what she'd seen and even more so by her reaction to it, she felt terrible. If she'd minded her own business and hadn't stared, likely Billy wouldn't have followed her gaze and the two would have gone unobserved.

Would Bethany be in trouble by him? He'd been so quiet on the drive home, and though she knew he wasn't angry with her or at her, it had still made her feel anxious and she wanted to get home. It felt like she was climbing a mountain, but finally she reached the second-floor hallway and walked to her door.

Retrieving the key they'd had made for her, she was about to insert it into the lock when the door flung open, a furious Wanda standing on the other side.

"You whore!" she growled, grabbing Mercy by the front of her jacket and yanking her inside the apartment before slamming the door shut. "You lied!"

The slap came so fast and so hard, Mercy was whirled around and slammed face-first into the wall, which sent her to the floor. Eyes wide, she looked up at the woman who stood over her. "I didn't!"

"You said Bethany would be there!" Wanda raged, lashing out at her again.

Mercy covered her face with her arms as she rolled away from her. "She was!"

"Then why did I see her in the soda shop with Helen not half an hour ago?"

Crying and peeking out to see if she was safe, Mercy lowered her arms when she saw her mother glaring down at her. "They left early," she said honestly. "I think Helen had to leave or something." No, not completely honest, but she didn't have the full story and she could never tell her mother what she'd seen and what had happened.

"How'd you get home?" Wanda asked, her voice deathly quiet as she eyed her.

"Billy took me home," she admitted. "Mother, we went from the creek directly here, I swear."

Without a word, Wanda walked to her bedroom, slamming the door closed behind her. Left alone, Mercy sat up. She was deeply shaken and her mouth and her eye hurt. She brought up a hand to her mouth and saw her fingertips coated in red. It was then that she tasted the coppery flavor of blood.

Chapter Five

Closing her bedroom door behind her, Bethany turned to face her bedroom as she shrugged out of her winter jacket. She was cold, tired, and still thoroughly pissed. She tossed the jacket to the bed as she unwrapped the scarf her grandma had knitted for her.

"Such crap," she muttered. She flopped down on the bed atop her jacket, bouncing slightly at the give of the bedsprings beneath her weight. Staring up at the angled ceiling of her attic bedroom, she didn't even see all the sketches taped to it, all her creations: people, buildings, cars, animals, and even a landscape or two.

Again, she saw Helen's face and the initial fear that had turned to absolute rage—that was, once she'd finally caught her after her girlfriend had hightailed it through the trees.

"Stop!" Bethany had growled, grabbing Helen's hand and whirling her around to face her. She'd never seen the lovely features contort to such anger. "What is your deal?"

"What is my deal?" Helen had nearly yelled. "That brat," she said, pointing back the direction they'd come. "Is going to tell the entire damn town!" The rage in those blue eyes turned to accusation. "Why was she even here, Bethany? She's not one of us. It's bad enough we have to drag your damn cousin everywhere we go."

Stunned, Bethany had just stared at her for what felt like a full minute but was likely a few seconds. Finally, she looked away. "Look," she said, forcing her voice to lower, knowing how voices carried in the woods. "Let's go get a malt and talk this out. Okay?" Truth was, she'd wanted to leave the blonde there and walk back to her brother and her friends. But, she'd felt it was best to remove Helen from the situation before damage could be done.

Bethany thought back over the past year that she and Helen had been together and realized that, far too often, rather than having fun at whatever they were doing, it ended with Bethany trying to smooth ruffled feathers. Honestly, it was becoming more work than it was worth, she thought.

A sharp knock at her closed bedroom door startled her. "What?" she called out, knowing full well who it was. Sure enough, her twin appeared.

Billy opened the door and slammed it behind him. He stood there, arms crossed over his chest and gaze focused on her. He said nothing, the siblings playing a game of visual chicken before he looked away. *Ha!*

Shoving off the door, he walked over to the small desk their father had made into the wall for her to do homework and draw. He turned the chair around to face the bed and plopped down into it. "We need to talk."

"About what?" she drawled, climbing off the bed. She decided it was the perfect time to hang up her jacket and scarf. That way, she wouldn't have to face the hurt and anger in his eyes.

"Why were you and Helen kissing?" he asked,

getting straight to the heart of the matter.

"Because that's what you do when you're dating," she muttered as if everybody knew that. When there was absolute silence, she glanced over at him. If the situation hadn't been so serious, she would have laughed. She was irritated. Really, really irritated. She finished her task and slammed her closet door closed. "What, William?" Hand on hip, she could feel her irritation turning to hurt at the judgment she saw in his eyes, the exact mirror of her own.

"Are you..." He cleared his throat and tried again. "Are you..." No more successful the second time, he faltered.

Bethany crossed her arms over her chest, feeling extremely defensive. "Like Grandma and Grandpa? Yes." She shook her head. "How dare you judge me, Billy?" She couldn't keep the hurt out of her voice. "Justice and Thea are both women, and you know that."

His jaw muscles bulged as he looked away. "Yes, but Justice looks more like a man—"

"Because she didn't have much of a choice! You know the story, so don't sit there playing dumb." She glared at him. "Or self-righteous."

He remained silent, that jaw muscle working again. "Well," he muttered, shoving up from the chair and storming over to the bedroom door. "That was shitty to leave Mercy there."

Left alone, Bethany stared at the door where her brother had just been. She was stung and she was confused. She needed her grandparents.

Bethany absolutely loved being at the old two-story farmhouse that her grandparents had lived in since they first moved to Wynter in the early 1890s. Apparently, it had been built by her grandmother's first husband and biological father of Rachel, Bethany's mother. He'd died long before Rachel was even born, and by that time, Justice had gotten her Angel back after a horrible train accident had separated them.

She loved hearing their story, even though she'd heard it a thousand times. So romantic, what they'd both done and gone through just to be together. The energy in their home was peaceful, calm, and filled with endless love and devotion to each other and all they cared about.

Bethany could only hope for that someday. Not only that, but her grandparents were the only people she could actually feel normal around. Being around them and their relationship helped everything make sense to her.

Of course she loved her parents, and of course she loved her older brother Ned and his fiancée Delores. She enjoyed spending time with both couples, but since both couples were heterosexual, she always felt like the odd person out, yet she could say nothing. She thought her mother suspected, as she'd dropped little hints over the last couple years, but Bethany wasn't quite ready to talk about it yet. She knew who she was and where her attractions lay, but she wasn't ready for any declaration.

"What's wrong, sweetheart?" Thea asked softly, glancing over from her portion of the quilt, which Bethany was helping her make. They sat at opposite ends of the dining room table, the large quilt spread out across it. It was nearly finished, the two working on it for the better part of two years.

Bethany glanced over at the woman whom she looked up to so much. She'd gotten her eyes, but many had said she'd also gotten her quiet poise, yet spunk when necessary. Thea wasn't afraid to speak her mind, and certainly didn't allow her gender to get in the way of her thoughts and opinions, nor define them, thanks in large part to her relationship with Justice.

"Huh?" Bethany said, knocked clear out of her thoughts.

Thea was now a woman in her late sixties, her golden hair mostly white, with some gold mixed in. The skin of her face and hands showed her advanced age, but her beautiful sky-blue eyes did not. It was so easy to see Justice's Angel, still there, still beautiful.

"You're troubled." Thea gave her a sweet smile. "I know my Bethany." Her fingers kept going, as though they had a mind of their own, even as her gaze stayed focused on the teen.

"Billy caught Helen and I today," Bethany finally said. When she heard nothing, she glanced over at her grandmother who was once again focused on her own task, the softest smile on her lips. "What?"

"How'd he take it?"

Bethany snorted. "He was a jerk. He was aggressive, confrontational, judgmental—"

"And hurt," Thea added softly.

Bethany stared at her. "But, you and Gran said I had a right to keep it to myself until I was ready," she said, referring to the special endearment she gave Justice while around family. She used Grandpa in public, as they'd been taught since children, but in private, she wanted to respect and honor all aspects of her beloved grandparent, including her femaleness.

"And you do," her grandmother agreed. "But," she added with a raised eyebrow. "Justice and I have found over the years that those who care about us most, who would support us, want to support us, are the ones that we need to keep close as our allies. Your Grandpa Jeramiah," she added, "God rest his soul, knew about Justice and me from early on and supported us publicly."

"Really?" Bethany said, surprised. Her father's father, and founder of the small town, had died when she was younger so hadn't known him as well.

"Absolutely. He told Justice flat out that he wanted her to run the saloon and brothel because of the perspective she could give the business." She gave her granddaughter a smile. "And the girls. Could advocate for them as no man could."

Bethany considered what she'd been told, hissing when her needle caught the pad of her thumb as her thoughts pushed out beyond the quilt. "So, you think I should have told Billy?"

Thea nodded. "The choice was yours, sweetheart, but the two of you have shared everything. Even a womb. My guess is, as with most men, they'd aren't good at expressing their hurt so it often comes out in anger or aggression. Part of him probably always suspected, but he was hurt to actually find out and know that you hadn't trusted him with it."

Blowing out a heavy breath, Bethany considered the wise words. "Crap."

⚜ ⚜ ⚜ ⚜

"Man, they did a number on it, didn't they?" Justice said, hands on hips as she and Bethany stood just inside the smaller house on the Kilkoyne property.

"I'm so sorry, Gran," she said, shaking her head. Justice and Thea now held more than six hundred acres of farmland, about a third of that Justice still ran herself, along with hired help. The rest of it was leased by local farmers who wanted to have their own land to farm but couldn't quite afford it themselves. Some of them rented the small two-story house, and the last family had just moved out.

Justice ran a hand through her hair, pushing the floppy bangs out of her face. "Well, kid," she said, glancing over at her granddaughter. "Guess we got some work to do, huh?"

She tossed a pair of work gloves to Bethany, who was also wearing a pair of Gran's trousers. That was one thing she loved about spending time with and working with Gran: she got to literally let her hair down and get out of the damn dresses!

"So, this place started out with three rooms?" she asked.

"Yup." Justice gave her a proud grin, her dark eyes twinkling. "This whole space here," she said, indicating what was now the kitchen, "was the entire kitchen and living space. Where the living room and bathroom are now, was where your uncle Nate and my bedrooms were. That was it."

"No bathroom?"

"Nope." She playfully tweaked Bethany's nose. "We weren't spoiled like you kids today."

"Whatever," she grumbled good-naturedly. "So, when was the second floor added?" she asked. "The two bedrooms and bathroom."

"Well," Justice explained, the two beginning to gather the trash that had been left by the previous tenants. Food trash, old, stained clothing, and broken furniture. "When Nate and Tabitha moved back to Wynter after he finished pharmacy school, they moved back into the house. But, they already had Franklin by that time and Tabitha was pregnant with Megan, so they needed more space."

"So, you guys added on at that point?" Bethany asked, grunting as she heaved a burlap sack filled with…something.

"Yup." Justice helped her. "Good lord," she muttered. "What's in here, a body?" She burst into laughter when Bethany suddenly gasped and let go, hands coming up in supplication. "I'm joking, hon," Justice assured. "Just more dirty clothes and such. Anyway, yeah, we added the second floor in, oh let me think, nineteen hundred, maybe? Ninety-nine." She shrugged. "Something like that."

"Wow," Bethany murmured. "So cool."

There was a knock at the door, and Justice walked over and opened it. To Bethany's dread, Billy stood on the other side. "Hey, Gran!" he greeted. "Grandma said you may need some help over here—" He stopped when he saw Bethany standing in the living room, collecting the pieces of a splintered wooden table. He shoved his hands into the hip pockets of his trousers and looked away.

"Absolutely!" Justice slapped the teen on the shoulder and stepped aside. "We certainly do. Tell you what," she said, looking from brother to sister and back. "You two get things cleared up down here and I'm gonna go see how bad it is upstairs." With a reassuring smile, Justice hurried to the stairs and up.

Thinking on it now, Bethany realized that Gran hadn't seemed all that shocked when they'd had a knock at the door. She muttered to herself, knowing damn well they'd been set up. She turned away from Billy and continued doing what she was doing. She had no idea what could have happened for that table to be in the bad shape as it was. If not for the oval-shaped top that was still in one piece, it would be tough to identify what the pieces of wood had once belonged to.

"Fancy seeing you here," he finally said.

Bethany could hear him messing with things on the other side of the room, as her back was to him. "Where else would I be?" she muttered.

He snorted. "Yeah, after you scampered off like a scared rabbit last night."

"You know what, Billy," she lashed out, whirling to face him. "Knock it off. I left last night because you were being a jerk and I sure as hell am not going to stick around here to put up with it today." He met her glare but quickly looked away. It was then that she saw in his eyes exactly what her grandma had suspected— hurt. Feeling guilt creep up on her, Bethany lowered herself to sit on the floor to start gathering the smaller pieces. "Um," she murmured. "Want to help?"

Moments later, he dropped whatever he'd been messing with and walked over to her, lowering himself to sit cross-legged near her. In silence, they began to clean up the mess. Billy said nothing, and she knew it was up to her to fix this.

"I knew when I was about nine," she said quietly, not looking at him. "Though, Grandma told me once that she saw me looking at an older girl with, as she put it, 'wide-eyed adoration' at church when I was about five, and she'd been suspecting since then."

After several moments, he asked, "When did

you tell them? Gran and Grandma."

"I didn't," she said. "I mean, yes, we've talked about it obviously, but Gran told me one day when I was about twelve that she wasn't going to ask me if a had a boyfriend, as Grandpa Jeramiah always used to do, even just in teasing, because she knew that wasn't for me."

He cleared his throat. "Did you tell Mama and Dad?"

Bethany shook her head, grimacing at some unidentified substance stuck to one of the wood pieces. "No. The only people in the family I've told outright are Gran and Grandma."

He finally looked at her, the hurt clear as day in the blue depths of his eyes. "Why didn't you tell me?"

She met his gaze, her anger flaring again from the night before. "Look how you reacted, Billy. Why would I?"

Heavy eyebrows fell but he said nothing for several minutes as they worked to clear out the broken table. Finally, he said, "I'm sorry about that. I was really shocked to see you guys and I was embarrassed that Mercy had to see that too."

She glared at him. Her anger turned to her own hurt, and she shoved up to her feet and stormed toward the front door. "Screw you, William!" She cried out in surprise when he grabbed her. "Let me go!"

"I'm sorry!" he exclaimed, trying to pull her into a hug. She pushed against him but he refused to let go. "I'm sorry," he said again as he held her to him. "I didn't mean that the way it came out."

She let him hold her, even if she was still deeply hurt. But, she'd never found anything that hurt more than being at odds with her twin.

"I didn't mean that." His voice was softer and he cradled her head against his chest. "I meant you kissing anyone, not the Helen situation. We weren't there for that...we were all there as friends, and I thought it was crummy. That's what I meant."

Bethany nodded, understanding. "I didn't want to leave the group," she said. "Helen insisted, and I've found with her, it's easier to just do what she wants. Less fighting."

"Why are you with her, then?" he asked gently.

She snorted. "A question I ask myself often." She pulled away and looked up at him. "I guess maybe I'm just worried I won't find another girl like me."

"Aw, sis," he said, giving her a loving smile. "There's more out there. There's gotta be. I mean, Gran and Grandma found each other. And, I know there's been others here too." He squeezed her arm. "Helen is..." He shrugged, dropping his hands away from her. "She's a difficult person just to hang out with. Can't even imagine trying to..." His eyebrows fell. "Have you..."

"None of your business," she said, pushing him away from her playfully, but her tone was firm.

"Sorry, sorry." He rolled his eyes.

Growing serious, Bethany asked, "Was Mercy upset?" She swallowed. "Disgusted?"

He shrugged. "I don't think so. I mean, she stopped me from running after you guys."

Eyes widening, she said, "Really?"

"Yeah. She was forceful. Told me to leave you guys alone." He rubbed the back of his neck. "Once we got back to the shore, I don't recall her really saying another word."

Bethany sighed. "Darn. Okay. I need to apologize

to her." She met his gaze again. "And to you. I'm sorry I didn't tell you, Billy." Their grandmother was right. "I should have trusted you."

He gave her a winning smile and a light punch to the arm. "We're good." He raised his eyebrows and pointed a finger at her. "Don't do it again." They shared a smile.

Chapter Six

It was Tuesday, no different from any other Tuesday. Billy had football practice, so the two rode together in the truck. After classes, Bethany would leave him at the school to go to work, then swing back by and pick him up once she got off, which coincided with him finishing on the field within a half hour or so.

Ned owned his own car, but the other three cars were swapped amongst the twins and their parents. With two very active and working teenagers, Henry and Rachel had decided to hold on to their two older cars—the Chevy pickup and old Buick—as well as their newer car, so everyone could get where they needed to go.

The Wynter's had wanted their children to form a confidence to be independent and make those sorts of decisions to learn, grow, and mature. When Billy was in football or basketball season, things got a bit tighter with schedules.

As they had the day before, the twins had stopped by Helen's house to pick her up for school, as Bethany did every day. And, as like the day before, she'd gotten a ride elsewhere. She'd been surprised the day before, but she knew at times Helen went in early for choir. But, two days in a row…something was off.

Billy said nothing as Bethany got back in the car after leaving Helen's front door and the news from her mother. They shared a quick glance and Bethany got the truck going again, headed on to school. "Well," she muttered. "Guess you won't need to climb in back."

Someone else she hadn't seen since Saturday was Mercy. She wanted to talk to her, to apologize to her, but had yet to see her. The day before, when the group had arrived at their table in the cafeteria, only Pops had been sitting there, meticulously emptying his lunch pail.

Arriving at the single-story brick building, the siblings got out of the parked Chevy and headed inside. "I may be able to get a ride with Gary after practice," Billy said. He met Bethany's gaze before they went their separate ways to their respective lockers. "I'll let you know before the end of the day."

"Sounds good. See you at lunch," she said, hugging her books to her as she walked down the busy hallway, barely missing being binged in the head by a flying paper airplane that somebody had let loose.

Reaching her locker, she glanced to her left, Helen's locker only four away. Sure enough, the other teen was there, but she wasn't alone. Quarterback and track star Phillip Wells was also there. He was leaning casually against the bank of lockers, his back to her though his name was splayed across her letterman jacket plain as day.

Helen was facing him, looking up at him as they chatted. Bethany could see her face over his shoulder, the tall, good-looking senior's bulk hiding the rest of her body. She could tell by Helen's expression and the way she was flashing those eyes at him that she was in flirt mode. Bethany was quite familiar with how Helen worked to reel in her prey.

Helen caught Bethany's gaze over the young

man's shoulder and held it, daring in those eyes for Bethany to say or do anything or even to look away. Choosing the third option, Bethany got the items from her locker for her first class then slammed the metal door closed and walked away.

⁂

The first half of the day had gone quickly, Bethany working hard on her academics to keep her perfect grade point average. Finally, the bell rang for the last class before lunch and she gathered her books, notebook, and pencil to hurry back to her locker to dump everything off and grab her lunch to head to the cafeteria.

She headed to their table, Pops there, of course, and some of Billy's friends. Her brother hadn't shown up yet, and again, no Mercy. She dropped her lunch pail on the table before taking a seat on the bench seating. "Hey," she said.

Pops glanced up from under the brim of his flat cap. "Good afternoon." He carefully staged the pickle he'd removed from a container atop the lid of the now empty and closed container. "I see Helen has found new friend stock."

Bethany glanced over her shoulder to follow Pops's nod. Sure enough, at the table with Philip and the rest of the sports group, sat Helen, nearly thigh to thigh with the varsity athlete from that morning. Sometimes Billy joined that table, but despite the fact that he was a talented athlete himself, he didn't like the culture of those who played.

Shaking her head, Bethany turned back to her lunch. "Have you seen Mercy?" she asked, needing to redirect her focus or get angry about Helen's behavior. Despite the fact that she felt things had been fine by time she'd dropped Helen off Saturday night, clearly that must not have been the case.

"I have not," Pops said. "I was going to ask you that, honestly. She wasn't at work last night, either."

Bethany met and held his gaze, clear concern within the brown depths. "And she normally works Mondays?"

He smirked, taking his sandwich in both hands, preparing to take a bite. "If she's not at school, she's at work."

"I see," Bethany muttered, looking down at her food, which didn't seem as appetizing anymore.

"Word has it," he continued. "The mother doesn't even let her keep any of her earnings."

Bethany felt her concern begin to rise. Yes, she knew Wanda was a single mother trying to survive. Her own few interactions with the woman had shown her to be a very serious person who often held a sour expression upon what would ordinarily be a lovely face. Her eyes were hard and looked down on whomever stood before her with suspicion or disdain.

For the time being, she'd finish her school day then head into work. Perhaps while in such close proximity to where Wanda and Mercy lived and worked, she could make sure everything was okay.

⁂

Taking in her reflection in the mirror above the sink, Bethany straightened the bow tie a bit, part of her uniform for the soda shop. She stowed the clothing she'd worn that day to school into the knapsack that had held her work uniform, then unlocked the restroom door and pulled it open.

She hurried through the shop to the door and the cold day beyond. October was nearly upon them and was certainly making its icy presence known. She trotted across the street to her truck parked in the parking lot and tossed her bag inside before heading back to the building for her shift.

Before she reached the door, she saw Wanda heading from the hotel to the side door in the building of the soda shop, which led to the apartments above. "Mrs. Faulkner!"

The older woman stopped, her hand on the door as she turned toward Bethany's voice. She waited for her. "Yes, Miss Wynter?" she said once Bethany reached her.

"Hello. I'm sorry to bother you," Bethany said, slightly out of breath from running once she saw Wanda. "I was just wondering if Mercy is okay. We hadn't seen her at school or at work, so…"

Wanda's hard gaze bored into Bethany's. Thin lips pursed into a bloodless line. "Perhaps if you'd been a bit more concerned for my daughter's safety and wellbeing on Saturday rather than leaving her to the mercy of the boys, we wouldn't be having this conversation and my daughter wouldn't have had to undergo punishment for disobeying me."

"Oh, no, Mrs. Faulkner," Bethany insisted. "She didn't disobey you. Helen and I were there the entire time. We had to leave for a few—"

"I saw you in the soda shop!" Wanda pointed past Bethany to the front window of the shop in question. "Perhaps your own parents should practice a bit of restraint in the freedoms of you and your brother. May better make for honest children." With that, she entered through the door and was gone, heading upstairs.

Bethany could only stand there and stare. "Wow," she whispered. Turning away from the closed door, she looked around, almost for inspiration of what to even think. One thing she did know was that her concern for the young woman who had come into their circle had grown substantially.

Shaking it off, as she had to get to work, she walked back into the building where she'd spend the next four hours, until closing. The after-school explosion would begin soon, so she had little time to get clocked in and her head in the game before they were swamped.

"Hey, kid," Henry said from the office where he sat behind the desk.

Bethany glanced over at him from the timeclock, which was stationed right outside the office. The hallway where she stood led to the back door and alley beyond where trash was dumped in the cans at shift's end. The employee bathroom was also there. "Hey, Dad," she said, punctuated with the loud *thwack* of her timecard being punched in the machine.

"You okay?" he asked, turning the wood chair on wheels to face her. "You look upset."

She replaced her card in the metal slot with her name written on it before she headed into the office. She plopped down into the chair across from him, shoulders slumped and hands dangling between her slightly spread knees.

Blowing out a breath, she met his gaze, not entirely sure what to say. After all, Wanda worked for him and Gran. She didn't want to cause problems or rock a boat that was pretty much none of her business. Finally, she said, "I just feel bad. I inadvertently got Mercy in trouble on Saturday."

"What did you do?" he asked, pen still poised over the page his hand rested upon.

Bethany looked down at her hands. "Um," she muttered, uncharacteristically shy. "Helen and I had a little…" She tried to think of how to put it without telling the whole story. "A little argument," she said, not entirely untrue. "And we left. I was intending to take her home and go back to The Hole with everyone, but Helen insisted on coming here to talk."

"Okay," Henry said, sounding as if he weren't entirely sure what the issue was.

"That left Mercy alone with Billy and the guys," she explained, looking up at him. "Which, you know and I know isn't a big deal. Billy would never let anything happen to her or anyone else. But Mrs. Faulkner only let her go with us if other girls were there too."

"Uh-oh," he said, as if understanding where she was going with her tale.

She nodded. "Yup. I just ran into Mrs. Faulkner outside and she's really angry. I don't know why, Dad," she said, sitting back in the creaky chair. She threw her hands up in exasperation and let them flop down to her lap. "Mercy was fine."

"Well, honey," he said, his tone conciliatory. "I get what you're saying, but she just lost her husband. Mercy is all she has now. My guess is, maybe it's made her a little more…" He looked as though he were searching for the word.

"Mean?" she muttered.

"Bethany," he admonished. "You won't understand until you're a parent. Do I agree with her anger? Not really. But, can I see where maybe she's coming from? Yeah." He smiled at her and pushed up from his chair. He walked around the desk and left a kiss to the top of her head. "Now, get to work, young lady."

She smiled at his pretend disciplinary tone.

With a grunt, Bethany lifted the last bag of trash into the last of the cans that would be picked up by the garbage men the next morning. She blew out a breath, which came out in a white puff of steam. Looking down first one side of the alley and then the other, she saw there was no one around, save for a cat that skittered out from beneath a parked car. No doubt it was waiting for her to go back inside so it could hunt the mice that sniffed around the garbage.

She turned back to face the back door of the soda shop, now closed, when she noticed the fire escape just to her left. Of course she'd always known it was there, but looking up, she saw there was a light on in the window. She knew the back apartment was one of the only two-bedroom units in the building, and her gut told her it was where Wanda and Mercy lived.

"Hey, you wanna walk out with us?" Mark asked, peeking his head out from the back door.

She met his gaze. "Nah. Got a few things to do before I head out. Have a good night, Mark."

"You too." He disappeared, the door closing behind him.

Left alone, she looked up again before walking over to the metal stairs. She placed her hand on the railing, chewing on her bottom lip for a moment before she made the decision to go up. She tried to be as quiet as possible, not sure what she'd see once she reached that window. For all she knew, Wanda would be sprawled out reading a book.

She reached the small landing that was just wide enough for her to sidestep around to the second set of stairs that weren't much more than a ladder. As she got closer, she was able to see into the small bedroom. The light was coming from a lamp on a bedside table, which illuminated a narrow bed against the wall, the headboard against the wall next to the window. There was a dresser, and that was about it.

Curled up on the bed was Mercy, a book in her hands. Bethany couldn't see a lot of her, mostly her raised nightgown-covered thighs and knees, bare feet poking out. She could see the open page of the book and just a bit of the side of Mercy's face.

Relieved, both that it wasn't Wanda's room and also to see that Mercy was okay, she considered what to do for a moment. Mercy didn't seem to know she was there, so she could easily backtrack, when suddenly Mercy turned and looked over her shoulder right at her.

Bethany gasped, falling back in shock at the ugly black coloring that surrounded her left eye and nasty bruise and cut on her lip. She was grateful for the railing, or she would have fallen backward off the stairs.

Mercy set her book aside and uncurled herself before she turned to the window and unlatched it, lifting it. "What are you doing?" she whispered.

"I'm sorry," Bethany whispered back, moving back to the window. "I wanted to make sure you were okay. After everything on Saturday, nobody had seen you in three days."

Mercy backed up from the widow, indicating that Bethany should climb inside. "She'll hear you out there."

As quietly as she could, Bethany climbed in through the window, grateful for the warmth inside as Mercy slowly pushed the window down to the sill. The two faced each other and again, Bethany was horrified by what she saw.

"My god," she whispered, emotion constricting the back of her throat as she stared at the horrible bruising upon the beautiful face. "Did she do that?" Mercy said nothing, simply looked down. "I'm so sorry. I'm so, so sorry." The tears were instant, burning hot as they trailed down her cheeks.

Mercy lightly touched her arm, so much caring in her beautiful brown eyes. "No." She shook her head. "It's not your fault." She looked like she wanted to hug Bethany, but just didn't seem to know how.

Bethany did it for her. She gathered the younger woman into her arms, feeling absolutely responsible for the injuries Mercy had taken, responsible for whatever the teen had undergone over the past three days. Based on the amount of anger that Wanda Faulkner still held in their brief meeting earlier, what on earth had it been like Saturday?

She held Mercy against her, so warm, yet she seemed so very fragile. She almost felt as though she were holding somebody made of glass or delicate china. As she held her, her tears still coming, though as silently as she could, she felt the smaller body trembling, almost as if she, too, were crying.

This immediately caused her to push her own upset aside, an intense need to protect Mercy coming over her. She held her, stroking her long, auburn hair, so soft. Finally, Mercy's body stilled and she began to pull away, so Bethany released her.

Looking into her face, Bethany used gentle fingers to brush long strands of Mercy's hair that had gotten stuck in tear streaks. "I am so sorry about Saturday," she said, just loud enough for the tiny bubble of space surrounding them. "All of it. Helen, us leaving, what you saw." She shook her head, feeling shame once again. "There's no excuse for any of it." She felt her tears threatening again. "I told you I'd keep you with us when you told me about your mom's issues. I failed you."

"No," Mercy said, shaking her head. "You had every right to have fun, Bethany. It wasn't right of me to put you in the position of babysitting."

Bethany gave her a sweet smile, using her thumbs to gently wipe away more tears about to roll down Mercy's cheeks. "You didn't. I offered." She dropped her hands away from Mercy's face, not wanting to chance hitting the horrible bruising with any more touches. "Are you okay?"

Mercy nodded with a shrug as she hugged herself. "I guess. I miss school." She gave her a sad smile.

"When is she going to let you go back?"

"Not until this is gone," Mercy said, indicating her bruised eye and lip.

Horrified, Bethany stared at her. "That will be like a week!"

Mercy nodded. "I know." She looked down, shame on her face.

"Tell you what," Bethany said, brightening her tone. "I'll grab your schoolwork for you, okay? Drop it off," she added, indicating the window. "Then I can pick it up in the morning if you want."

Mercy's head shot up, a bit of hope in her eyes. "You'd do that?"

"Of course." Bethany gave her a lopsided grin. "And," she added, growing a bit more serious. "From here on out, you're with me. Got it? Not letting you out of my damn sight."

Mercy gave her a shy smile. "Now you are trying to babysit."

"No, I just want you to be able to have a normal life, friends, fun." She used two fingers to lift Mercy's chin, which had fallen again. "Okay?" When she got a small nod, she smiled. "Okay. I better go before I get you into trouble again." She moved back to the window, easing the window up, stopping to listen, making sure there was no movement either outside or in the apartment beyond the closed door. All clear, she slowly climbed back out into the cold night.

"Bethany?" Mercy said, stepping up to the open window.

"Yeah?"

Mercy chewed her bottom lip for a moment before meeting Bethany's eyes. "Thanks."

Bethany gave her a winning smile before she began to make her way down the stairs, the quiet slide of the window and quiet thud of it making contact with the sill meeting her ears.

Chapter Seven

"Thank you, Mrs. Moses," Bethany said, flashing a bright smile. "I'll absolutely make sure she gets these."

"Thank you, Bethany," the older teacher said. "It's very kind of you to gather her assignments for her. Do tell her I hope she feels better soon."

"Yes, ma'am, I will." Bethany tucked the pages she'd been given into her bag before shouldering it and heading back out into the swarming main hallway of the school where Billy waited for her. He shoved off the locker he'd been leaning against and the two made their way toward the double doors to go outside.

"I'm going with you," he said stubbornly.

She sighed. "No, you're not. We talked about this."

"Yes, and you've still not given me a reason why. She's my friend too."

"I know she is, Billy," she said, passing through the door he held open for her before he followed. "But," she continued, glancing over at him. "Despite everything, I know that her mother needs her job. I need my job," she said, placing a hand over her own chest. "You need your job, and our family doesn't need a murder conviction."

"Murder conviction? Wait." He stopped their progress with a hand to her arm. "Is she hurt? I thought she was sick."

"I never said that." Bethany opened the driver's door of her truck and tossed her bag inside before climbing in after as Billy did on the passenger side. No practice today, she had time to drop him off at home and change for work before heading to the soda shop. No, she'd never said that to him, but had essentially left it vague.

He studied her as she got them moving. "So, she's not sick?" Bethany said nothing. "Is she hurt, Bethy?"

She cleared her throat and said, "Her mother was rather upset Saturday." She met his gaze, hoping that simple statement would give him enough to drop it.

He looked away, jaw muscle clenching and unclenching. "Is she okay?"

"She'll be fine. She'll probably be back in school Monday—"

"I'll tear that woman a—"

"You'll do no such thing!" She glared at him. "She needs us, Billy. I promised her that she was with us and that we'd support her." She turned her focus back to the street. "Got a strong feeling that we've got to play our cards right with her mother or we'll never see her."

❧❧❧❧❧

Night had fallen and her shift was once again over. Armed with Mercy's makeup assignments, Bethany once again climbed the metal staircase. This time, however, she knew that Wanda was next door working a night shift in the hotel restaurant. She still stayed quiet, as she didn't want to alert any of the other apartment residents, but wasn't as concerned as the night before.

Reaching the small railed-in platform at the top, she peeked into the window. As she'd been the night before, Mercy was reading on the bed. She tapped lightly on the window, getting the other young woman's attention. Mercy's smile was instant as she tossed her book aside and climbed off the bed.

"Hi," she said after pushing the window up enough for Bethany to climb under. "She's at work."

"Yeah," Bethany said, shivering as the warm air from the bedroom hit her frozen body. The nights were definitely getting colder and the smell of snow hovered on the air. "How are you doing?" she asked. She studied Mercy's face, noting that the bruising was basically what it had been the previous night, but at least there was nothing new.

"I'm okay," Mercy said absently, studying Bethany's shivering form. "My goodness! Where's your jacket? You're shivering."

Bethany nodded. "It's really cold out there and I had to clean up dumped trash cans that raccoons got into." She gave her a sheepish grin. "And, my jacket is in my truck."

Mercy raised her eyebrows. "Good place for it." She took the pages from Bethany's trembling hands and placed them on the dresser top. "Thank you," she said. "I truly appreciate this." She lightly took Bethany's arm and tugged her toward the bed. "I don't have an extra blanket, so we'll do this." She pulled her quilt back to reveal a blanket and sheet. "Sit." She patted the still-made bed.

Bethany did as told, her booted feet still on the floor. Mercy reached around her and pulled the quilt back up and around her shoulders, the heavy material draping over her front. She nearly moaned in pleasure as she pulled the quilt around her. Its warmth quickly began to seep into her bones. "Thanks."

"Of course." Mercy grabbed the pages from the dresser and sat next to Bethany, careful not to tug the quilt off her shoulders. "This is just for today?" she asked, looking through the small stack.

"No," Bethany said, finally beginning to warm up. "After I explained that you'd be out the rest of the week, they all gave me your assignments that you've already missed and what you'll miss. You can give it to me Thursday night and I can turn it in for you Friday, if you want. No late grades that way."

Mercy nodded. "I can do that." She gave Bethany a shy smile. "That gives me tonight and all of tomorrow." She nodded. "Yeah, I can do that," she said again.

"Are you okay, Mercy?" Bethany asked again, her tone serious. "Do you need anything?" She looked around the small room. "Are you allowed to leave this room?"

Mercy followed her gaze around the space and nodded. "I am, and do a little when she's gone. But..." She shrugged as she looked back to Bethany. "Mostly I've just stayed in here."

"How long will she be working?" Bethany asked, an idea sparking.

Mercy shrugged. "Another couple hours, at least. She's working tonight because they have some folks coming in late and they requested dinner service with their room rental. I think it's a pretty pricey group, so your grandfather okayed it."

"Sooooo, you like ice cream?"

Mercy looked at her, eyebrows drawing in confusion. "Yes, of course. Why?"

❧❧❧❧

Bethany was thoroughly amused at the wide-eyed look on her companion as she turned on the light in the kitchen. She didn't dare turn on any lights in the storefront, as they didn't need any unwanted attention, particularly from Wanda Faulkner.

"Have a seat," Bethany said, patting one of the stools at a work surface that was often used to cut up fruit and nuts and such to put in sweet treats.

She walked over to the walk-in, where all the vats of ice cream were stowed overnight and while the shop was closed. She pulled out two basic flavors, vanilla and chocolate, and carried them to the working space. She smiled at Mercy's widening eyes. "I'm going to make you the best sundae you've ever had," she said. She grabbed containers of this, that, and the other thing, popping the lids open to even bigger eyes from her companion. She smiled, absolutely loving the excited look on Mercy's face. She hadn't seen that light in her eyes since their fun at The Hole Saturday, before Helen had started her nonsense.

She was surprised Mercy hadn't asked her about that, but then again, her quiet friend seemed to keep a lot inside. She wondered if she'd ever ask about it, or perhaps she just didn't care.

"Can I ask you a question?" Mercy said, watching with interest as Bethany worked.

"Of course. Cherries?"

"Please." Mercy was quiet for a moment before she said, "Why are you being so nice to me?" She met

Bethany's gaze. "You don't really even know me."

"No," Bethany said with a shrug. "Fudge?" At Mercy's nod, she explained. "My Grandpa Jeramiah founded this town, which you probably know. But see, he grew up in a super religious family back in Indiana, white Christians who thought white Christians ruled the town, state, country, and I'm sure, world."

Mercy nodded, grabbing a halved peanut that got away from Bethany and popped it into her mouth. "I know the type."

"Exactly, so he didn't agree with that. He used to call it 'preaching hate.' So, as a young man, he set out west. Ended up in the region and struck it big in the mines." She shrugged again. "Decided if this was going to be *his* town, he was going to do it *his* way."

"What was his way?"

"His way was including everyone. He didn't care what color you were, what god you worshipped, or even gender." She gave her a winning smile, proud of all her grandfather had been. "As long as you were a good person, who worked hard, he'd find a place for you in Wynter."

She studied her friend sitting across the prep space from her for a moment, trying to decide if she should divulge just *how* inclusive her grandfather had been. Mercy Faulkner was clearly a quiet, soft-spoken young woman, seemed to keep her thoughts to herself, and Bethany couldn't even imagine her judging a fly. Even so, though an open secret in town, it was Justice's secret to tell—not hers.

"So," Mercy said, breaking into Bethany's train of thought. "All of you were instilled with that same kindness and compassion?"

Deciding it wasn't the right time, Bethany nodded. "Exactly." She wiped her hands on a towel before walking over to the containers filled with clean spoons, forks, and knives. She grabbed one of the long-handled spoons and walked back to the sundae that looked gorgeous in its crystal goblet-type bowl. She eased the spoon into her creation and slid it over to Mercy with a smile. "Here you go, madam."

Mercy wrapped her fingers beneath the bowl part, the short stem between her fingers. She turned it this way and that. "Oh my," she murmured, shaking her head. "There is no way I'll be able to eat this whole thing." She chuckled. "You have to help me with this."

Bethany reached over and plucked one of the cherries from the top. She popped it into her mouth, teeth crushing the skin of the red fruit as juice squirted into her mouth. "Helped," she mumbled around the fruit.

Mercy laughed. "Not hardly!"

Amused, Bethany grabbed a second spoon and began to dig in with her companion. "But," she said, her thoughts returning to their conversation. "With all that I said, I don't want you to think that Grandpa Jeramiah taught us charity toward others. He didn't see it that way." She shrugged. "It was just about being a good person."

Mercy nodded, her jaw moving as she rolled around the bite of ice cream, fudge, and halved peanuts she'd just put into her mouth. After a moment, she swallowed and said, "My dad was like that. You would have loved him."

It hurt Bethany's heart to see the profound sadness return to those brown eyes. "What was his name? And, what happened?"

"His name was Arthur, but most called him

Art. Um, he worked at the steel mill in Pueblo. A chain snapped and a load from a crane fell on him." She stared down at the sundae for a long moment, her entire demeanor changing.

"I'm so sorry, Mercy," Bethany said. "I'm sorry I brought it up."

"No, it's okay." Taking a deep, shaky breath, the seated girl looked up at her. "I don't really get to talk about him, so it's kind of nice."

Eyebrows drawing, Bethany said, "Your mother doesn't talk about him with you?"

Mercy shook her head, taking in another bite of the cold treat. "Can I be honest?"

"Of course you can."

"Obviously she had nothing to do with his death. It was a horrible accident. But I don't think she's very sad that he's gone." She tapped her spoon lightly against the glass lip of the bowl before adding. "I honestly have no idea why they got married, how they met, any of that, but I think my mother is the type who should have gone into a convent or something. Focused on a singular thing, no men or children, any of those things that she just doesn't seem to want any part of."

Bethany was quiet for a moment as she ate more of her creation, trying to decide what she wanted to say. A lot of things were filtering through her mind, including the fact that she wanted to beat the crap out of Wanda Faulkner.

"Has she always been violent?" she finally asked.

"No," Mercy said. "Honestly, she's never hit me before." She stared down into the remains of their dessert. "I'm not sure what's going on with her. Stress, maybe. I just don't know."

Bethany nodded. After a moment of contemplative silence between them, she met Mercy's gaze. "Well, we'd probably better get this cleaned up and you back to your cell." They shared a smile.

❧❧❧❧

Autumn was in full swing and gearing up for winter. The town certainly lived up to its name at times. Thanksgiving was over and now they were trucking on toward Christmas. It was the first week of December and it was a cold one. With nearly a foot of snow on the ground, driving was a slow and cautious venture.

Bethany was gathering her books and jacket when somebody walked up to her. She was stunned to see that it was Helen. Looking quite sheepish, the blonde met her gaze but said nothing. "What?"

"Uh," Helen finally murmured, eyeing the kids passing them before looking back to Bethany. "Can I come over tonight? I need to talk to you."

Bethany stared at her. "About what?" She shrugged into her coat and shouldered her loaded bag before slamming her locker door. "We haven't spoken in more than two months, Helen. I don't have much to say."

"I know," Helen said, looking sheepish. "And we can talk about that too. But I really, really need to talk to you." Her face brightened. "Maybe I could get a ride home? We could talk on the way if tonight won't work for you."

"No room in the truck. I'll be home after seven." With that, Bethany turned and walked away to find Mercy to give her a ride home.

Later that night, Bethany felt extremely defensive standing in her own bedroom. Right at the appointed time, Helen had shown up. She sat on Bethany's bed, the very place where they'd lost their virginity together. That seemed like a lifetime ago now, as Bethany leaned against the wall with her arms crossed over her chest.

"So," she said. "What's this all about?"

Helen looked down at her lap, where her hands fidgeted with her purse. She took a deep breath, then looked up at Bethany. "I'm pregnant."

Bethany snorted. "I'm good honey, but I'm not that good."

"I'm serious, Bethany!"

"Me too." Truth was, Bethany felt absolutely nauseous. She knew it. Helen had freaked out and, rather than just talking to her like a rational adult instead of all her demands over malts, she'd turned to Phillip. They'd been nearly inseparable, up until a couple weeks ago. She squeezed her eyes shut for a moment to try and ground herself, then said, "Why are you telling me this? Shouldn't you be telling Phillip?" She quirked an eyebrow. "I assume it's his."

Helen nodded. "It is. And what am I supposed to say? 'Gee, Phil, I really messed up and left the woman I love but guess what? We're having a baby!'"

Bethany heard that word—love—but didn't react to it. She absolutely knew Helen didn't love her. She wasn't entirely sure the extremely selfish young woman was capable of it. "Yes," she agreed. "It's his kid. Why are you here telling me?"

"Because I need your help, Beth." Helen looked over at her before she pushed up from the bed, setting her purse where she'd just been sitting. She walked over to Bethany, as beautiful as ever, as dangerous as ever. "Please help me."

"Do what?"

Helen, standing less than a foot away, stared at her like she'd lost her mind. "Get rid of it!"

Bethany gasped at her. "Just what exactly do you expect me to do, Helen? I'm not a doctor. I'm not a magician. I can't just snap my fingers," she said, doing just that, "and make it all better."

"No," Helen conceded, taking a small step closer and into Bethany's personal space. "But you can go with me. I've been asking around and know of somebody. I can easily get the money," she said, her parents some of the wealthier in town and blindly generous with their three children. She placed her hands on Bethany's hips. "Please, baby," she murmured. "I only trust you with this."

Bethany looked into blue eyes, feeling rather disgusted at their proximity and Helen's touch. She knew that if Helen had this child, Helen had not one clue or tool to be a mother. No doubt that child would suffer greatly or, as had been rumored about her father's business dealing clear back in Prohibition, end up in the flow of the black market.

She swallowed, disbelieving what she was about to say. "I'll help you," she said quietly. "But I am no longer your 'baby.'" She gently pushed Helen from her. "Don't touch me again."

Chapter Eight

Mercy had been very surprised when Bethany had asked her to not only accompany her and Helen for something that needed to be done in the nearby town of Tunston, but also if she could spend the whole weekend, this first of December, with them both.

She'd had no clue what the plan was, but had cleared it with her mother, assuring her that she'd get a ride to the hotel for her shift. Bethany had said she'd needed her to do this for her, so without question, she'd done it. There wasn't anything she wouldn't do for her. After the situation a couple months before, with Bethany's unending kindness and compassion, Mercy had found herself drawn to the older teen.

She couldn't quite put her finger on it, on what she felt. Certainly, Bethany was very beautiful, and more than once Mercy had found herself having to look away from her eyes for fear of getting lost in them, even if she didn't fully understand what that meant. Surely, as had been with other peers and women she'd seen over the years that caught her attention for this or that, she simply admired Bethany, wanted to be more like her. Surely.

No matter what she'd been thinking, nothing could have prepared her for why she'd actually been needed this morning. Bethany had arrived right on time, at nine in the morning, driving the old Buick that Billy usually drove. Sitting in the passenger seat was a quiet and somewhat somber Helen. Mercy had climbed into the back and was given a quiet greeting and smile by the driver before they were on their way.

They'd taken the hour drive to Tunston, which was roughly the same size as Wynter, though it had a hospital and some other businesses—legitimate and not as legitimate—that their town did not. Wynter had a medical facility and a local doctor, but if surgery was required or any sort of substantial injury, patients were taken to Tunston.

They, however, were not going to a hospital. They arrived at a small house on the outskirts of town and were met by a short woman of an advanced age who was nearly as round as she was tall. She'd ordered the three young women inside, the house cluttered but not exactly dirty. Helen had pulled out some folded bills, handing them to the woman who then took Helen by the arm and led her into another room of the house, closing the door behind them.

Mercy and Bethany were left sitting alone in the living room where the old woman had pointed for them to stay. Confused and antsy, she'd become downright worried when she looked over at Bethany to see her knee bobbing and fingers tapping on her thighs. She'd said nothing, simply waited for what was next.

What was next was where they were currently. After an hour at the small house, Mercy was cradling a crying and groaning Helen in the back seat while Bethany drove. They were headed back to Wynter and, apparently, a little empty farmhouse on the Kilkoyne property. There, they'd spend the day and night with Helen and make sure she survived this.

"It hurts," Helen whimpered.

"I know," Mercy said, holding the reclining woman's upper body in her lap. "We'll be home soon." She brushed sweaty blond hair out of her lovely face. Her heart softened at the look of pain and fear in that face. Now understanding what had happened, she knew that the past didn't matter right now. They had to make sure she didn't end up with a horrible infection that could easily take her life, let alone the bleeding that they'd been warned about.

"Is she okay?" Bethany asked, glancing back at the reflected back seat in the rearview mirror.

Mercy met her gaze in the mirror. "She's in a lot of pain, but I think she's okay."

They pulled up to a small two-story house surrounded mostly by farmland. There was a larger farmhouse half a mile away, which Bethany explained was where her grandparents lived. The smaller house needed some work, a coat of paint, and what looked as though may have been a front yard at one point had pretty much gone to seed. She could easily imagine a nice, expansive front yard, with the wash hung out to dry on the existing clothesline.

"Do they know we're here?" Mercy asked as she gently nudged Helen to a sitting position. "We're here," she said to her.

"They do," Bethany affirmed. "They just don't know why." She met Mercy's gaze as she opened the driver's side back door. "I hate lying to them, but..."

Mercy nodded, understanding. She'd had to lie to her own mother, so she understood they were all out on a limb with this one. "Okay, let's get her inside."

Neither strong enough to carry Helen, they'd

done what they'd done in Tunston. Each of them had taken a side, one of her arms flung over their shoulders, and had made slow but steady progress. Once inside, given the option to go upstairs or stay downstairs on the couch with a hearty fire in the fireplace—which would be built once she was settled—Helen had chosen the couch.

"Do you know how to build a fire?" Bethany asked.

Mercy slowly shook her head. "My father always took care of that, and we don't have a fireplace at the apartment."

"Okay, no worries. Why don't you grab the bags from the car and get the tea started that Mildred gave us for Helen, and I'll get started on the fire," she said, indicating the cut logs stacked in the wood holder near the hearth.

Mercy nodded. "Got it."

Within an hour, the house was warm and cozy and Helen was tucked in on the couch with a warm crocheted blanket covering her. She reclined against a pillow and the arm of the couch, her hot herbal tea mug held in her hand. She was pale and still a bit weepy. She seemed to be doing better than she had initially, but she was still emotional from time to time.

Mercy sat in a rocking chair, slowly rocking to and fro as she stared into the flames. It was relaxing, the flickering heat helping to clear her mind. Bethany had gone back into town to pick up a few groceries for their meals.

"You think I'm a monster, don't you?"

Mercy glanced over at the couch to see Helen looking at her. "No," she said, shaking her head. "I don't. I'm not you, Helen, and don't know what your circumstances were to make you feel this was the right decision for you, but it was yours to make." She shrugged. "I just hope you don't regret it someday. I imagine that would be a horrible burden to have to bear."

Helen said nothing in response for a moment as she took a sip from her hot tea. "Did you know that Bethany and I were a couple?" she asked at length. "Before that day in the woods."

Mercy shook her head. "No. I had no idea. Clearly, the two of you were close friends, but honestly," she added with a sheepish grin. "I didn't know two girls could kiss."

Helen smirked. "Oh, we did far more than just kiss." She looked into the fire, her smirk morphing into a sexy little smile. "We used to hurry home from school before she had to go to work, barely getting her bedroom door closed before we were naked and panting."

Mercy felt her chest tighten at the words, though she honestly wasn't sure why. She felt a bit disgusted at the imagery it brought to mind, though that had most to do with the woman who said them. Again, she had no idea why.

Helen snorted again, but this time with derision. "Should have stuck to that," she murmured, looking down into her cup. "She's amazing in bed and I wouldn't have had to deal with this nonsense." She indicated the cup, herself, and the house around them. She glanced over at Mercy. "Don't have sex with a man unless you're really sure, Mercy," she said, voice hard. "Trust me, they'll say anything to get you in that position. When they're done with you, they'll say anything to get themselves *out* of that position."

Mercy had no idea what to say. She was surprised by the candor and by the bitterness she heard in Helen's voice.

Helen looked back to the flames. "Had more pleasure in five minutes with Bethany than in a whole month with Phillip," she muttered.

Absolutely no clue what to say, Mercy turned back to the flames. She was insanely relieved when she heard Bethany's car pull up to the house. However, she knew the heat in her cheeks wasn't just from the fire.

⁂

After eating a little something, Helen had decided she wanted to sleep, so Bethany and Mercy had opted to go for a walk so the house would be quiet for the recovering woman. It was cold, but the sun was out, making the afternoon near blinding as it shone down on the pristine layer of snow that blanketed the land.

"Can I ask you something?" Mercy asked as they strolled.

"Sure."

"When you were gone, Helen spoke to me a bit." Mercy snuck a look at her companion. "You two are no longer together?"

"No," Bethany said, her tone guarded.

"If you don't want to talk—"

"No, no it's okay." Bethany smiled at her. "Sorry. Just not really used to talking about this." She took a deep breath, which was released in a white plume of steam. "It wasn't a breakup, per se," she said. "The week after we all went to The Hole, she just made it very clear that she'd moved on." She smirked. "To Phillip the football player."

Mercy nodded, absorbing what she'd been told. "So, you guys were like a couple. Like, girlfriend-boyfriend, couple?" At Bethany's nod, she again grew quiet, considering. "Well, then I'm sorry all this happened, Bethany. I mean, I'm guessing it was because Billy and I saw you guys. I'm just…I'm really sorry. I should have minded my own business."

"Please don't take responsibility for something that you had nothing to do with, Mercy," Bethany said gently. "Helen was a bomb waiting to go off. Honestly, I'd been unhappy for a long, long time."

"Why did you stay?"

Bethany shrugged. "Guess I worried I'd never find another woman."

"Who was attracted to other women?"

"Yeah. I mean, I know they're out there, but in this small town." She gave Mercy a sad smile. "You know?" Bethany chewed on her bottom lip for a moment then met her gaze. "I'm going to tell you something, but you can't say anything, okay? I mean," she amended. "Lots of people here know, especially the old-timers, but certain people, just not a good idea."

"Okay," Mercy said. "I won't say a word."

"My grandparents, Justice and Thea, they're like me. Or," she added with a lopsided grin. "Guess I should say I'm like them."

Mercy's eyebrows fell in confusion. "What do you mean?"

"Justice is a woman, Mercy."

Stunned, Mercy looked over at her with huge eyes. "What?"

Bethany nodded, obviously proud to be talking

about someone she loved and admired so much. "Yup. She was never the girly-girl type of person, even as a little girl or teenager. As she put it to me once, 'I'm a Justice.'"

Mercy thought about what she'd just been told, thinking back to that initial time she'd met what amounted to one of her bosses. "You know," she said. "That makes sense. I thought there was something about Justice that seemed…off, I guess. I couldn't put my finger on it." She looked over at Bethany. "Did your grandmother know? When they initially met?"

Bethany nodded. "Yup. I don't know the whole story, I don't think, but she knew from the first time they met." She smiled. "Love at first sight for them both."

"Wow. I think that's amazing." Her eyebrows drew. "Then wait, where did your mom come from?"

"Again, not entirely sure about the whole story, but they were separated for a bit and my grandmother ended up getting married. She doesn't like to talk about it," Bethany added. "I get the picture that it was sort of a situation where she didn't have a choice. You know? Not a lot of options for her."

Mercy nodded. "Sure. Sadly, it happens a lot."

"Yeah, it does. Anyway, he was killed in the mines here, I guess, and Justice and Thea raised my mom together as her parents."

Mercy was astounded, and honestly found the whole thing to be amazing. "So," she asked, her tone brightening a bit as her curiosity grew. "Is that what you want? To find a woman to be with, like them?"

Bethany didn't respond for a moment, but a slow, wistful smile spread across full lips. "Yeah," she finally said. "Not so sure a baby would be in the picture, though I'd love that. But absolutely." She shrugged and let out a contented sigh. "I'd love to find that right girl and just be happy."

Mercy nodded. Somehow, that made sense to her.

❧❧❧❧

"Okay," Bethany said, hands on hips. The fire was built up, the lower level of the house nice and toasty. Helen had been given more of the tea, which made her sleepy. They'd also had dinner. "So, do you need anything else?"

Helen shook her head, eyelids drooping. "No."

"Sleep well, Helen," she said. "Call out if you need us. We'll be just upstairs."

Helen nodded and mumbled something even as her eyes fell closed. Mercy watched this, wondering if maybe one of them should stay downstairs with her, or if Helen should be moved upstairs to the only bed with Bethany. She would happily take the couch. She was about to open her mouth to suggest such a thing when Bethany tugged on the sleeve of her sweater.

"Come on. Let's go to bed."

Mercy took one last look at Helen then followed Bethany through the house, only lit by the flames in the secured fireplace. The higher they climbed, the cooler it got. The house currently had no other working heat, as there were no tenants. She'd noted the thick quilt on the full bed when she'd dropped off her overnight bag earlier. And, with the two young women sharing a bed, they'd probably stay warm enough throughout the night.

"Which side do you want?" Bethany asked, nodding at the bed once they reached the bedroom.

"Um, by the door?" Mercy said, meeting Bethany's gaze. She gave her a sheepish smile. "I tend to have to pee at least once, so…"

Bethany chucked. "So advised."

Bethany took the bathroom first, doing her nightly routine and changing into her night clothes while Mercy changed in the small bedroom. This was one of two, but the only one with any furniture in it. It had been explained to her that, though the house wasn't generally rented furnished, when it was vacant as it was now, they kept a few basics on hand in case somebody needed quick access to shelter or for emergencies.

Turns out the planning was fortuitous, as they were now one of those such parties in need of shelter to get Helen through this situation. Once Mercy, too, had finished with her nightly routines in the bathroom and returned to the bedroom, she saw that Bethany was already in the bed with its antique brass headboard and footboard.

She was lying on her side of the bed, hands tucked under the pillow her head rested on. As Mercy entered the bedroom, making sure to leave the door open in case Helen called for them in the night, she spared a glance to her bedmate. Her hair was brushed down and shiny, such a rich dark color, usually put up in some way.

But now, with the darkness of her hair against the paleness of her face and bedding, it was so stark, and the sky-blue eyes popped in a gorgeous, vivid shade. It reminded her of a precious gemstone. Those eyes swung to her as she climbed in beneath the quilt. She noted, with a smile, that her pillow had been fluffed.

Wearing her cotton nightgown, she slid onto the mattress and pulled the covers over her. The bed was small enough that she could feel the heat coming off Bethany's body and her right leg just barely grazed Mercy's left. The simple, innocent, and accidental touch sent little shives through her belly, and she had no idea why. So often around Bethany, she felt things that she just didn't understand. It could be nauseating, dizzying, and certainly unsettling.

"Do you have enough room?" Bethany asked. She turned on her side, facing Mercy. "Should give you a little more."

Mercy looked over at her to see those brilliant blue eyes already on her. "What do you want to do after high school?" she asked. For so many young women, it was a simple answer—get married and have children. Obviously, for Bethany it wasn't that easy.

"I want to go to nursing school," Bethany said. "Get a career, something I can grow with, you know?"

Mercy nodded. "I think that's wonderful." She gave her a shy look. "I feel like such a kid next to you and Billy. You guys seem so far ahead of the game, know what you want, who you are."

Bethany smiled. "Don't sell yourself short, Mercy. I think once you're away from your mother, however that happens, I think you'll blossom." She studied Mercy's eyes. "You'll be what, sixteen this summer?" At Mercy's nod, she said, "But your eyes, they tell a very different story."

"What do you mean?" Mercy asked, a bit nervously.

"They're ancient," Bethany said. "You're an old soul with innate wisdom."

Feeling super shy at such a compliment yet feeling as though she could fly off that bed, she tried to hide her smile. "What am I, Pops, Jr.?"

Bethany grinned, shaking her head. "You're not grumpy enough." Her grin widened into a beautiful smile at Mercy's bark of laughter. "Turn over."

Mercy did, her back to Bethany, who to her surprise spooned up behind her. For a moment, she couldn't breathe, but then as her heart settled to a somewhat normal cadence, her eyes slid closed and she fell into a deep, dreamless sleep.

Chapter Nine

Mercy moved from the back seat to the front seat as Bethany helped Helen walk to the front door of her house. She was walking okay but had asked for a steadying hand. Mercy wondered if perhaps it was simply to get some time alone with Bethany, even if just a few moments. That morning at the farmhouse, when Helen had awoken clearheaded and not drowsy from the tea, she'd seemed less than thrilled that the two had shared a bed the night before.

Clearly their brief moment of solidarity the day before was gone, as Helen eyed Mercy with the same hard, suspicious glances she had since the day she'd spotted the two women kissing in the woods. She didn't understand the seeming dislike or even disdain for her, but Mercy was determined to not let it affect her friendship with Bethany, which seemed to be growing deeper.

She was truly grateful for Bethany and Billy, and even Pops. The friendship of the three kinfolk, and the way that they welcomed her into a tightening, close group of four, meant everything to her. Nobody, certainly not an ungrateful and spiteful young woman like Helen, was going to take that from her.

Mercy had lost enough in her young life, and she wasn't going to lose Bethany and the others. She watched as the two stood at Helen's front door for a moment, seeming to talk. Helen took Bethany in a very long and very tight embrace, a full-body hug, no less.

As so many things did lately, Mercy's feelings about it confused her. She felt…angry. She felt like Helen had no right to do that, no doubt because she now more fully understood the history between her and Bethany. Hadn't Helen lost that right when she'd walked away from Bethany and straight into the arms of Phillip Wells?

Never even being close to dating anyone, let alone being intimate on any level, she had no idea how it all worked and, she reasoned, no right to have an opinion. She forced herself to look away. Bethany had left the car running, as she said she'd be right back, and as it was a bitterly cold late Sunday morning, and she'd left the heater running as well.

Still struggling with thoughts and emotions that she just couldn't name or understand, Mercy decided to turn on the car radio. She needed to be distracted, as her mind wanted to wander into what Helen may be telling Bethany and, maybe worse, how Bethany was responding.

"None of my business," she told herself.

She bobbed her head and tapped her fingers along with a favorite, "Dolores" by Tommy Dorsey and his orchestra. She quietly sang along, feeling herself relax into the music and fun lyrics. She looked out into the day, bright with the snow of two days before. It struck her that the snow had maintained its pristine whiteness, since in Pueblo it would have turned dark with soot from the traffic and belching smoke from the steel mill within hours of falling.

Suddenly, the music stopped and a news broadcaster began to speak:

We interrupt this program to bring you a special news bulletin. The Japanese have attacked Pearl Harbor, Hawaii by air, President Roosevelt has just announced. The attack also was made on all naval and military activities on the principal island of Oahu. We now take you to the White House...

Eyes huge and her hands coming up to cover her mouth, the other man's voice who began speaking drifted off into an echo inside of Mercy's head. Her head snapped to look in the direction of the driver's side when the door opened and Bethany plopped down behind the wheel, a wave of frigid air with her.

"Sorry about that," she said with a heavy sigh, slamming her door closed. "That damn woman just doesn't get it." She glanced over at Mercy. "What's wrong?"

Mercy couldn't speak, tears already welling in her eyes. All she could do was nod toward the radio. Bethany listened and it took a moment for her to understand what had happened as the flower of understanding slowly bloomed across her face.

"Oh my god," she whispered. "Oh my god! Leo!" She got the car moving, flying out of Helen's driveway and onto the street, headed toward her house. Once she screeched into her own driveway, things seemed to hit Bethany hard.

Mercy took the sobbing young woman into her arms, even across the awkward expanse of the front seat. She slid across the slick bench seat to get a better hold as she cradled the sobbing woman against her. She stroked her hair and her back, able to feel the hot tears against her neck.

Something caught her eye and she saw Henry Wynter heading out of the house and to them. His handsome face, usually filled with smiles or mischievous grins, was anything but. Clearly he'd heard the news as well. He looked deadly serious, even somber.

"Your dad's here," Mercy said softly, gently lifting Bethany's head from her shoulder. She smoothed long strands of dark hair away from Bethany's tear-streaked face and tucked them behind an ear.

Bethany nodded, her face red and ruddy from her upset. She looked deeply into Mercy's eyes for a moment, then turned away as her door was pulled open.

"Come on, sweetheart," Henry said, taking his daughter's hand and urging her out of the car. As soon as she was standing, he engulfed her in a big hug. He looked down at Mercy, who still sat in the car. "You're with us too, hon," he said, nodding toward the house.

Mercy nodded and climbed out of the car. She followed father and daughter up the pathway to the front door, which opened as soon as they neared it. Rachel stood there, tears freely streaming down her cheeks. Bethany instantly went into her arms once she reached her. The two women clung to the other, crying together.

"Come on," Henry said, gently maneuvering Mercy around the two with big hands on her shoulders.

The radio that sat on the mantel in the living room was on, a fire popping warmly in the fireplace beneath it. Mercy walked over to a chair and sat down, not entirely sure what to do. After a few moments, Bethany and Rachel entered the room, the two sitting on the couch, side by side, Rachel holding her daughter's hands in her lap as if her life depended on it.

"What does all this mean, Henry?" Rachel asked, her voice thick from emotion.

He stood near the fire, hands tucked into the hip pockets of his trousers. "Well, I'd wager Roosevelt will declare war and we'll be entering a second world war." He looked away, clearing his throat as emotion hung on the final word. He took a moment before looking back to the three women looking back at him. "I served in the first one, Rachel dealing with everything here, including our first born, Leo." Again, he cleared his throat and brought up a hand to rub at his chin.

"Is he okay, Daddy?" Bethany asked, her voice so small she reminded Mercy of a little girl.

"I don't know, sweetheart," he said. "Just don't know. But I do know that things will probably change, and they'll probably change huge."

❧❧❧❧

Despite Henry's explanation when he dropped Mercy home, Wanda wasn't interested in details, as usual. Mercy could see that her mother's anger was simmering, and she knew it was merely a matter of time before it would boil over again. She was grateful that Wanda had constrained herself considering the gravity of what had happened that day.

Now, night had fallen, and after a grueling night of Mercy needlessly scrubbing the apartment from top to bottom, Wanda had secured her pound of flesh for this perceived slight. So be it. Freshly bathed and in a clean cotton nightgown, Mercy lay in her bed. It was a cold night, snow expected over the next couple days.

She stared up at the ceiling and tried to clear her mind, but it just wouldn't. Thoughts tumbled from the attack on Pearl Harbor to Bethany's brother Leo stationed there and from whom the family hadn't heard since the attack, to Helen and her situation, and to the night before. No, she pushed that out of her mind. She skipped to the next image, once again the idea that the United States may be going to war. According to Bethany's father, it was inevitable.

Mercy was dragged from her morose thoughts by the sound of light tapping on her window. Lifting her head, she looked to see the very woman she'd just shooed from her thoughts standing on the other side. Pushing the covers back, she rolled out of bed and to the window, quickly unlatching it and sliding it up.

Bethany said nothing as she climbed in, quickly and quietly closing the window behind her. She turned to Mercy and didn't need to say anything. Mercy could see it in her eyes and on her face bathed in the moonlight. She took the older woman into a hug, feeling Bethany immediately fall into it.

Mercy's eyes fell closed as she held her, able to feel the sadness radiating off Bethany in waves. After a long moment, she pulled away and tugged lightly at the wool jacket Bethany wore. "Take that off," she whispered, so as not to be overheard.

Bethany shrugged out of her jacket and tossed it to the corner near the window before she, too, got into Mercy's bed. The younger woman was on her side with her behind and back against the cool, plaster wall, Bethany lying on her back. She was lying slightly diagonal as her booted feet hung off the bed. Mercy covered them with her covers to warm up her friend.

"Was your mom mad that we got you home a bit

late?" Bethany asked, glancing over at Mercy.

Mercy could still feel the sting of the slap and hear the sharp report of her hand. She pushed it all out of her mind. "It's fine," she said. Right now, there were bigger things to be concerned about. "Did you guys hear from Leo?"

Bethany studied her for a long time, almost as if trying to see the events of the night between Mercy and her mother through Mercy's own eyes. Finally, she looked away. "No. Mama is really scared but Dad is trying to stay positive. He told us he knows how chaotic things are likely to be there in Hawaii right now."

"I really hope he's okay, Bethany. I'm so sorry. So very scary." She reached over beneath the covers and lightly squeezed the soft hand that lay there. She was moving her hand away when, to her surprise, Bethany wrapped her fingers around it.

Bethany gave her a sheepish smile. "Sorry I'm being a bit needy, but I'm so anxious about everything."

"It's okay," Mercy assured. "I don't mind." Outside of her father, she'd never known such an affectionate family as the Wynters. Even Henry always squeezed her arm or playfully tugged at her hair when he saw her at the hotel.

Art Faulkner had never been inappropriate with her in any way, but his affection with her had always been limited to when they were alone, be it when he came to say goodnight in her bedroom or if the two of them went to run errands without Wanda. Based on that, Mercy had come to understand that affection wasn't something to be done in public, even the most basic version of it.

Now, pushing sixteen years old, she was being

rewired to understand that her father had acted that way in order to not anger his wife, who felt affection was taboo. In her mind, it wasn't about showing love or caring, but something dark or dirty. Now, as she held Bethany's hand and had received endless hugs and squeezes from both Henry and Rachel earlier that day, she knew it was Wanda that was dark and dirty, not love and caring.

She had no idea what made her do it, but she moved the short distance over to her friend and rested her head on her shoulder. As the understanding of just how broken her mother was settled into her consciousness, Mercy found herself craving affection and the normalcy of wanting it.

"Lift," Bethany said, releasing Mercy's hand. She wrapped her arm around Mercy's shoulders and urged her back to lie against her, which she did. Her fingers lightly played in dark auburn hair. "Ned said that, if war is declared by the US, he's going to sign up for the army." Bethany's words were quiet, of course, but they were also flat, as though she was trying her level best to not feel.

Mercy felt her heart drop. "Do you think he'll do it?" Not entirely sure what to do with her top arm, she tucked her hand in the small bit of space between their bodies. She lost her breath when Bethany grabbed it and tugged until her hand rested on Bethany's stomach. She swallowed, hard. Her hand in a place that normally wouldn't be where her hand would be sent little bolts of lightning through her hand, up her arm, and down into her lower belly.

"Oh yeah," Bethany said, not missing a beat. She was clearly unaware of the issues Mercy was having as she began to run soft fingertips up and down Mercy's forearm. "Your skin is so soft," she said. "You have such little hair on your arms. Like a little Chihuahua."

Mercy grinned. "Don't they have hair, though?"

"Yes, and so do you, but it's so soft and fine that it makes your arms all soft and addictive."

Again, Mercy's breath was stolen from her. She had no idea what she meant by that, but the words had hit her in a place that she just had no clue what to do with. Yet again, she felt like such a child next to Bethany. She'd done, seen, and experienced things that Mercy hadn't even considered or known was possible until recently. Not that she had any interest in any of those things, of course.

⚜ ⚜ ⚜ ⚜

As he'd done since Mercy had returned to school after her weeklong absence a few weeks before, Sam had shown up outside of the door to Mercy's building to walk with her to school. His flat cap in place, the two walked in companionable silence. She glanced over at him from time to time, as it felt he had something on his mind.

"Are you okay?" she finally asked. "You seem really troubled."

He nodded, not looking at her as they continued on. He had his book bag hitched on a shoulder and his hands tucked into the pockets of his wool trousers. He always seemed like he belonged in a time long ago to her, somehow. "I am troubled," he finally said.

"Want to talk about it?" she asked, the two stopping to wait for a car to pass before crossing the street.

He shrugged and let out a heavy, steam-coated

breath. "I just have this horrible feeling that we've been living in a dreamworld." He glanced over at her. "You know? Like, everything was good, fun with friends, our family, all of it. But now, everything is about to change. Like, we're about to wake up into what's really a living nightmare."

"That's really dark, Sam," Mercy said.

Again, he nodded. "These are dark times, Mercy."

For reasons they hadn't been told, the student body was instructed to head to the cafeteria just before ten thirty that morning. Their friend base gathered at their regular table, Mercy and Sam already there. Bethany slid onto the seat next to Mercy, Billy plopping down on the table next to her, his feet on the bench.

"What's this all about, anyways?" one of the boys in their group asked.

"The *Post* said that President Roosevelt will be speaking to the full Congress," Sam said.

"The *Post*?" the same boy asked, glancing over at him with a raised eyebrow. "You read the newspaper?"

Sam's own eyebrows fell. "Don't you?"

Billy chuckled. "Such an old man, Pops."

"Attention, students," came the voice of Principal Rodriguez booming over the public address system. The chatter in the cafeteria immediately came to a stop. "As many of you know, this nation faced a sad situation yesterday with our young men being attacked at Pearl Harbor in Hawaii. As such a historical event plays out before our eyes, we felt it was instrumental for you young people to hear what our president has to say to the joint session of Congress. Your attention, please."

There were a few clicks and bumps following his

words as it sounded like he was moving the microphone he used for announcements over to a radio. Within moments, it began. Mercy felt her stomach twisting as her nerves set in. Her knee was bouncing under the table matching the steady beat of her anxiety.

Enthusiastic applause and cheers were followed by the introduction of the president. Mercy took a shaky breath as she awaited what he had to say. The deep, accented voice of the president acknowledged those before him, Mercy's hands growing sweaty. She rubbed them on her skirt-covered thighs. The words he said next got her heart racing.

"Yesterday, December 7, 1941—a date which will live in infamy—the United States of America was suddenly and deliberately attacked..."

She glanced across the table at Sam to see that his gaze was downcast though silent tears streamed down his cheeks. A look over at Bethany and Billy showed the twins holding hands.

"...The attack yesterday on the Hawaiian Islands has caused severe damage to American naval and military forces..."

Instantly Leo came to mind, and Mercy moved her leg just enough so that it touched Bethany's. The older girl looked over at her, her eyes filled with so much emotion as she reached under the table and grabbed Mercy's hand, holding on to it as it rested on Mercy's thigh.

"I regret to tell you that very many American

lives have been lost."

Soft crying reached Mercy's ears. It was Bethany. Billy leaned over and cradled her head against his own, forehead to forehead. Mercy's eyes fell closed and her own silent tears began to fall along with the sounds of quiet crying and gasps from her fellow students in the cafeteria as the president asked Congress to declare war on the Japanese Empire.

Chapter Ten

Appetite gone, Bethany played with her food as she listened to the angry argument between her father and Ned, not daring to look up at them. Wisely, she kept her eyes and thoughts to herself.

"Damn it, Ned!" Henry Wynter growled, slamming his palm on the dinner table. The fork jumped off his dinner plate. "You have no idea what you're saying. No idea what you've done."

"I did what Leo did and I did what you did, Dad!" the second-oldest brother exclaimed, equal anger in his own voice. "A man sacrifices for his country and his family."

Bethany glanced up when a heavy silence met her brother's declaration. Ned was glaring at their father and Henry glared right back. She was waiting for them to sprout horns to clash.

"Hasn't this family sacrificed enough?" Henry said, the anger gone, profound sadness replacing it.

"We don't know that he's dead," Ned said, his voice still holding an edge. "And even if he is, isn't that all the more reason for me to go? Avenge him? Those goddamn Nazi bastards have to pay! And the Jap—"

"Enough!"

Bethany started when her father banged the table again to underscore his demand. She glanced over to her mother, who was quietly crying. She glared at Ned before pushing back from the table and moving over to her. "It's okay, Mama," she whispered, hugging the blond head to her chest. "Nice going, Ned."

He gave her a contrite glance before he, too, pushed back from the table and slammed out of the dining room and then the house. Bethany glanced over at Billy, who was looking down at his own dinner, only partially eaten. It seemed the heated discussion between father and son had made them all less than hungry.

Rachel Wynter sniffled, then let out a heavy sigh. She reached up and cupped her daughter's face before moving away from her. "I'll get this cleaned up," she said. "Clearly dinner is finished."

"No," Bethany said, moving away from her. "Billy and I will get this, Mama."

Ten minutes later and a coin flipped, Billy stood at the sink filled with warm, soapy water, dish towel in hand. Bethany took the newly washed dishes and rinsed them in clean water before drying them. A stack of dried dishes waited to be put away on the counter. She kept glancing over at him as she felt he had something to say but knew better than to push. He'd speak when he was finished navigating the maze that was his mind.

"I'm going to enlist, Bethy," he said at length. His voice was quiet, for her ears only as their parents were in the living room listening to a radio program as their father read the *Post*. "I can learn a trade while fighting for our country. And," he added, seeming to need to get it all out in one go. "I want you to come with me."

She stared at him, her stomach roiling at the news and the huge ask. "Wait, what?" She nearly dropped the plate she'd been drying, so she quickly set it and the dish towel she'd been using on the counter. "What?" she asked again.

"Think about," he said. "Girls from all over Europe have already been enlisting, I hear. They're getting trained for jobs they'd never be able to do otherwise, No doubt it'll be the same for American girls too." His eyebrows were raised in excitement. "Maybe you could even get trained as a nurse. Then, when all this is over," he said, a hand held out in a random gesture. "You could come back home and get on with the hospital in Tunston or with Doc Stone here, whatever."

Bethany turned away from him, needing to absorb all that he was saying. Finally, she turned to look at him. "After how angry Dad just got at Ned, you want to do this too? You want to put them through that?" She pointed toward the living room.

"Ned is a hothead," he said. "He wants to go purely for some macho need to prove himself." He met her gaze, pleading in his blue eyes. "For me, this is about serving and defending our country and what those bastards have done, yes, but also to plan for a future. And," he added, looking uncharacteristically shy. "I'm going to ask Mercy if she'll wait for me."

Her breath knocked out of her all over again, she said, "What?" for the third time in their short conversation.

"I know." Billy's shy grin grew. "She's young now, but by time I get back, she'll be older, around eighteen, probably." He turned his gaze back to his soapy water. He began to wash the dishes again. "There's just something about her," he explained. "So beautiful. And, she's so smart, such a calm about her, you know?"

Bethany nodded, returning to her own chore. "I do," she murmured. She felt distinctly uncomfortable by how distinctly uncomfortable Billy's voiced intention had made her feel.

"So, I figure if I'm over there doing my part, it would be great to get letters from her, you know? She could become my girl over time."

She nodded. "No doubt." She placed the plate on the stack. Needing some space from him, she tossed the damp drying towel to the counter and began to place the dishes in their correct cabinets.

"So," he pushed. "Will you go?"

"Billy—"

"Bethy," he interrupted. "We've done everything together, literally from conception on." He paused until she met his pleading gaze. "I don't wanna do this without you."

"We wouldn't be placed together, Billy," she said. "Probably not even in the same country."

"Yeah," he conceded. "But we'd leave together. Get on that train together." He shrugged. "Maybe even get to come home together too."

"Yeah, in a lovely wooden box, William." She glared at him. "And, we're not eighteen, and I sure as hell am not leaving school until I graduate."

"Well, of course not!" He quickly dried his hands on the towel she'd discarded before walking over to her. He placed his hands on her shoulders, staring down into her eyes. "We'll graduate in June and then turn eighteen in July." He shrugged a shoulder. "We'll go then, or in the early fall."

Looking into her brother's eyes, she knew there was little in life she'd ever deny him, nor had she thus far. But this…this was a horse of not only a different color but a totally different species. She forced herself to look away for fear she'd say yes just to make him happy. "Let's finish this," she said quietly, turning back to her dishes.

❧❧❧❧

Bethany sat at a table by herself. It was late evening, so the hotel restaurant was fairly quiet. Most of the staff was in the kitchen cleaning up after the dinner rush. She'd not ordered anything to eat but had the Coca-Cola she'd been sipping sitting on the table with her sketch pad in her lap, the back braced against the edge of the table. She was sketching the intricate detail of the bar front, as well as the brass bar that ran along its length just above the floor. At one time, when the place had been a saloon, the cowboys or miners would rest a booted foot on the brass bar as they waited for their drinks or while chatting.

She'd always been drawn to the bar itself, the history of it and all that it had seen over the decades. It made her proud to no end that Justice had literally helped build the building in which she sat. She'd been asked by her very own grandfather, Jeramiah Wynter, to manage the saloon from almost day one. The ironic thing was, her mother Rachel hadn't even been born yet, Thea still pregnant with her.

So, in asking Justice to help run his business, Jeramiah had no clue he was already bringing Justice and Thea into his family before his son would eventually marry their daughter. Bethany smiled at her thoughts, absolutely loving how life could be such a spiderweb of happenstance, coincidence, or maybe no coincidence at all, but meant to be.

"Hey."

She glanced up from her sketch and instantly a smile came to her lips. "Hey, yourself."

"Are you drawing something?" Mercy asked, her hand resting on the back of one of the three empty chairs at the four-top where Bethany sat. Her apron was in place and hair pulled atop her head to keep it from falling into plates of food, no doubt. Bethany had to do the same at the soda shop.

"I am." She nodded toward the bar. "I love the detail work."

"Can I see?" Mercy asked, interest in her voice.

"Sure." Bethany raised the sketch pad to the table, turning it so it faced the standing young woman.

Mercy took the pad in hand and brought it up, her gaze scouring the detailed pencil sketch. Her eyes widened. "This is amazing, Bethany!" She looked down at the artist, who felt a bit shy. She rarely let anyone outside of her family see her work.

"Thanks."

Mercy looked back down to the sketch then to the real-life bar and back again. "Absolutely amazing." She gave Bethany a bright smile before handing the pad back to her. "You're incredibly talented. Have you done anymore?"

"Oh, yeah, I have a million sketch pads and pages at home. This is the first one in this book, though," Bethany said, tapping the pad with the pencil she held.

"I'd love to see them," Mercy said, hope in her voice and her eyes.

"Well," Bethany drawled, a little grin on her lips. "Guess you'll have to come to my bedroom, then." She smirked. "I've snuck into yours enough." She could not believe the flirtatious words and tone that left her lips, seemingly without even a quick consultation with her brain. When she saw a slight blush that eased up into Mercy's cheeks, she silently berated herself. Then she noted the smile that Mercy was clearly trying to suppress.

"Yes, well," Mercy said, her fingers once again gripping the back of one of the chairs, her gaze on them. "I guess I'll have to visit your bedroom, then."

Bethany's grin grew. "I'll make it worth your while." *Stop it! Stop it right this minute!* "Lots of sketches and stuff to show you, you know," she added lamely.

Mercy nodded, her suppressed smile still in place. "No doubt." Clearing her throat, she looked at Bethany, seeming to push their previous conversation aside. "Well, I get off soon and finally will get to my homework, so before I go, do you need anything else? Refill?" she asked, indicating the carbonated drink that was left in Bethany's glass.

"No, I'm okay." She glanced at the delicate gold watch upon her wrist that had belonged to her great-grandma Ninny, Justice's mother, whom they'd lost a few years before. "I should get too." She sighed. She'd come to the hotel to hang out after school because she was trying to avoid Billy. She wasn't ready to give him the answers that he kept bugging her for. She was off today and honestly felt like a loser for hiding, but it was a massive decision that would change the trajectory of her entire life.

Mercy stepped away from the table to give Bethany room to get out of the little corner she'd tucked herself into. "Finished?" she asked, indicating the drink. At Bethany's nod, Mercy grabbed it in the capacity of a waitress. "I'll go run this to the kitchen then meet you at the register, okay?"

Bethany met her gaze and nodded. "Absolutely." Mercy hurried away and she gathered her things, tucking the sketch pad into the knapsack she used to keep it from getting dirty or wet when sketching away from the house. She also shrugged into her winter jacket. Shouldering her bag, she walked over to the register, digging out a few coins for her drink. Her parents had never let her or any of her siblings—or Pops—have a free lunch, literally or figuratively.

A moment later, as promised, Mercy pushed through the swinging door and hurried over to the cash register. She accepted the coins Bethany handed her. "Big spender," she commented, sparing a glance to Bethany as she punched in the appropriate code into the register.

"Completely," Bethany acknowledged. "This place would go under without me."

Mercy allowed the smile she'd unsuccessfully tried to conceal earlier to blossom. A full-on smile like what graced her face at the moment was so rare… Bethany hadn't realized just how incredibly beautiful it made her already lovely face. Something about her was different today, Bethany thought. Perhaps more aptly, something between them was different today.

When she'd gone to Mercy's bedroom window the last time, Sunday night after the attack, something had changed between them. Perhaps a deepening in their friendship? Perhaps she was beginning to see Mercy Faulkner for the really amazing young woman she was rather than a young girl who had just undergone a horrible situation and was starting over in Wynter with her equally horrible mother.

That had admittedly been her thoughts and feelings initially. She'd wanted to help her get settled, as she was working for her family business and renting housing from her family. She figured once Mercy had made a few friends her own age, that would be the end of it. Over time, she'd grown to genuinely like her, respect her, and now she realized Mercy had become a bit of an emotional confidante for her.

That last thought consumed the hell out of her. Hadn't that always been Billy's place? Truth was, she hadn't had many female friends in her life at all. Reason number one was that it had always been her and her twin. Reason number two was that she'd known since she was very young that she was attracted to other girls, so it made her feel uncomfortable around them, always worried she'd give something away if she had a crush on a friend.

So, she'd been shocked that Billy hadn't figured it out when suddenly Helen was around her like flies around honey. Further, she and Helen had been extremely sexually active, so she was surprised—and, she supposed, relieved—that it hadn't been evident to those in her life, particularly her twin.

Now, as she placed the coins in Mercy's palm, she worried she may be in trouble. In their large circle of friends, all the Wynter kids knowing each other, she'd never been truly connected to any of them other than as buddies, Helen a distinct exception. But for some reason, this newcomer was becoming important to her, even more important than Helen had been, and she cared about what happened to her.

She cared about the treatment from her mother and was actually finding herself getting more and more angry about it. She suspected there had been more violence than that horrible time that kept Mercy out of school for a week. Perhaps Wanda had just gotten smarter about it, realizing going too far could get her into trouble.

"Bethany?"

Shaking herself from her thoughts, Bethany realized that Mercy was trying to give her her change. "Sorry." She gave her an embarrassed smile as she took it and dropped it into the pocket of her jacket. "Heading out too, huh?" she asked.

"I am." Mercy slammed the cash drawer shut and stabbed Bethany's bill down on the little metal spike that held a whole pile of impaled tickets, proof they'd been paid and closed out. "Been a long day. Honestly, I have no desire to do homework," she said, leaning against the bar for a moment. "Just want to crash." She rubbed at her eyes with her hands before they fell away as she sighed.

"I understand." Bethany knocked her knuckles on the bar top. "Go grab your jacket and things and I'll walk you the thirteen feet to the door."

Mercy chuckled and nodded. "Be right back."

A few moments later, Mercy reappeared, shrugging into the wool jacket that looked like a quilt of different colored patches in style. "Ready?"

Bethany held her arm out, lips quirked in a smirk. She delighted in the laugh that earned her.

"You are in rare form tonight, Miss Wynter," the younger woman said, shaking her head as she laced her arm in Bethany's.

"Yeah, well when I'm stressed, either I shut down, become a total jerk, or get silly." She glanced over at her companion as they strolled to the door. "Guess silly won out."

"I'm sorry you're stressed," Mercy said softly, waiting as Bethany pulled open one of the double doors that was the entrance and exit to the building.

"Not your fault," Bethany murmured. "I know all of us are anxious right now." She patted the bag slung over her shoulder as they stepped out into the cold night. "One of the reasons I was sketching."

They walked the few yards to the apartment entrance, a narrow alleyway separating the buildings, just wide enough for a person to walk. "That helps you?" Mercy asked. "To sketch things?"

Bethany nodded. "Yeah. Always has." They reached the side door of the building that would lead up to the second-floor apartments. "Since I was little, I'd draw or paint, something."

"I really do want to see your other sketches," Mercy said, all teasing from their earlier conversation in the restaurant gone. "I have absolutely no artistic talent whatsoever, so I really admire those that do."

"Okay," Bethany said, removing her arms from Mercy's. She shoved her hands into the pockets of her jacket as a frigid breeze blew between them. She saw a shiver go through Mercy. "Get you inside," she said, nodding toward the door a couple feet from Mercy. "Don't want you to catch your death out here."

Mercy nodded, tugging her jacket a bit closer to her body. "I'd invite you up, but my mother is there," she said with a tired sigh.

"It's okay," Bethany said, a cheeky grin on her lips. "I know other ways to get in."

Mercy grinned and nodded. "Yes, you do. Well." She reached out and tugged lightly on the bottom of Bethany's jacket. "See you tomorrow at school."

"Yes, ma'am." Bethany clicked her heels and

stood erect, bringing her hand up in a stiff salute, which made Mercy laugh. It was a sound she was beginning to like.

"Thank god I found you!"

Bethany was snapped out of her mirth by the panicked voice of one of her coworkers, still dressed in his striped soda jerk uniform. He was leaning out of the open door of the soda shop.

"What's wrong, Dan?" she asked, concerned.

"Your dad called, looking for you," he said. "You need to get home, Bethany. Leo's been identified."

Chapter Eleven

She was out of tears and felt so numb as she stood there. People had mostly filed out of the small cemetery known as Miner's Hole. The funeral proper had been held at the small white Presbyterian church in town, Father Waylan delivering a moving service over the American-flag-draped casket.

The graveside ceremony had been left for family and close friends. Her brother had some school friends that had attended, along with an old girlfriend who Bethany suspected had never gotten over her first love, Leo Wynter. She'd often wondered if Leo and Martha would have reunited once his service was complete. But, alas, they'd never know.

Bethany stood at the freshly turned earth, the narrow white marble headstone denoting the military service of the man buried there. She read his name, branch, rank, and life dates, all etched into the stone. He would have turned twenty-four next month.

She started when she realized she wasn't alone. Glancing over, she saw Mercy stepping up beside her. She and Wanda had joined the somber events of the day. Though she wore a simple black dress, her colorful wool coat was a bit of a bright spot in the day. Bethany gave her as much of a smile as she could muster.

"Hey."

"Hi," Mercy responded. "Your family is about

to leave."

Bethany nodded. "'Kay." She took a deep, shaky breath, the cold, fresh air filling her lungs. She brought one of her hands out of her coat pocket and kissed two of her fingers before placing them atop Leo's headstone. "Love you."

Turning to face Mercy, she saw so much compassionate understanding in the brown depths of her eyes. She had to look away or come undone all over again. *Damn it!* Too late. She tried to turn away, but Mercy gently eased her into an embrace. She allowed herself to be held as the tears flowed. She honestly didn't think she had any left.

"It's okay," Mercy whispered, stroking her back. "I'm so sorry."

Bethany buried her face in soft, auburn hair, somehow the feel of this young woman holding her bringing her a peace and comfort that confused her. She realized that there was something about Mercy that reminded her of her grandmother, Thea possessing that same quiet calm, that same ability to make you believe everything will be okay with a simple touch, a simple look.

Ironically, it had been that same simple look, that same simple touch that had aroused her emotions all over again. After several moments she calmed, the tears easing to sniffles and finally burning, tired eyes. She was loath to release Mercy, but she had to. There was no other reason to continue the physical connection between them.

"Sorry," she muttered, her voice thick from so many hours, so many days of crying. She pulled away from Mercy, bringing out the tissue from her pocket to wipe at her eyes and nose. She smiled sheepishly at the seemingly unending patience of the young woman standing in front of her.

"You don't need to apologize, Bethany," Mercy said. She squeezed Bethany's arm before letting her hand drop and taking a small step away from her, out of her personal space. "Anything I can do?"

Bethany sniffled again and shook her head as she shoved the soiled tissue back into her pocket to discard later. "You're already doing it," she said. "I truly appreciate you being a friend in all this, Mercy. I mean that."

"Of course." Mercy looked pleased by the words, a little sparkle in her eyes. "And," she added. "Your parents invited Mother and I over for lunch, and my mother said we can."

Bethany's smile was instant at the news. "Excellent." She took one last look at her eldest brother's grave, then turned back to Mercy and nodded in the direction of the wrought iron gate that served as the entrance and exit of the cemetery. "Let's go."

❦❦❦❦

Lunch had been more of a talkative affair than Bethany had expected. She had little to say, but Billy, their father, and Justice were discussing plans to shut down the hotel and transition it into a small textiles factory. The government had begun to call on businesses to help in any way they could.

There would be a huge need for uniforms, flags, parachutes, and any number of other essentials for the boys heading off to war. Not only were Justice and Henry being patriotic, it made solid business sense. Bookings would drop off, they figured. Much of their clientele was young men working at the lumber mill, and no doubt most of them would be called to head off to war.

When Billy grew quiet, she looked up to see that he was looking at her from across the table. Through their silent twin communication, she knew exactly what he was asking her. She shook her head, so subtly that only he would be able to see it.

Why not?

Today isn't the day, Billy.

Why? It's the perfect time.

We just buried our brother!

His jaw tightened as he looked away from her. Damn it, Billy. She pushed away from the table. "Excuse me," she muttered, then left the dining room, hurrying up the stairs to her bedroom. There was no way in hell she wanted to be around to hear the uproar when he made his announcement.

Slamming the bedroom door, she threw herself onto her bed. She was a molten volcano of emotions. She felt angry, sad, upset, and profoundly grief-stricken on so many levels. She felt like her world was imploding and she had not one ounce of control over any of it. She wanted to cry, wanted to laugh, and wanted to scream, all at the same time.

Why did Billy have to do this? Why did he have to push her to do this with him? It was crazy and it was unnecessary. She was so afraid that it would destroy their parents. Leo's death at Pearl Harbor, wasn't that enough? Ned heading off in a couple weeks, wasn't *that* enough?

She felt like she was about to burst out of her own skin. She wanted to go run a couple miles just to get rid of some of this energy. She felt antsy yet didn't want to leave her bedroom. She felt completely out of control of her own life in that moment. A heavy, dark, ugly obligation hung over her head, and she resented the hell out of Billy for putting it there.

She glanced over to the door when a knock sounded from the other side. Rolling her eyes, she climbed off the bed and yanked open the door. For the rest of her life, Bethany would never be able to explain exactly why it happened. When she saw Mercy standing on the other side of that door, she grabbed her hand and yanked her inside the bedroom, closing the door behind her.

As if in a dream, the next thing she knew, Mercy was shoved up against that door and, with one hand buried in her hair and the other on her hip, Bethany took her in a demanding kiss. At first, Mercy's hands pushed at her shoulders, a shocked whimper eaten by Bethany's mouth, but within a few short moments, the kiss was returned. Though Mercy's hands remained on Bethany's shoulders, the firmness of them pushing against her had weakened significantly.

After a moment, Bethany was brought back into reality, horrified by what she'd done. She stumbled back away from Mercy almost as if those hands had indeed pushed her away. They were both breathing heavily, though Mercy, still against the door, was looking at her with wide, stunned eyes.

Bethany's own eyes bulged as realization hit. Her hands came up and covered her mouth as she stared at Mercy, who looked incredibly shellshocked. "Oh my god," Bethany whispered, taking a few steps backward, feeling the need to get as much space between her and Mercy as possible. "Oh my god." Tears instantly sprang to her eyes at what she'd done.

She'd never forget the look on Mercy's face in that moment. She looked afraid of her.

Turning her back to Mercy, Bethany buried her face in her hands. She was crying again, though for a very different reason this time. Mercy had been nothing but a friend to her, there for her and her family through the most difficult time of their lives. Yet, look what she'd done to repay her.

She was so utterly disgusted with herself, so lost in self-recrimination that she didn't hear Mercy walk up behind her. Instead, Bethany was nearly startled out of her mind when there was a soft touch to her upper back.

"Bethany," Mercy said, her tone so soft and gentle, Bethany's tears came harder. "Hey." Mercy used a firm touch to turn Bethany around to face her. She said nothing more as she wrapped her arms around Bethany, who still cried. She held her against her, gently rocking her as she cupped the back of her head.

Bethany held on, letting herself go. The strange thing was, as much crying as she'd done in the two weeks since they'd found out Leo was dead, so much emotion had built up inside that she hadn't yet dealt with. Now she understood it was because she'd been crying only to deal with him, compartmentalizing her emotions only to her immediate grief.

Now, everything else had pushed its way to the surface in a violent explosion. After many minutes, her tears slowed, though the dread in her belly was as raw as ever. "I'm so sorry," she murmured, pulling out of the hug. Tears continued to fall down her cheeks as she looked at Mercy. The fear was gone, now replaced with her seemingly unending compassion. "I'm so sorry, Mercy."

"Shhh," Mercy said, her hands coming up to wipe at Bethany's tears with her thumbs. "It's okay," she murmured in a soothing voice. Bethany's eyes fell closed as a soft kiss was left to her forehead "It's okay," Mercy said again.

This time, the softest of kisses was left on her lips, a bit more than a peck, but certainly nothing of a romantic nature. Bethany felt it was probably her way of letting Bethany know that it was, indeed, okay, and she wasn't afraid of her.

Relieved, Bethany nodded.

The snow crunched beneath their boots as they made their way deeper into the woods. Bethany was quiet, feeling more like she was on autopilot than on a little adventure with family and friends. She knew the old barn was just up ahead. She and Billy had found it when they were eleven years old, and ever since Billy had been obsessed with it.

"Coming up now, gang," he called back, leading the pack. Bethany pulled up the rear, Mercy and Pops walking together in the middle.

Since the day of Leo's funeral more than two weeks ago, the day she had essentially attacked Mercy, something in her had changed. Losing control of herself so badly, so violently, something in her had shut down. Now, she was walking through life one expectation at a time. Expected to wake up and go to school, done. Expected to do her assignments and keep her perfect grade point average, done. Expected to go to work, be a smiling face to the customers, done.

Truth was, she felt nothing inside. One too many traumas, including the one she'd incited, had broken her. She felt overwhelmed and unable to cope. Yes, Mercy had said she'd forgiven her, and Bethany believed that she had, but she hadn't forgiven herself. Mercy Faulkner was a precious soul to be protected, and she'd failed miserably.

As they walked, she felt eyes on her. Glancing ahead and to her left, she saw Mercy looking back at her as she walked with Pops, who was still yapping away about God only knew what. Bethany could see the concern on her lovely friend's face, a question in her eyes. Bethany had no answers for her.

"Here we are!" Billy crowed.

The old structure, likely built around the beginning of the town, was a two-story barn made of wood. Time had weathered and darkened it. There were the two traditional huge doors that could be opened to allow for large animals or equipment. To the right of those was a human-sized door. The window above suggested a loft.

"Who on earth builds a huge barn in the middle of the woods?" Pops asked sensibly.

"And that's exactly why we haven't shown you this before. Leave it to you to take away the magic with a logical question. Who the heck knows?" Billy chuckled, using his shoulder to push the human-sized door open, the sharp splintering sound speaking to the fact that the door needed to be replaced. Every time she and Billy had gone there, they'd struggled with that door.

Inside, the quartet found themselves in a huge, dark space. It had been cleared of debris long ago by the twins. Now, what remained were the chairs they'd brought over time, a table they'd created using some wood planks and a bale of hay, and the fire ring they'd made.

"Um, is that a good idea?" Pops asked, nodding to that very thing as Billy hurried over to it, squatting down with the book of matches he'd pulled from his pocket.

"Bethy, grab a couple logs," he ordered, nodding to the stack that had been there since the previous year when they'd cut down a small tree and split it into logs. Nobody knew about their hideout, so what they'd brought in once remained until they removed it.

Bethany headed to the woodpile and began to stack logs in her arms. Mercy joined her to help. For just a moment, their gazes met, and it hurt Bethany to see the confusion in those beautiful brown eyes. She looked away, grabbing another log.

"You're going to smoke us out of here," Pops said, hands on hips as he watched the other three arrange the logs the two young women had carried over.

"Nah," Billy assured, on his knees. "This place has got so many holes in it." He grinned, indicating the structure and bits of the overcast sky able to be seen in holes and cracks. "We'll be fine."

"What about a fire?" Pops challenged.

"What about one?" Billy asked, his features exploding into shades of orange and gold as he got the fire lit.

"We're in an old barn that is likely fifty or sixty years old," Pops pointed out. "Essentially a structure of kindling."

Billy glanced up at him. "Simple. Don't stick

part of the wall in the fire."

A small smirk crossed Bethany's lips as she lowered herself into the chair she always used when they were in the barn. She unbuttoned her jacket and removed the bag of large, fat marshmallows she'd brought. She set them in her lap as she tugged off her gloves, shoving them into the pockets of her jacket.

"Pass out sticks, will ya?" Billy asked Pops, moving away from the fire to his own chair, which sat to Bethany's right, Mercy taking the one to her left and Pops in the one to Mercy's left, finishing the circle. The sticks were nearest Pops's chair.

Pops did as asked, handing two of the long, thin sticks to Mercy for her and Bethany and one over to Billy, keeping one for himself.

"So, why are we here?" Pops asked. "What did you guys want to tell us?"

Bethany said nothing, simply tore open the bag of marshmallows and handed one to Billy. She held the open bag toward Mercy who, again, met her gaze. So much in those damn eyes. She could see the wheels behind them spinning and Bethany had to look away. She hated how much those eyes were able to affect her, affect her emotions.

"Pops?" she said, holding the bag out past Mercy for her cousin to retrieve his own marshmallow as well.

"Well," Billy said, carefully easing the soft sweetness onto the pointed end of the thin stick. "Bethy and I did something last weekend," he began, sending the marshmallow end of his stick toward the small fire, just large enough to warm the small circle of people around it and toast their goodies.

Bethany prepared her own marshmallow and

stick, her face expressionless as she wouldn't allow herself to feel anything.

"Okay," Pops drawled, looking over at him then at Bethany and back to Billy.

Bethany noticed that Mercy wasn't looking at anyone. She was simply staring into the flames, her stick across her lap and marshmallow still held between her fingers. She looked to Mercy's profile—nothing. Mercy wouldn't look at her.

"We wanted to tell you guys first," Billy continued. His voice was a mixture of nervousness and excitement. "We, Bethy and I," he said, indicating his twin and himself with his hand. "We feel we need to stand up for what's right, defend our country." He gave Pops and Mercy, who still stared into the fire, a big smile. "We enlisted. We head out the day after we turn eighteen."

Chapter Twelve

Mercy looked down into her lap, her bottom lip tucked beneath her top teeth as she tried desperately to hold in the tears that were threatening. She set aside the stick and marshmallow. "Um, I'll be right back," she murmured, popping up from her chair and hurrying away from the warm circle of the fire.

She felt like she was suffocating and desperately needed the cold air on her face and in her lungs. She pulled open the door, which Bethany hadn't closed fully so there wouldn't be any sticking issues when they tried to leave, and burst out into the January day. She ran once she was out, hair flying back behind her.

The cold air felt so good on her heated face, both from the fire but also her tears, which were so cold upon her cheeks. Finally, she stopped, her hand resting on the thick trunk of a tree as she tried to catch her breath, which was hard when the tears wouldn't stop. Her head fell as her shoulders slumped.

She felt so lost, particularly since the events in Bethany's bedroom, events that had replayed in her mind—and her dreams—so many times. It had been a moment of surprise and admittedly, fear, but she'd come to realize later that it was because it had been so unexpected and aggressive. Seeing Bethany's devastated reaction to what she'd done, Mercy had a different perspective, and had been able to see it for what it was—a hurting young woman trying to reach out and connect in any way she could.

Mercy understood that all too well. So many times she'd changed that moment in her mind to one where it hadn't been such a shock but instead expected, and she'd been able to take comfort from Bethany's touch, her kiss. The very thought of it made her stomach tumble all over again.

She raised her face to the overcast sky, the smell of snow yet to fall in the air. She tried to calm herself, knowing there was nothing she could do about any of this. And frankly, it was the story of her life. She'd learned long ago and in some pretty profound ways, to not get attached to anything or anyone, or try not to, because it would be taken away.

The tears came back, making her angry at herself. Though she knew this lesson, she could never accept it. She was a sensitive and deep person; she thought deep, cared deep, loved deep. She was the complete opposite of her mother and proud of that fact. But now, as her chest felt heavy and her heart literally hurt, she thought maybe Wanda Faulkner had it right. If you don't care, you don't get hurt.

Who was she kidding? She used the sleeve of her jacket to wipe at her eyes and face, even as the tears kept coming. She didn't know how to turn her emotions off, her heart, her caring. And now, two of the people who had come to mean a lot to her, Bethany and Billy, particularly Bethany, were leaving. And they weren't just leaving, they were heading off to war.

Fresh tears. "Darn it," she muttered, wiping frantically at her face, but it did no good. She was surprised when she was gently turned around and found herself enveloped in strong arms. Those arms, however, didn't belong to the person she wished they did. They belonged to Billy.

"I know," he cooed, cradling her head against his chest. "This whole situation sucks and there really are no right answers."

She nodded into the hug, in full agreement there.

"I promise," he continued. "We'll come back." He pulled away just enough to look down into her face. "Will you write to me?" he asked, his voice uncharacteristically shy and unsure.

Mercy could feel a difference in his energy but wasn't entirely sure what the change was or meant. "Of course," she said. Why wouldn't she?

His smile was broad, the confidence she was used to returning. "Great." He used his fingers to wipe away some of her tears. The touch, a bit intimate, made her slightly uncomfortable. "Come on," he said, hand falling away as he grabbed hers in his, lightly tugging. "Let's have some roasted marshmallows."

❧❧❧❧

Spring was upon them as was the final semester for the seniors. After the holiday break, things at school had become remarkably different. Almost overnight, many of the teachers had disappeared, mostly the younger men. They'd enlisted and were on their way to Europe leaving devastated families behind.

It was a strange time, as Mr. Meloney's class had become Mrs. Meloney's class, and Mr. Edwards, Mrs. Edwards. The wives of the departing men had been allowed to come in as temporary stand-ins until a more permanent situation could be put into place. Some former teachers were coming out of retirement to help fill the vacancies left by the newly enlisted.

Now, on a mild day in March, Mercy walked out of the building to meet Sam so they could walk home together. The transformation of the hotel was in full swing and all hands were on deck for it, including kitchen staff and hotel workers. Everywhere a person looked in town reflected the war effort, be it businesses changing such as the hotel, or simply Old Glory waved from every house, every building, and even smaller flags from cars.

The streets of Wynter, and likely every other American town, ran with the red, white, and blue of patriotism. Once a month Wynter was holding a parade where those who were heading out soon marched to the cheers, and often tears, of the townspeople. A tribute to the bravery of the youth, and for some, the last images of their hopes and dreams for the future.

It was a hard time.

Mercy didn't find Sam by the flagpole, where he usually was, but instead noticed he'd walked over to the high fence surrounding the ball field. It was after-school practice for the baseball team, and player number eleven had the name Wynter blazed across the back of his jersey. She noticed Sam wasn't watching his cousin, however.

As she studied him, she saw that he seemed to be transfixed by a junior named Harry Pilner, number nine on the field. The handsome boy with dark blond hair and deep dimples was out in right field. He stood in the typical stance, feet wide and hands on his thighs, waiting for the pitch.

She'd had him in a couple of her classes, a sweet kid with an easy smile and dark blue eyes. But, looking at him now, she had no clue what had Sam so focused on him. His uniform was fine, nothing out of place, no holes or anything strange.

Mercy walked up to the fence beside the fresh-man, glancing over at him. "Hey," she said, startling him. "What are you looking at?"

"Nothing!" he exclaimed, body language imme-diately stiffening in a defensive posture. "Why would I be looking at anything?"

She was surprised by his response, almost as though she'd caught him stealing the proverbial cook-ie from the cookie jar. "Um," she stuttered. "Because you were."

"That's absurd," he muttered, looking away. He fished his watch out of the pocket of his vest, worn beneath his winter jacket. He flipped it open and sent an accusatory glare her way. "I was bored, wasting time as you're late."

Amused, as there was clearly something he was trying to hide, she shook her head. "No, I'm not," she teased. "I'm two minutes early."

"Let's go," he muttered, irritation in his voice as he reached up and readjusted his flat cap.

She left it alone and the two friends began their two-mile journey. As they walked, she glanced over at him. The newly minted fifteen-year-old looked troubled. Now, he always looked like he had the weight of the world on his shoulders, but today it seemed a bit more so.

One thing she did note, however, was he was beginning to mature into a fine-looking young man. His jaw was beginning to square up, his features becoming more like a man than a boy. He'd already grown to be a head taller than she was in the months since she and her mother had arrived in town.

"What's going on?" she asked conversationally.

"You seem troubled, Sam." She playfully bumped his arm with her shoulder. "Hmm?"

He remained quiet for so long that she thought he wasn't going to answer her question, but finally he did. His voice was very quiet, very shy. All unusual behavior for a young man who seemed to so often have no filter or no problem speaking his mind. Finally, he opened his mouth to speak, but then closed it again, teeth literally clamping together.

"Sam," she said. "It's okay." She gave him a reassuring smile when he looked over at her.

He nodded and cleared his throat. "You know about Bethany, right? Her penchant for other females."

Mercy blushed deeply. "Yes," she said. "I do."

"So, wouldn't it stand to reason that there are males like that too?" he pushed.

"Well, of course," she said. "We may have some differences on the outside, but at the end of the day, males and females are essentially the same species."

"Exactly," he agreed enthusiastically. "So, that cleared up, what if…What if…"

She could see he was struggling to say it, though she suspected what he wanted to say. "What if you are one of those males?" she asked gently.

He cleared his throat again and reached up to adjust the collar of his shirt, buttoned to the tippy top. He removed his cap and ran a hand through his hair before replacing it. He was clearly nervous and completely uncomfortable with the direction of the conversation, even though he'd brought it up.

"Sam," she said, stopping their progress with a hand to his arm. He faced her but refused to meet her gaze. "Listen, you seem like you're about to jump out of your skin. I'm absolutely not going to judge you, I promise. You can tell me what you want to, or don't. I think I get what you're inferring, and it's okay." He spared her a glance and she rewarded it with a bright smile. "It really is. You are who you are, just like Bethany." She shrugged. "Just like me and Billy and Elmer and…" She shrugged again. "Fill in the blank. We're all exactly who we're supposed to be."

Samuel Popperton literally looked like he was about to melt in relief. Even as his shoulders slumped as the weight seemed to be lifted, they straightened, and he stood tall and his chest puffed a bit. Yes, she did believe he was a natural stick-in-the-mud, but she did see some of that ease. How much of that was fear of being truly seen?

She smiled at him. "Any guy would be really lucky to have you, Sam," she said quietly. Though they were alone on the sidewalk, she wanted him to understand she respected his privacy in the matter and would hold his confidence.

He reached out and lightly squeezed her fingers before moving his hand away as they got walking again. She smiled, understanding that was his way of showing his gratitude. She decided a change of subject was due, as it felt he was finished sharing for the day.

"Speaking of Bethany," she said. "Do you know if she's mad at me or something?"

"Mad at you?" he asked, sounding surprised. "For what?"

"Well, I don't know. That's the problem." Despite what he'd just shared with her, in his roundabout sort of way, there was no way in heck she was going to tell him what had happened between them the night of Leo's funeral nearly two months ago. "I rarely see her anymore. I mean, Billy is around all the time," she said, perhaps a bit more irritation in her voice than she intended. "But other than seeing her in the halls now and then, she'd just kind of vanished. She doesn't even sit with us at lunch anymore." She felt so sad as she told him this. And, Bethany hadn't come to her window since way back in December.

He nodded. "Yeah, I've noticed she's pulled back a lot too. I mean, she can do this from time to time, but this is pretty severe for her. I know she was really close to Leo. Next to Billy, he was the closest person to her. She and Ned never really got along all that well." He paused. "Come to think of it, not many do. Anyway, I think losing Leo hit her really hard." He glanced over at her. "I wouldn't take it personally, Mercy."

She nodded. That made her feel better, but just a little.

❧ ❧ ❧ ❧

Mercy glanced at her alarm clock again, fingers tapping nervously on her thighs where she sat on the bed. The soda shop closed in three minutes. She blew out a breath and decided she should head down. Pushing to her feet, she stood near the window, listening. Nothing. All was quiet, her mother still at work next door.

She pushed up her window and glanced out, seeing nothing in the alleyway behind the building. She hiked up the skirt portion of her dress in order to climb out onto the small landing, then, leaving the window open, slowly and quietly made her way down the metal stairs. She made it to the ground below. The back door of the soda shop had remained stubbornly closed.

She lowered herself to sit on the bottom step of the fire escape and waited. Within a few moments, the door opened and Bethany butted her way out, loaded down with bulging bags of trash. She made her way to the cans, not seeming to notice she had an audience of one.

"Hey, stranger."

Bethany whirled around with a gasp of surprise. When she spotted Mercy, her hand went to her heart and she looked away for a moment. "Jesus!" she hissed. "You scared the crap out of me."

"Sorry," Mercy said, though she didn't much sound it.

"What are you doing out here?" Bethany asked, looking from Mercy up to her open window and back again.

Mercy shrugged, remaining where she was. "You seem to be avoiding me, so I came to you."

Bethany looked decidedly sheepish. "I'm not avoiding you," she mumbled.

Mercy smirked, pushing to her feet and walking over to her. She began to help load the trash into the cans. "No?" she challenged, an eyebrow raised. She placed the lid on the trash can, perhaps a bit harder than need be. "I think we both know that's not true. It may not be just about me, as you seem to be avoiding all of us, but I can't help but feel like I've done something wrong."

Bethany didn't look at her as she placed one of the other bags in another of the trash cans. She placed the lid back on and shook her head. "You've done nothing wrong, Mercy." Her voice was quiet, tinged with sadness.

"And," Mercy added softly. "We established that

you didn't, either."

Bethany met and held her gaze for a long moment before she looked away. There was so much in those gorgeous eyes that Mercy couldn't read, but they were definitely troubled. Bethany nodded, tossing the final bag of trash. "Yeah."

"Look," Mercy said, no idea where the confidence was coming from but taking Bethany's hands in her own anyway. "You've become an important friend in my life, an important person."

Bethany said nothing, but it was clear she was listening, so Mercy continued on.

"Maybe I read you wrong, as I don't know you crazy well. But, I don't think so." She looked deeply into sky-blue eyes. "Something is bothering you and it's driving me nuts that you won't let me help or at least listen."

"Sorry," Bethany murmured, looking down at her shuffling feet like a little girl.

"Hey," Mercy said, waiting until Bethany looked at her again. She gave her a sheepish grin. "I'm not trying to give myself more importance in your life than I no doubt have, but I care." She shrugged, looking down at their hands before she released Bethany's. "I do. And we're running out of time before you and Billy go off and do this crazy thing." She took a deep, shaky breath as her profound sadness of Bethany's leaving threatened to surface again. "I don't want to waste what time we have left." She bit her lip, looking down. "You may not come back."

"Hey." Bethany waited until Mercy looked at her again. "I promise you," she said softly. "I'll come back. And, you're right." She glanced up into the dark, star-filled sky before meeting Mercy's gaze again. "You're right," she said again. She leaned against the brick wall that was the back of the building.

Mercy walked over to the wall and leaned her shoulder against it a couple feet away, arms crossed over her shoulder. She felt Bethany had more to say, so she remained silent.

"Sometimes when I don't know what to do or really who I am, I shut down, close myself off." She looked over at Mercy, mirroring her position, arms crossing over her chest. "I feel like I'm in this horrible limbo right now, Mercy. Not a kid, yet don't know anything about being an adult. Does that make any sense?"

"Oh, absolutely!" Mercy needed to touch her and didn't fully understand why, but she went with it. She reached out and placed her hand on Bethany's arm. She was pleased when chilled fingers rested upon it. "Bethany, yes, you are an incredibly responsible young woman. You have a job, carry perfect grades, wear your halo proudly, all of it." She smiled at the small bark of laughter at that. "But you've had a pretty smooth life. By that I mean, a good family, strong support, nothing too crazy."

"And then all this happens," Bethany added. "Leo, Pearl Harbor, the war..."

Mercy nodded. "Exactly. A lot coming at you at one time. No wonder you feel lost, Bethany. You're literally not the same person you were on December sixth."

Bethany stared at her for a long time before shaking her head. "How the hell did you get so damn wise at fifteen?"

Mercy shrugged. "I've been there. And hey," she added with a smirk. "I'll be sixteen in three months."

Chapter Thirteen

Mercy did her level best to focus on what she was being shown in her mother's full-length mirror. Wanda had allowed the two to use it in her bedroom. It was for work, after all.

"Okay, so you see the two ends here," Bethany was saying, standing behind Mercy with her arms essentially wrapped around her shoulders as she held the material of the undone red bow tie at Mercy's throat. "Now, watch."

Again, Mercy did her level best to focus, but she could feel the heat from the body behind her that grazed her periodically as she worked. It was a completely innocent moment, though quite intimate in its confines. Even so, Mercy was struggling to breathe at times.

"You're gonna flip this over this way," Bethany was saying.

Crud. Mercy realized the bow tie was halfway tied and she'd missed some steps. "Wait." She gave Bethany's reflection a sheepish smile. "Sorry. Can you start again, please?"

Bethany smirked and nodded, undoing her handiwork. She rested her chin on Mercy's shoulder and gave her a stern look through the mirror's reflection. "Focus."

Mercy nodded. "Yes. Sorry."

Finally, that torture finished and Mercy was

turned around to face the similarly dressed woman. "Okay, you look sharp," Bethany said, straightening the bow tie a bit and smoothing a few wrinkles free from the striped button-up.

"How do you get used to this?" Mercy asked, tugging a bit at the collar.

Bethany smiled. "Takes time, and I won't lie, I still look forward to yanking this thing off after every shift." She patted the center of the tie with her finger. "So, are you excited?"

"I think so," Mercy said, looking down at herself quickly before meeting Bethany's gaze again. "I'd much rather be moved over to the soda shop than the sew shop, so yes."

"You'd be far better to learn at the sew shop," Wanda said from the bedroom's open doorway. "Life lessons, far more important than scooping ice cream."

Mercy looked over Bethany's shoulder to her mother, who leaned a shoulder casually against the doorframe though there was nothing casual about her expression or body language, her lips tight and arms crossed tightly over her chest.

"Mother," Mercy said, feeling herself shrink back a bit inside herself. "I don't have the skill set or availability Mr. Wynter needs for those working there. I have school." She swallowed as she continued. "Plus, with Bethany leaving in a few months as well as some of the others, they need Sam and I to take over their shifts next door."

Wanda pushed away from the doorframe and turned to walk away. "Ice cream," she muttered.

Ashamed, Mercy turned away but was stopped by two fingers under her chin. She was gently urged to look at Bethany. Knowing speaking wasn't an option with Wanda not far away, Bethany simply rolled her eyes and screwed her face up in an expression of, *whatever*. Mercy smiled, getting the message. She nodded.

The two left the bedroom and headed to the front door of the small apartment. Wanda stood in the kitchen, making herself a sandwich. Mercy glanced over at her. "Thank you for letting us use your mirror, Mother."

Wanda didn't respond to that but said, "When will my daughter be home?"

Apparently her question was posed to Bethany, so she answered. "She'll be working a bit later shift than she did next door, Mrs. Faulkner. She should be home around nine. We close at eight, but it takes a little time to do closing duties."

"So," the older woman said, hand on hip as she faced the two young women. "When exactly will she have time for homework and house chores?"

"Well, ma'am," Bethany said reasonably. "I've worked here since I was fourteen and have straight As and handle my responsibilities at home as well. She'll just have to shuffle her schedule a bit and adjust when things are done. And," she added with a smile. "Her hours won't be closing every night. I just need to get her trained."

Wanda glared at the two but again said nothing in response. She turned to her task, her back to them. Mercy glanced at Bethany, embarrassed by her mother's rude behavior, but knew there was nothing she could do. So, instead, she followed Bethany out of the apartment.

Though she lived above it, Mercy hadn't been inside the soda shop but a couple of times. They didn't have the extra money to spend on such things and she felt she had no real right to be in there if she wasn't buying something. She didn't feel it was right to go in simply to say hello to Bethany. After all, she had a job to do.

They trotted down the stairs to the door at the bottom only to make a quick right to enter the soda shop. "Well," Mercy said as Bethany held the door for her. "I guess instead of having thirteen steps to my front door, I'll have three."

Bethany chuckled. "I have to admit," she said, grinning at her friend. "It's weird leaving through your front door."

They both snickered as Mercy was led to the back where they'd punch in. She was, of course, familiar with the process from the hotel, and in fact her timecard had been brought over and a new label stuck over the business name to reflect her current position. Clocked in, the very long day began.

Bethany was an incredible teacher. She knew that job like the back of her hand. She was patient, invited questions, and allowed Mercy to learn things her own way, which was to watch once then do herself. A few times, it was to watch three times then do twice. Bethany never left her side and introduced her to every single person they came into contact with, customer or coworker.

"Okay, let's head to the basement," Bethany said. "We need to grab some more sugar."

Mercy nodded. "Right behind you, boss."

Bethany smirked. "Boss, huh?" she nearly purred, just loud enough for her little shadow to hear. "Don't you forget that."

Mercy swallowed and nodded sagely. "'Kay."

Bethany burst into laughter. "Come on," she said, tugging on Mercy's sleeve.

❧❧❧❧

More tired than she'd expected to be, Mercy made her way to the door, Bethany shutting off lights behind her as they went. Together they'd taken out the trash and finished all the closing tasks, the other employees sent home early. Bethany had wanted Mercy to perform all tasks alongside her so she'd get a better grasp on her duties.

"What do you think?" Bethany asked as they stepped out into the cold night, the streets largely empty.

"A lot more physical than the hotel," Mercy said. "I had no idea vats of ice cream could be so heavy."

Bethany nodded, locking the front door to the store. "Oh, definitely. But they're huge, so it's not just a little ice cream," she said, glancing over at her friend, who stood huddled close by on the wooden sidewalk. "What I found—"

Her words were cut off when they both started at the *BANG* that sounded not two feet from where Mercy stood. She literally jumped back away from the glass and metal door that led up to the apartments.

"Oh my god." She hurried over and eased the door open. A man lay at the bottom of the stairs and his body was shaking violently. She recognized him as the young man who'd moved in across from she and her mother at the beginning of spring. She knelt down next to him. "It's okay, Riley," she said, placing a hand on his arm.

Bethany stepped over the man and knelt on the

stairs side of the small entryway. She met Mercy's gaze, looking absolutely terrified.

"He has epilepsy," she explained.

Bethany nodded, looking relieved at the information. Together, they stayed with him, waiting for the tremors to stop. Mercy had spoken to him a few times in passing, but he'd informed all the neighbors about his seizures so as not to "scare the heck out of anyone," as he explained it.

Finally, his body began to calm down and the tremors stopped. He was breathing heavily as he lay on his side in the entryway, body curled up in an awkward position. Mercy lightly squeezed his arm to let him know they were there as he still seemed to be out of it.

"Are you okay?" she asked gently.

Bethany smiled down at him as he was facing her. "Hey there," she said. "What day is it, Riley?"

"Uh," he muttered. "Wednesday? No, Thursday."

Bethany's smile widened. "Good job."

He groaned as he turned to his back and slowly sat up. He groaned again when his hand came up to his head. "Ow."

"Do you need to go to the doctor?" Mercy asked, looking into his face. He was a handsome young fella, looked to be somewhere in his early twenties. His dark brown hair was cut short, as was the style, though his bangs draped over his forehead at the moment, making him look more like a little boy. "You took quite a tumble."

It took a moment, but finally he responded to her question. He shook his head and met her gaze. "Don't think so."

"Can you stand, Riley?" Bethany asked. At his

nod, the two women helped him to his feet, though it took a couple tries. "Were you headed upstairs or down?"

"Up," he said, the slender man a head plus taller than his companions.

"Okay," she said, glancing past him at Mercy. "Let's get him upstairs."

Mercy nodded, Bethany moving behind him to join Mercy. The stairwell was too narrow for the passage of more than one person at a time, so they'd be there to keep him steady as his large hands braced himself on the walls on either side as the trio made upward progress.

Once they reached the top of the stairs, Bethany moved around front. "Give me your apartment key."

He reached into his trouser pocket and retrieved his keys, sorting through them in slow, almost dreamlike movements until he found the correct one and handed it to Bethany. Mercy helped him with her arm at his back, his slung over her shoulders as Bethany hurried down to the apartment Mercy told her was his.

The door opened, Bethany returned to Mercy and Riley, taking his other side as the hallway was wide enough to accommodate all three. "Almost there," Bethany said softly. It was clear the young man was hurting and seemed utterly exhausted after his seizure.

The apartment was very small, a one-bedroom and a bit cluttered, though not dirty. "Where do you want to go?" Mercy asked. "The couch or bed?"

"Bed," he muttered.

"Want to go ahead and turn down the bed?" Bethany asked, nodding at the narrow doorway.

Mercy agreed and abandoned her post at his side to do as suggested. The bed was made, so she pulled down the thin quilt that topped it and blanket and sheet. It was so strange being in the bedroom of a stranger, let alone a man. Her mother would flip, she thought.

"Okay, plant it there," Bethany said, getting the tall man turned around and in position to sit, which he did. As if in silent agreement, both women took a booted foot, unlacing and removing the footwear so the young man could turn himself to get correctly positioned on the bed. "Are you okay?" Bethany asked Riley. "Do you need some water or anything?"

He shook his head, brown eyes closing as a wrinkle formed between his heavy eyebrows. "No," he murmured. "Thank you so much for your kindness." His eyes opened a bit. "Um," he said, looking to the window. "Would you mind pulling the shade?" he asked. "I get the most awful headaches after an... episode. I'd be real grateful."

"Of course." Mercy hurried to the end of the bed, the side of which was pressed against the wall like her own, to make more room in the small bedroom. She had to lean across it to reach the bottom of the shade. She pulled it down, trying to make as little noise as possible. She knew how much light would come streaming in through the window come morning.

"Thank you," he murmured thickly, his eyes already falling closed.

Bethany met Mercy's gaze, a look of concern in her eyes. Mercy nodded, agreeing. But, they'd done what they could do. The keys were left on the small kitchen table and the doorknob was locked before they left the small apartment, closing the door behind them. They headed back down the hallway and the stairs to the entryway where Riley had landed after falling down the stairs when his seizure struck.

"Poor guy," Bethany said. Her voice was quiet, even as they could speak down there without worry of bothering those upstairs.

Mercy hugged herself, a bit unsettled by what she'd seen. "Yes. He told all of us about his seizures when he moved in not long ago. Nice guy, I guess. Keeps to himself."

Bethany smiled at her, reaching up and tucking some auburn strands behind her ear that had come out of her updo while helping the young man. "You did good." She leaned in and left the softest of kisses on Mercy's cheek, dangerously close to her lips. The kiss lingered a bit, soft fingertips caressing Mercy's check before she moved away. "I need to get home," she murmured, her eyes downcast.

Mercy could feel a heavy tension between them, a need coming from Bethany that she, too, felt, though she didn't fully understand what it meant. All she did know was that she didn't want her to leave. "Oh!" she said, finding a reason, as flimsy as it was, to keep her there, if only for a moment longer. "How do I undo this?" She reached up and lightly tugged on her uniform bow tie.

Bethany grinned. "You're halfway there." She reached up and took the front bow between the thumb and forefingers in her left hand and the back of the bow with her right. "Lightly tug," she instructed, doing it as she said it, the bow coming undone and the two ends flopping down from the collar. "Then," she said, a teasing tone in her voice. "You do this." She began to unbutton the top buttons of the shirt.

Mercy gasped, batting her hands away. "Excuse me!"

Bethany gave her a devilish grin, dropping her hands away. "Well, I need to get. Don't want you getting into trouble on my behalf."

She knew Bethany was right. Nodding, she said, "Okay."

She chewed on her lower lip for just a moment in uncertainty before she went with her instinct and gave Bethany a hug. The two held each other for a long moment, clearly both loath to let go or say goodnight. But, reality was a thing, especially when Mercy heard one of the apartment doors open upstairs.

Bethany's hand stroked down her back before the hand fell away, as did the woman herself. She took a step back in the confines of the entryway and met Mercy's gaze. "Goodnight, Mercy."

"Goodnight." Mercy watched her go, waiting to make sure she reached her truck safely where it was parked across the street in the lot, as usual. They shared one last look and wave before Bethany climbed in and got the truck started. The headlamps disappeared into the darkness as she drove away.

Feeling sad, her heart heavy, and frankly feeling like part of herself had just driven away into the night, a confused Mercy headed up the stairs. Luckily it hadn't been her mother opening their door in search of her but one of her other neighbors to use the community phone in the hallway. She nodded a greeting at the older man as she passed him and headed to her own door.

She was glad that her mother was already in her bedroom when she entered, locking up behind her. She was tired and tired of smelling like a walking, talking ice cream cone. She looked forward to a bath and bed.

Entering the small hallway that led to the bedrooms and bathroom, she walked to her mother's closed bedroom door. Using the backs of her fingers, she lightly rapped on the wood. "I'm home, Mother."

"Good. Get to bed," was called from inside the room.

"Yes, ma'am."

Chapter Fourteen

It was the first weekend of no snow, not even sodden ground after it had melted. It was early May, and though more snow would likely fall before winter called it quits and turned to summer, the four friends were enjoying the warm day.

Pops and Billy were standing in the middle of the shallower part of the creek with pant legs rolled up fly fishing. Bethany and Mercy were back on shore, Bethany with her sketch pad and Mercy reading a book.

It was glorious. Bethany's eyes were hidden behind her dark sunglasses, so Mercy had no idea that they were on her, sketching her. She studied Mercy's face, relaxed as she held the book flat against her raised thighs as she leaned back against one of the logs arranged around the stone ring that would hold their campfire later—if they stayed that late.

She glanced down to the pad that, like Mercy's book, rested against Bethany's raised thighs. She used the edge of her hand to smear the graphite line she'd just drawn into shadows that were made by the overhead sunlight beneath Mercy's breasts, lovingly cupped in her bra and short-sleeved blouse.

Something had changed over the last few months, and it made Bethany extremely uncomfortable. She was finding herself more and more drawn to the young woman who sat just a couple feet away. Certainly,

Mercy was absolutely stunning in such a natural way. Mercy could have just rolled out of bed, her long, auburn hair sticking up in every direction, and still be stunning.

She surreptitiously scanned her face, the long lashes that currently hid the downcast expressive brown eyes. The light sprinkling of freckles across the creaminess of the skin of her face. Full lips, naturally rosy and just a bit pouty. She knew firsthand just how soft those lips were, how soft her face was.

She knew it was absolutely not okay that she wanted to sample their softness again, but if it would ever happen again, she knew the circumstances would have to be different and that she would need to take her time in approaching Mercy. She wanted to test the passion that she suspected Mercy was capable of. It was usually the quiet, shy ones that, when given the chance, blossomed into the most addictive and beautiful flowers.

Mercy was already doing that, already opening her petals and, unwittingly, pulling Bethany closer and closer to smell her fragrance. As much as part of her wanted to hate Billy for what he had done, blanketing her with his guilty twin logic that he knew damn well she wouldn't be able to turn away from, Bethany was also partly glad she was leaving in just over seven weeks.

It was getting harder and harder to keep her hands off Mercy, to keep her thoughts to herself. She knew she had a terrible poker face, and she was so afraid that she'd scare the hell out of Mercy again if she saw just how much Bethany wanted her. But what scared Bethany was that it wasn't just a physical need. She craved her presence, her calm, her energy, her sweet smile.

She focused on those lips now in her sketch. There was the softest smile upon them now, as if Mercy were enjoying what she was reading, or simply enjoying the time with her friends. Bethany couldn't help but allow that same smile to spread across her own lips. If Mercy was happy and content, so was she.

"Do you think we'll do this again?"

Pulled from her thoughts, Bethany blinked several times, then looked over at Mercy from her sketch. "Do what?"

"This," Mercy said, indicating them, the boys in the water, and the gorgeous cloudless sky.

"Of course we'll do it again," Bethany said, carefully closing her sketch pad. She wasn't comfortable with Mercy or, god forbid, Billy seeing her sketch. She smirked. "Probably tomorrow."

Mercy looked down at her book, then shook her head. "No," she said, looking back to her, sadness in her eyes. "I mean, when you guys get back. I'm worried things will change."

Bethany studied her for a moment. "What would change?" she asked gently, clearly seeing how unsettled Mercy was.

Mercy fingered the pages of her book as she shrugged. "I don't know," she murmured, looking down at her fingers.

Bethany put her sketch pad and pencil aside and pushed to her feet. "Come on." She held out her hand. "Let's go take a walk."

Mercy glanced up at her, then placed her bookmark between the pages and closed her book, setting it on the log she'd been leaning against before taking Bethany's hand. She got to her feet and the two headed toward the trees.

"Billy," Bethany called out. "Gonna take a walk." He gave her a salute of acknowledgment before returning his attention back to his casting.

They walked in companionable silence, the shade of the woods feeling good after enjoying the warm sun for so long. Her skin felt warm and a bit tingly. Perhaps she'd gotten a bit too much sun on her winter-paled arms. They both looked up when birds began to squawk down at them. She smiled.

"Thinking we're not welcome guests." She looked over at Mercy, who was looking up into the tree. She nodded, meeting her gaze.

"Perhaps we should move on before we get pooped on."

Bethany tugged on the hand she still held, leading them in a different direction. She knew she should release the soft, warm hand in hers, but she just couldn't. And, in fairness, Mercy hadn't pulled hers away, either. As it was getting closer to graduation and closer to the time when she and Billy would leave, she could sense an air of…what was it? Sadness? Fear? Worry? Desperation, maybe? Truth was, though, she wasn't entirely sure if it was coming from Mercy or if it was coming from her. Perhaps both.

They continued on in silence, just enjoying the day, enjoying the peace, quiet, and company. Finally, Bethany knew she needed to respond to Mercy's question and concern. "I imagine things will change," she finally said. "Mainly because we'll all get older, mature. Well," she snorted. "Some of us." They met gazes and shared a smile.

"And then there are those of us who are already fifty," Mercy added.

"Pops," they said in unison, chuckling.

"But seriously," Bethany said with a heavy sigh. "I think this war is going to change everyone, Mercy. Whether you head off to fight or stay put in your hometown."

"The town has already changed," Mercy said. "You can feel it. Everything seems so heavy, so much uncertainty on everyone's face. Not so long ago," she added, their hands lightly swinging back and forth between them as they strolled. "I used to see people so excited to go into the soda shop. You know?" She looked to Bethany who met her gaze. "A sweet treat on a random Saturday. Now, it's almost as if they're saying, 'I better get this now because I may never get it again.'"

"Yes," Bethany agreed. "I feel it too."

"And those parades." Mercy's voice broke and she pulled her hand away. She turned away, face buried in her hands.

Damn you, Billy! She walked over to her and gently turned her around to face her. "Come here." She enfolded the smaller young woman into her arms, her eyes closing as she rested her head against that which rested on her shoulder. She said nothing, as there was nothing to say.

She couldn't say for sure that neither she nor Billy would be killed, though she'd tried to reassure Mercy before. She couldn't tell her everything would be okay, because she didn't know that, either. She couldn't apologize, because at the end of the day she could have said no. She could have let Billy go on this fool's errand by himself, but she hadn't. It was one of the few times in her life she'd ignored her own heart and had gone along.

Instead, she held Mercy as she cried, another crack forming in her heart with every tear that fell against her neck. She brushed her fingers through Mercy's hair and rubbed her back. As much as she'd like to think the tears were for her, no doubt they were for every single young person that was leaving Wynter to find their destiny on the battlefield or in a field hospital somewhere in a distant, foreign land.

As much as she'd like to think it was she that Mercy would miss, no doubt it was all of them in the tight-knit foursome that was their friend circle. The other friends that she and Billy once had were peripheral and had drifted away outside of school hours. The four of them, that was all they needed, and now two of them were leaving.

"Do you think your mom would let you spend the night tonight?" Bethany asked into the hug once the tears began to slow. "No school tomorrow, and we don't go in until noon," she added. "We could swing by your place and you can get your stuff for work and just go in with me."

"I can ask," Mercy murmured.

"We can stay up stupid late and eat junk and giggle like little girls," Bethany said, smiling at the chuckle she heard and felt against her neck. "Sound good?"

Mercy nodded. "Very good."

⁂

To both Bethany and Mercy's astonishment and joy, Wanda had agreed, though she hadn't looked happy about it. Bethany always worried that Mercy would pay for her mother's acquiescence in other ways. Mercy never complained, never said how things were when they were alone at home, but it was always a fear. Bethany trusted that woman as far as she could throw her.

But for the time being, they had just pulled up in front of the Wynter house. She hadn't even asked her own parents as she knew they adored Mercy and would welcome her with open arms. She hadn't been disappointed as Mercy was met with hugs and kisses and big, welcoming smiles and enthusiastic greetings.

"Honey," Rachel called out to the teens as they were about to head upstairs. "I need you to take that dress mannequin back to your grandma tomorrow before you go to work."

"Will do," Bethany called back, leading the way up the stairs. When they got to her bedroom, she stood at the open door and hurried through the darkness to her bedside table and switched on the lamp so Mercy could enter without running into anything. "Welcome to Chez Bethany," she said with open arms. Though Mercy had been there once before, things had gotten a little…complicated, and spending time in the room or looking around hadn't exactly been part of it.

Mercy smiled and gave her a little bow. "Why, thank you." She shrugged the strap of her overnight bag off her shoulder and set it on the floor near the foot of the bed. "I finally get to see all your drawings."

"Ah yes," Bethany said, rubbing the back of her neck as she looked up at all of them that were on her ceiling. "You do."

"Oh wow," Mercy gasped, walking over to where Bethany stood and looking up. "Those are amazing."

"Thanks," Bethany said shyly, tossing the sketch pad she'd been using at The Hole earlier that day to the bed, along with the pencil and her purse.

"Why do you put them up there?" Mercy asked. She indicated the bed. "May I?"

"Sure." She watched as Mercy climbed onto the bed until she flipped over to her back and looked up at the spread before her, hands resting on her stomach.

Bethany moved her belongings from the bed to the bedside table and joined her. She wanted to see what Mercy saw, through her eyes and perspective, as it were. They were nearly shoulder to shoulder on the bed. It wasn't as narrow as Mercy's, but wasn't huge, either. "See that one," she said, raising her hand and pointing.

Mercy moved her head so that it rested against Bethany's, the two nearly sharing a pillow. "Yes."

"That was our dog, Edgar."

"Edgar?" Mercy asked, amusement in her voice.

"Hey, now. I was like, five. I named him after the mailman." She grinned at the laughter that earned her. "And that," she said, pointing to another sketch. "That's my dream house."

"It kind of looks like the one we stayed at with Helen that weekend," Mercy said, cocking her head a bit.

Bethany considered that. "Yeah, I can see that. It's actually more like Gran and Grandma's. You'll get to see that tomorrow when I drop off the sewing thing before we head to work." She sat up. "Okay," she said, climbing off the bed. "I need to pee, then I'm going to grab us some snacks. Be right back, 'kay?"

"Yes, ma'am," Mercy said from where she lay on the bed. "I'm just going to stargaze." She nodded toward one of the sketches that was of a landscape and night sky, filled with moon and stars.

Bethany chuckled and left the room. She hummed to herself as she trotted down the two flights of stairs to the main floor. She paused when she saw her parents sitting together on the couch, her father reading something amusing from his *Reader's Digest*. As she watched, her mother kicked off her shoes and curled her legs up to the side, leaning into him. As he read, he absently stretched his arm around her shoulders.

Smiling, she turned away and continued on to the kitchen. That was what she wanted. That beautiful love and affection. After so many years—well, a lifetime for them—her parents were still deeply in love. Neither had been with anyone else in any way. And, as her Grandma Thea had told her, nor had they ever wanted to be. First best friend, first fight, first day of school, first kiss, first love.

Her father, two years older than her mother, had once joked, "Those first two years of my life were the loneliest."

In the kitchen, she was surprised to see Billy making himself a peanut butter and jelly sandwich. She shook her head, amused. "Don't you ever get enough?" When he said nothing but seemed to ignore her, her eyebrows fell. "What's wrong?" She grabbed a couple bowls from the cabinet, intending to fill one with potato chips and the other with nut mixture they kept around.

"Why didn't you tell me you were bringing her here to spend the night?" he asked, voice flat.

Confused, she said, "What? Who?" She walked over to the pantry to grab her intended goodies for them to munch on.

"Who do you think," he said, glaring over at her.

She quirked an eyebrow as she carefully tore open a new bag of chips, not wanting them to fly out everywhere. "I wasn't aware I needed your permission."

"It's not right," he said, slamming the jar of homemade strawberry jelly down on the counter, startling her. He turned to her, hand on hip. "You bring her here, shoving it in my face that I'm not allowed to spend time with her."

"Billy," she said with a tired sigh. "You spent all day with her today. The Hole? Fishing? Picnic lunch? Ring a bell?"

"Yeah, with you and Pops there too. I can't just spend time with her alone. Just because you're a girl, you can. Her mother is so freaking weird with whatever issues that she won't even allow her to go on a double date with me and Elmer and his girl." This time the peanut butter jar got slammed. "It's not right that just because of my gender I'm pushed aside."

Bethany looked up from her own task for a moment. "Hmm, sounds vaguely familiar," she muttered. "Sorry, bud, you got no sympathy from me on that one."

He clicked his tongue in irritation. "Hardly the same thing, Bethany."

"No? Okay." She set the chips aside once the bowl was filled and popped open the can of nuts.

"Damn it, Bethany! You know damn well I like her! Yet, you swoop in—"

"No," she said, angry. She turned to face him, fire in her eyes. "No. That is not what happened because honestly, Billy? Nothing happened. We're friends, and will remain so." She hated the words that were so bitter on her tongue, but she knew they had to be true "Yes, I know her mother has issues, lordy do I know. But has it ever occurred to you to ask her what *she* wants?"

"Huh?"

Hand on hip, as he had done moments before, Bethany used her other hand to point in the general direction of their parents. "You need to take some notes from Dad. He has never treated Mama with anything short of respect and never treated her as anything less than an equal."

"What does that have to do with me and Mercy?"

"Did you ask her if she was interested in you, Billy?" she asked. "Did you ask her if she'd like to go out with you, or did you just assume she would because you're you? I know you asked Wanda Faulkner if her daughter could go on that double date with you—"

"Which she said no—"

"Did you ask Mercy if she even wanted to?"

His mouth was open as if to say something but quickly snapped shut. He stared at her as if it finally hit him what she was saying. Rubbing the back of his neck, he turned back to his sandwich.

"Billy," she said gently. "You're an athlete. You know how it works with a game. You show up, play hard, and if you win, it's because you fought to win. You don't get a victory just because you showed up." What she said next hurt, but she'd known for a long time he was interested, and she was going to do the right thing by him—as usual, even though it was getting harder and harder for her. "If you like her," she said. "Win her because you gave it your all. Don't claim victory or possession because you think you can or are entitled to it." With that, she finished her task, cleaned up her mess, and left the kitchen.

Chapter Fifteen

A nd so," Bethany said, looking out over her fellow graduating seniors from where she stood behind the lectern. "In conclusion, I wish for you, my fellow members of the class of nineteen forty-two, go forth into this very uncertain time. Be brave, be bold, but never forget who you are. We are Wynter strong!"

Those in the school's gymnasium erupted into applause at the valedictorian's speech. She gave the room at large a smile, then moved back to her seat on the dais where the faculty involved with the ceremony sat. Soon enough it would be time for the seniors to be called one at a time to get their diploma.

Seated again, she surreptitiously looked around the room, the graduates sitting in chairs on the floor of the gym while parents and friends sat in the bleachers. She smiled when she saw her parents and grandparents. Even Uncle Nate and Aunt Tabitha were there. She felt a quick hitch of emotions at the absence of her older brothers, Leo in the ground and Ned off in the Pacific somewhere.

There was somebody else missing too. Mercy had volunteered to work, as much of the staff was gone from the soda shop, many of them seniors or siblings of them. Bethany's attention was pulled out of her thoughts when Principal Evers began to speak again, a few remarks before diplomas were doled out.

Congratulations given and hugs and kisses thrust onto the newly minted high school graduates, Bethany and Billy were loaded into the car to be driven to the start of the parade route. It was their turn, and Bethany dreaded it. Since the day they'd told their parents what they were doing, it hadn't been discussed again.

At first, she'd been surprised by the silence, as her parents, particularly her mother, were extremely keen on communication. One night, it had hit her: her family was on overload from the attack on the country to the loss of Leo and by proxy Ned, then the twins. There wasn't a day that her guilt didn't eat her alive. There wasn't a day that she wasn't angry at Billy—and herself.

They'd already lost Leo. What if she or either of her other brothers didn't make it back? What would that do to her mother? As she watched the scenery go by, so familiar to her, houses and buildings she'd seen her entire life, she considered that. She also considered what would happen if she simply didn't use that train ticket sent to her by the United States government. Would she go to jail?

With just over three weeks before they left, she knew she'd do the "right thing," but damn it all, she didn't want to.

"Okay, you two," Henry Wynter said, pulling the car to a stop. "Here we are."

Bethany shook her thoughts away as she looked around. Sure enough, there was the fire truck and school marching band that would be heralding what she thought was the parade of the walking dead. How many of those unloading from the cars around them to join in would never make it back home?

"What's the matter?" Billy asked, grabbing her arm.

She stared at him, looked him long and hard in the eye. "This is a fool's errand, Billy," she said, then turned away and walked to the man who held up his hand and was blowing a whistle to get everyone to go to him.

She reached up and straightened her mortarboard as she went, readjusting some of the bobby pins to make the fit a little more secure. She felt her brother walk up beside her. She could tell he was irritated, though he said nothing. In the weeks since everything had happened, and since Mercy had entered their lives, she and her twin had been at odds more than at any other time in their lives. She hated it. They'd turn eighteen in a matter of weeks, and she felt more disjointed from him than she had in the entire seventeen years prior.

"When are you gonna knock this off?" he finally said, muttering just loud enough for her to hear above the chattering all around them.

"Knock what off?" she asked, not looking at him.

"Blaming me for this."

She wasn't sure how to answer that. Her instinct? Forever. But she'd agreed to go. Honestly, she wasn't sure who to be more furious with, him or herself. "You don't think you hold any part in this?" she asked instead.

"Well, I do," he admitted. "To a point. I didn't twist your arm, Bethany," he bit out.

"No?" She glared up at him. When he wouldn't meet her gaze, she knew he understood that she would never have gone had he not laid it on thick, using their own twin dedication against her.

"You still could have said no," he muttered stubbornly.

The conversation was cut short when they were positioned in rows, Billy right behind her. There were very few young ladies heading out, so Bethany and the few others were put in a row by themselves, all the males in rows behind them.

With instructions to begin marching once the fire truck blew its horn, Bethany felt her stomach doing flips and flops. She was hot, the graduation gown she wore heavy and bulky, and honestly, she just wanted to be at home. She wanted to be lying on her bed on her stomach sketching. It was her escape, to create whatever world she wanted to.

She took a deep breath, noting that the air was a bit heavy, muggy. She could see some clouds coming in from the west. Perhaps their parade would get rained out. Perhaps Wynter was gearing up, yet again, to cry for her leaving children.

The marching band headed out, the talented group of young musicians making her smile for the briefest of moments. That was something she wished she'd done in school—gone out for band. She'd just stayed so focused on her academics and worked a lot of hours at her family's businesses.

She allowed herself to get into the music just a bit, fingers tapping lightly against her leg as she waited, baking under the afternoon mid-June sun. She started when the fire truck's horn belched out into the day, delighting those lined up along the parade route but making Bethany want to throw up. She began to walk, along with the others that would soon be marching off in a very different kind of uniform than that of graduation.

Those around her waved, were excited to be the focus for the mile of their journey that would end downtown. She didn't wave, she didn't smile, she didn't rejoice in such a patriotic send-off. People along the route were standing on the sidewalks, on their lawns, sitting on their car hoods, all waving American flags.

They passed a group of children, who couldn't be any older than six or seven, so excited, jumping up and down and cheering. She saw one little boy who did none of those things. His little face was scrunched up as tears slowly streamed down his cheeks. The woman standing with that group of kids hugged him from behind, whispering something into his ear.

Bethany looked away. She saw a police cruiser parked at a corner, the uniformed officer standing at the open driver's door, his hand to his forehead in salute. A woman was watering her flowers with a watering can. She glanced over at them, then quickly away. Bethany couldn't tell if the look on her face was one of sadness or disgust. Not everyone thought the United States belonged in the war, despite Japan's attack.

Finally, they were heading into downtown proper, the rows of businesses on the main street coming into view. Again, people lined the sidewalks, leaned out of second-floor windows, even a few atop a roof or two. They were getting near the hotel and soda shop. She saw all the women who were working at the transformed hotel and now making uniforms, standing outside of the building.

She saw Wanda Faulkner. She stood toward the side of the building, arms crossed over her chest and her expression tight. She met Bethany's gaze, her own hard. Bethany looked away when she saw the familiar uniforms, the red and white stripes and bow ties. She did smile a bit at that. All her coworkers were standing outside the soda shop, as well as what looked to be all the customers.

Her friends and classmates that she also worked with were cheering, yelling, and making general fools of themselves on their behalf. That is, all but one. Mercy leaned against the corner of the building, hugging herself. She looked as if she was one moment away from breaking. She met Bethany's gaze, which held for a moment, and apparently that was all it took.

Mercy's face scrunched up as she began to cry. She quickly turned away from the street and ran down the alleyway. Without a thought, Bethany broke from the parade and took off after her, her graduation gown billowing out behind her as she shoved her way through onlookers and finally down the alleyway.

"Mercy!"

The younger woman was sobbing behind the soda shop building, not far from the fire escape. Bethany reached her, out of breath and shocked she didn't roll an ankle running in the heels she wore, even though they weren't terribly high.

She said nothing, nothing to say as she placed her hand on Mercy's shoulder. The crying young woman looked up at her. "I don't want you to go."

Bethany brushed some auburn strands of hair out of her tear streak. "I know," she said softly. "We'll be back—"

"No!" She fully faced Bethany, so much pain and sadness in her eyes. "I don't want *you* to go." She looked away from Bethany. "I'm so tired of crying," she whispered.

Bethany brushed more hair out of her face before she cupped her face, gently urging her to look at her. Mercy's eyes were an endless brown pool of pain. "Sweetheart," Bethany murmured. Mercy leaned into the touch.

"Bethany," Mercy said, pleading in her tone and her eyes.

Understanding to the pits of her soul, Bethan was about to take a small step closer when Billy rounded the corner, out of breath. "Oh, thank god," he panted. "I was so worried!" He grabbed Mercy, pulling her against his chest.

Bethany nearly stumbled backward at his sudden appearance. She watched as he cradled her head against him, though Mercy's gaze never left hers. She was sickened as he murmured soft words to the woman he held, assuring her they'd be back before she knew it, that he'd bring her amazing things back from Europe, as though he were heading off on vacation.

Disgusted, Bethany turned away and left the alley.

❧❧❧❧

Fingers tapping on the steering wheel, she had no idea if Mercy was going to show up or not. When she'd entered the soda shop that afternoon to wish Mercy a happy birthday, she'd had no idea what to expect after the encounter with Billy in the alley. Her fears were put to rest the moment she looked into Mercy's eyes, however. Mercy had immediately come out from behind the counter and gathered her in a hug, muttering an apology for Billy interrupting their moment after the parade. While kids were gathering in the shop to celebrate Mercy during her shift, Bethany had suggested a private outing after Wanda fell asleep, and to her surprise, Mercy had agreed. She understood that it was dangerous, and that it was entirely likely that she could change her mind or, god forbid, get caught. She glanced up at the clear, cloudless sky, the full moon overhead.

She'd decided to take her own advice to her brother. No, she wasn't asking Mercy what she wanted, because at this point, it didn't matter. What Mercy was making very clear was that she wanted to spend more time with Bethany, and Bethany wanted that, too, so… She let out a heavy sigh of relief when she saw the figure sprinting across the street and to her truck.

The door was yanked open and a heavily breathing Mercy threw herself inside. Her eyes were wide and she looked somewhere between scared and liberated. "Sorry I'm late," she said, closing the door and getting herself situated as Bethany got them moving. "I had to wait for her to turn on her fan, which honestly I don't think she'd hear a tornado over, plus once she turns it on, I know she's ready for sleep."

"It's okay." Bethany grinned, reaching over and patting Mercy's leg. "You okay?"

"Yes," Mercy blew out. "I can't believe I just snuck out."

Bethany gave her a devilish grin. "Hey, with you already celebrating your birthday with us today at the soda shop, there was no way in hell she was going to let you come out with me tonight."

"No," Mercy admitted. "No way." She looked around. "Where are we going?"

"Well," Bethany said, heading toward the outskirts of town and into the woods. "I figure, the full moon landed square on your sixteenth birthday, so it was a sign."

"A sign for what?"

"A sign that you were supposed to come swimming with me."

"Wait, what?" Mercy gasped. "Swimming? Bethany, it's after nine o'clock!"

"Why, yes it is," Bethany agreed. She burst into laughter at the uncertain look she got. "It'll be fine, I promise you. I brought us some towels," she said, patting the two folded items sitting on the bench seat between them.

"But I don't have a bathing suit," Mercy protested.

"You got a bra on?" Bethany asked, holding the wheel with both hands as she slowed on the uneven wooded path that jostled them.

"Yes."

"You got underwear on?"

"Yes,"

"Then you're good to go. I mean," she added, teasing in her voice. "You could just go in the buff, but I don't see that happening." She laughed again at the gasp that one caused. "Teasing. Listen," she said, more serious as she pulled to the regular parking space at The Hole. "If you don't want to get into the water, you don't have to, but it's a warm night and will be beautiful." She met Mercy's gaze. "Okay?"

Mercy, who looked a bit relieved, nodded. "Okay."

Truck parked, Bethany grabbed the towels and the two climbed out. It was an absolutely gorgeous late June night. The sky was crystal clear, black velvet with stars twinkling like diamonds upon it. The moon was so bright, sitting over the water, shimmering in the gently lapping waves.

"My goodness," Mercy whispered as they stepped out of the trees to the shore. She looked up into the night sky, eyes wide. "So amazing. Look!" she exclaimed, pointing. "A shooting star."

Bethany stepped up beside her, watching. "Wow," she whispered. "Make a wish." She closed her eyes and made her own wish. *Let me return home to Wynter and be happy.*

Mercy's eyes fell closed and her lips moved, though no sound came out. Bethany studied her profile. Her face raised to the sky. Her hair fell down her back and her throat, so graceful as her head was arched back, her features so lovely. Bethany fought the urge to run a fingertip down along the rounded line of her forehead and along a straight nose to full lips,

She forced herself to look away and ultimately, move away. She plopped the towels down on one of the logs and began to unbutton her dress. She allowed the garment to fall off her shoulders and felt she was being watched. Turning to glance over her shoulder, she saw Mercy looking at her.

A shiver ran down her back and through her body. The intensity in those eyes nearly took her breath away. She knew that likely Mercy had no clue she was even doing it, so Bethany didn't act on it. But damn, it was hard. She looked away and let the dress fall before stepping out of it. She was left in bra and panties.

She wanted this to be fun and refreshing for them, so once she had her dress folded a bit and set on the log, she ran into the silver-tipped ripples, splashing her way to the deeper water. She groaned in satisfaction as the cool water enveloped her. She dipped below the surface, shooting across the waterway, which wasn't any more than five or six feet deep at its deepest, but certainly deep enough for a good swim.

When she broke the surface, she saw that Mercy had removed her socks and shoes and had made her way out onto the huge boulder that sat at the edge of the deeper water. Billy and Pops often dove off it. She had her legs submerged to just below her knees, feet lightly kicking this way and that.

Bethany swam over to her, noting how calm and serene she looked. She pulled herself up onto the boulder and plopped down next to Mercy. She glanced over and met her gaze. "Did I make a mistake bringing you here to swim?" she asked, apology in her voice.

"No. Not at all." Again, the peaceful smile as Mercy looked out over the night. "It's so absolutely gorgeous here, like a different world at night." She grinned at Bethany. "Thank you so much for bringing me here.

Pleased, Bethany gently nudged Mercy's shoulder with her own. "Happy birthday. Again."

Mercy's smile was so sweet. "Thank you," she said softly. Their gaze held for a moment before she looked down at her hands, which rested on her thighs, partially exposed as she'd pulled the skirt of her dress up so as not to get it wet. "You know, my father died just a couple months after my birthday last year, and I truly thought I'd never have a good birthday again, left with my mother." She smiled, though still kept her gaze downcast. "I was wrong."

Bethany grew very serious as she felt such a need wash over her, a need to protect this precious creature she sat next to, a need to make sure she was happy. "As long as I'm around," she said. "I will make it my absolute mission in life to make sure you have a wonderful birthday from here on out." She gave her a little smirk. "And, when I'm not physically around, I'll still make it happen." She studied Mercy's eyes. "Got me?"

Mercy nodded. "Yes, ma'am." They shared a smile before Mercy looked away again. When she spoke, her voice was so quiet, Bethany almost missed what she said. "Want to know what I wished for?"

"Sure, if you want to tell me. Though," she warned sagely. "May make it not come true, as they say."

Mercy nodded with a little shrug. "Yes, but I figure it will or it won't, regardless."

"True. So, what did you wish for?"

"I wished that you'd kiss me."

Bethany's heart melted and her clit seized, but she ignored the second one as best she could. She brought up her right hand and, using a gentle touch, urged Mercy to look over at her. She smiled at her. "Your wish is granted."

Mercy's face was soft beneath her fingers, but it had nothing on the softness of her lips. Bethany took her time, reading Mercy's reactions and responses. She wasn't going to push anything that wasn't wanted, wasn't going to take or claim. She wanted to show Mercy what it meant to hold the reins, even as she was led. To show her that she was respected, yet wanted.

Mercy responded, meeting Bethany's lips, moving against them. Their kiss was soft, slow, allowing exploration and plenty of opportunity for Mercy to pull away if she wanted to. She clearly didn't want to, as the softest sigh escaped as Bethany deepened it a bit, opening the door for a more intimate caress.

Mercy's hand tentatively rested on Bethany's thigh, which sent a jolt through her. Bethany released a sigh of her own to let Mercy know that the touch was not only okay, but desired. Another sigh at the first soft touch of tongue sliding against tongue, though Bethany wasn't sure which of them it had come from.

After several wonderful moments, Bethany felt Mercy begin to pull away a bit, so she slowed the kiss and brought it to a natural end. She left a final soft kiss on her lips before moving away enough to be able to look into her face, flushed like her own.

"Yes," Mercy said at length. "Best birthday ever."

Chapter Sixteen

Y ou're so sweet, Evelyn," Bethany said, looking down at the little kerchief the older
woman had given her, Bethany's initials stitched to
the corner. The woman, who'd known her Gran for
decades, had worked for the family for about twenty
years. She'd been a wonderful wing for newcomers to
be taken under at the soda shop. "I'll carry this with
me wherever I go."

The older woman, who was several inches
shorter than Bethany, took her in a bone-crushing
hug. "You be safe,' she whispered in Bethany's ear.
"You come back to us." She'd lost her son in the first
world war, so she knew what she was talking about.

"Yes, ma'am," Bethany said into the hug, returning the squeeze she got before she was released to
move on to the next uniformed soda shop employee.

She steadily made her way down the line,
accepting hugs, kind words, and trying to soothe a few
tears. The following day was her and Billy's eighteenth
birthday, and they would ship out the day after that.
Today was her final day working at the soda shop, and
her shift had come to an end.

She'd been part of the goodbye line herself more
than once as other employees had left to find their
fate overseas. Finally, she reached Mercy. Their gazes
met and, without a word, Bethany was taken into her
embrace. Though she didn't want to let go, propriety

was alive and well as she knew they were being casually watched by the others there. They all knew the two were close friends, but still.

"Come over tonight," Mercy whispered into the hug. Bethany nodded.

Later that night, Bethany was in her bedroom, packing. Their birthday was strictly a family affair, including just their parents, grandparents, aunts, uncles, and cousins. A big birthday to be sure, but a final send-off. The next day, she and Billy would be driven to Denver to catch their train.

"Come in," she called out at the soft knock to her door. She watched as her mother entered, a small smile on tight lips before the door was closed again. Bethany remained standing at the foot of her bed, folding the clothing she was told to bring with her and placing it in the one regulation-size duffel bag she was allowed to bring. "Hey, Mama."

"Hey, sweetheart." Rachel looked haggard, soul-tired. She had since Pearl Harbor. It absolutely pained Bethany's heart to see it, almost as though her beautiful mother had aged overnight. Again, guilt niggled at her. Rachel sat on the bed, watching her daughter work. "How are you feeling about everything?"

Bethany shrugged, placing the panties she'd just folded up into a small square atop the others. "Nervous," she admitted. She spared a glance to her mother before returning to her task. "Guilty."

"No," Rachel said, reaching out her arm and placing her hand over Bethany's, who was picking up another garment to fold. She left it there until Bethany met her gaze, blue eyes so troubled. "No," she said again. "This is a very scary and dangerous time in our country and our world right now, Bethany. We need the courage of our youth to save democracy for all of us." She gave her a sad smile. "Just like your Dad marched off some twenty-five years ago."

Bethany nodded, agreeing, but was still concerned. "Will you guys be okay?" she asked. "I mean, *really* okay?"

Rachel smiled and pushed to her feet. She walked over to her daughter and gathered her in a tight hug. "I'll be really okay when all my babies are back home," she said softly into the hug. She squeezed before releasing her. "Are you going to Mercy's tonight?"

Bethany nodded. "Yeah."

Rachel eyed her for a moment, crossing her arms over her chest as she leaned back against the wall. "Honey," she began. "I can see some tension between you and your brother. It's been building for a while now. Does Mercy Faulkner have anything to do with it?"

Bethany could only stare at her, stunned. "Why would you ask that?" she asked slowly.

"You forget," Rachel said sweetly. "I grew up in what amounted to a lesbian household. I know what I'm looking for. I wouldn't choose it for you because I know it'll make your life that much harder, but I understand that it's who you are." Sadness flashed through her brown eyes. "But, honey, I've never seen you and Billy be angry at each other for more than an hour." She brushed some hair out of Bethany's face. "I don't want to see you both angry at each other as you leave us."

Bethany stood there for a moment, chewing on her bottom lip before asking, "Should I just leave Mercy alone?"

"Is that what she wants you to do?" Rachel challenged, a honey-colored eyebrow raising.

Bethany shyly met her gaze and shook her head. "No."

"Then you need to be honest with your brother. I know the twin obligation, I've seen you two do it your whole lives." Rachel smiled again and kissed her daughter's cheek. "But, at the end of the day, your life is about you, Bethany. Billy will do what's right for Billy." They shared a smile at the truth of those words. "So," Rachel concluded, giving Bethany a final tight squeeze. "Do what's right for Bethany."

Bethany stared at her after the hug, stunned by the words, but she nodded. "Okay," she said, deciding her mother was absolutely right.

❧❧❧❧

The night was warm but quiet as Bethany made her way to the back of Mercy's building. She glanced up, noting that Wanda's bedroom window was open, as was Mercy's. She decided to remove her shoes before making the climb, worried that any noise might alert Mercy's mother to her presence.

She was up to the first landing when she noticed a figure sitting on the step of the second set of stairs on the twin fire escape. The glowing orange tip of a cigarette caught her eye. Her breath catching initially, she realized it was the fire escape on the other side of the apartment building, those across the hall from Mercy's side.

Realizing that it was Riley, she placed her hand on her chest. In the dimness of the light in the alley, she could just barely see him raise a hand in a wave. She returned it, and smiled when he brought his fingers to his mouth, pretending to run a zipper across his lips. Relieved, she continued on her way, finally reaching the open window where Mercy was waiting for her.

Without a word, she handed Mercy her shoes so she had both hands to climb in through the window. Once she was in, Mercy leaned into Bethany, whispering in her ear.

"She should turn on her fan any minute, then we can shut my window and talk."

Bethany nodded in understanding but pulled the smaller woman to her. She held her tightly to her, needing to feel her. Mercy seemed to understand or need it too as she held Bethany just as tightly. Their bodies were flush, and all Bethany could do was close her eyes and bury her face in soft, auburn hair.

Her body was coming alive, and she was angry at herself for it but couldn't help it. Her heart was racing and her skin was singed at every point that touched Mercy's warm flesh. Apparently Mercy was feeling it too, as Bethany felt her warm breath against the side of her neck and then her cheek.

As if of their own accord, Bethany's lips sought out the soft ones that moved against hers once they met. Mercy's hand moved into Bethany's hair as they kissed. In that moment, she thought of her mother's wise words. Yes, she needed to do what was right for her. Just because Billy was a boy did not mean he automatically had the first rights to anything.

She'd already given up too much by going along with him, a price she would be paying in just twenty-four hours. For now, she was going to live her truth and whatever that was for the young woman she was kissing. She had no idea where this would lead, if anywhere, but for the time being, this was where she belonged.

The kiss came to a natural end, both breathing heavily. She looked into Mercy's flushed face, not sure what she'd see there. She certainly hoped not fear or uncertainty. She saw neither of those things, only a want that she wasn't even sure Mercy realized she was revealing. Bethany cupped her beautiful face and left one final kiss before moving out of her personal space.

They shared a smile before both their attention was garnered by a sound. Looking toward the window, Bethany heard what sounded like a little mini hurricane. She looked to Mercy for an explanation.

"She turned her fan on."

"Good lord," Bethany murmured.

Mercy walked over to her bedroom window and eased it closed so their voices wouldn't drift out and through Wanda's window, despite the fan. "It may get a little warm in here," she said, looking at Bethany. "I can turn on my fan, but it's pretty noisy too, and we wouldn't be able to hear if she was near my door." She met Bethany's gaze. "Your call."

Bethany glanced at the fan then the closed bedroom door. She saw Mercy's point. "Let's leave it off for now, see what happens."

Mercy nodded. "Okay. My thoughts too. So," she said shyly, sparing a glance to Bethany as she walked over to her dresser. "I have something for you. For your birthday tomorrow."

Bethany watched as Mercy opened her underwear drawer, pulling the garments forward until she reached the back of the drawer. She pulled something wrapped in fabric out. Drawer closed, she set the package atop the dresser and carefully unwrapped it.

"My father gave this to me for my last birthday,"

Mercy explained, carefully untangling something before she lifted it up. It was a necklace, a small pendant dangling. It was too dim in the room for Bethany to tell what it was. Mercy walked over to Bethany, holding the two open ends of the chain in the fingers of both hands. "He used to call me his little angel," she continued, reaching Bethany. She held it up to reveal the tiny, angel pendant. "So, I figure between my father and I, we can keep you safe."

Bethany was so touched she was moved to silence. She turned around as she was urged to do, the chain lowered in front of her face and into place, the pendant falling just below the hollow of her throat. She lifted her hair and Mercy clasped the necklace into place.

"Are you sure?" she asked, turning back to face Mercy, her hand going up to touch the cool metal against her warmed skin. "Your father gave this to you."

Mercy nodded, looking down at where the pendant rested. "Yes." She met Bethany's gaze. "You can always bring it back to me," she said with a little grin. "Incentive to come home."

Bethany returned the grin. "Any other reasons I should want to come home?"

Mercy looked down for a moment, her fingers lightly playing with the pendant, unwittingly sending crazy thrills through Bethany's body. "Well," she said softly, a little shy. "Perhaps this will answer your question." She met Bethany's gaze again. "There's something else I want you to have for your birthday. And," she added, a small smile and shrug punctuating her words, "in general." She took one of Bethany's hands and placed it upon her right breast, warm flesh beneath the thin material of her nightgown.

Bethany was stunned, yet somehow not. She was humbled as she looked into Mercy's eyes, seeing a bit of nervousness there but also absolute certainty. She smiled at her, a look, she hoped, that showed Mercy just what this gift meant to her. She initiated another kiss, this one different from any they had shared. Mercy responded, sighing into the kiss when Bethany's hand gently squeezed the firm flesh her hand covered.

Understanding that she was being given a huge responsibility, Bethany took it very seriously. She pulled out of the kiss, looking deeply into Mercy's eyes, making sure one last time that there was no hesitation or regret, or discern if Mercy was simply offering herself because Bethany was leaving.

Seeing none of these things, she urged her the few short steps to the bed and lowered herself to it, tugging Mercy down with her. Mercy lay on her back, Bethany on her side with the back of her body against the wall, and their kiss began again. She was amazed at just how different it was with Mercy compared to Helen.

Clearly at this point Helen had slept with a man, but when they first got together more than a year before, neither of them had been with anyone in any way, not even kissing. But they'd embarked in full exploration mode, seemingly in heat as they couldn't get enough of each other. It had been erotic, sloppy, and at times, dangerous as they'd almost gotten caught more than once.

But with Mercy...Yes, Bethany was on fire and absolutely wanted to do anything and everything with her, but it was lifetimes different. Just the kissing they were doing now was so precious to her. It wasn't because she was introducing Mercy to physical love, whereas she and Helen were figuring things out together. It was deeper than that, and in some ways that terrified her. She had to admit that she loved Mercy.

Somehow, the quiet little redhead had wormed her way into Bethany's heart in a very short amount of time. Hell, she had with all of them. Even Pops seemed affected by her, softened by her. She could see why her father had called her his little angel. Mercy Faulkner truly was an angel on earth. *Her* angel.

She pulled back from the kiss, her hand stroking Mercy's flushed cheek and running slowly down to cover her breast again, her gaze never leaving Mercy's. Her fingers lightly tugged and twisted the hardening nipple, which made the young woman gasp.

"Can I take this off?" Bethany asked, tugging lightly on the thin material of the nightgown.

Mercy nodded, doing a little tugging of her own. "This too?"

Bethany smiled and nodded. They both sat up, removing their respective garments. Now the nervousness in Mercy's eyes really geared up as she lay back, fully exposed and utterly stunning. "You are so beautiful, Mercy," she whispered.

"So are you," Mercy whispered back. Her gaze fell from Bethany's eyes to her breasts, bared to her.

For the first time in her life, Bethany felt shy, Mercy's attention so intense. Again, her mind went back to Helen. The blonde was such a superficial, surface person that it had been all about sex, learning what felt good physically. Now, certainly those things played a factor, but she cared what Mercy thought. She cared that she was pleasing to her. She cared, full stop.

Bethany brought Mercy's hand to her own breast, giving her permission to explore, to sate the curiosity that was so evident in her eyes. It felt wonderful to be touched by her, but Bethany kept her responses quiet as she wanted Mercy to explore freely without worry that she was doing something wrong.

Bethany's eyes fell closed and her head rested against the wall as Mercy leaned up, experimentally peeking her tongue out, just barely touching it to a hard nipple. Bethany's fingers buried themselves in Mercy's hair, gently urging her closer. She couldn't suppress her moan as her nipple was enveloped in the warmth of Mercy's mouth.

Body on fire, Bethany knew their time was limited. They could be discovered at any moment. Wishing she could let Mercy explore her all night, she knew that wasn't an option. At this point she knew without question that they were on the same page, and she no longer worried about scaring Mercy or taking her somewhere she didn't want to go.

She pushed Mercy to her back, the surprised and worried look in her eyes disappearing as Bethany took her in a deeply passionate kiss. She moved atop her, both moaning into the kiss as their naked skin came into full contact. The kiss ended and she saw her own desire reflected back in Mercy's eyes.

As much as she wanted to explore every inch of Mercy, show her every example of pleasure, she knew they didn't have time. She urged Mercy's thighs apart with her knee, and when they were spread for her, she settled her hips between them, adjusting herself so that her most private place rested against that of the woman beneath her.

Mercy looked up at her with so much trust in her eyes, which became hooded as Bethany began to slowly move her hips, slick, hard need rubbing against slick, hard need. Her movements were slow and measured, partly to make the pleasure last, but also because the bed springs squeaked terribly and she didn't want to garner unwanted attention.

Mercy's eyes slid closed as her fingers roamed over Bethany's back and upper shoulders. The little noises of pleasure she made were incredible and shot to Bethany's clit each time. She loved the feel of their bodies together, the feel of Mercy's softness. She couldn't wait for the day when they could truly spend time together, truly take the time to show Mercy what being loved by a woman was all about.

She kissed Mercy, though it didn't last long as they were breathing too hard as the pleasure built. Mercy's hips were moving with Bethany's, thrust and counterthrust. Unable to contain her moans, Bethany buried her face in Mercy's neck as she was held tightly, almost painfully tight. Mercy gasped, her back arching her breasts into Bethany's as she panted in Bethany's ear.

Her own orgasm rushed through her, making her shiver in response. Bethany ground her hips into Mercy's, making the woman in her arms gasp a second time, a small shudder go through her body. She could feel the back of her head cupped by Mercy's hand as she breathed hard, trying to calm her pulsing body.

It took several moments, but finally Bethany was able to raise her head. She looked down in Mercy's painfully beautiful face. She smiled when she saw a look of wonder there, as though Mercy had no idea what had just hit her.

Chapter Seventeen

Grabbing yet another article of clothing, Mercy tossed it into the laundry basket. She noticed a stocking sticking out from beneath the bed and got down to her hands and knees to grab it. It was then that she noticed something shiny farther beneath the bed, the scent of the fresh bedding she'd just put on it hitting her nose.

Nearly on her stomach, Mercy reached out as far as she could, her fingers just barely getting a grip on the cool, smooth object. She pulled it out and pushed up to her knees to see it was an empty glass bottle, and the label upon it read *laudanum*. No clue why it was there, she tossed it to the trash can her mother kept in the corner of her bedroom by the dresser. She'd be emptying it out later, anyway.

Laundry gathered, Mercy grabbed the basket and carried it to her bedroom to add her own clothing so all could be washed together. She wasn't working at the soda shop that day, but her mother was at the sewing factory next door and had left her a list of chores. She was fine with it, honestly. Her mother was so tired all the time, apparently the long hours weighing on her. But also, and mostly, it was a good distraction.

Halloween was just around the corner, and Bethany and Billy had been gone for pushing four months. She missed them both, but it literally physically hurt how badly she missed Bethany. She'd heard nothing from her, and that scared her a bit. She promised she'd write when she could, but Mercy had no idea where she'd been sent, what she was doing, or how much time or opportunity she'd have to write.

She'd considered asking her family if they'd heard from her, knew anything, but had stayed away from them. She figured they had so much they were dealing with, what with one child dead from this god-awful war and the other three in the thick of it. The last thing they needed was her nosing around.

Basket set on her bed, she spared a glance at the bed at large. It was the absolute most bittersweet feeling in the world, knowing such incredible pleasure and joy on that bed with Bethany yet not knowing if it would ever happen again or if she'd ever see Bethany again.

So many times over the months she'd relived that night in her mind. The feel of Bethany's lips on hers, hands on her, breasts pressed against her own. Her eyes fell closed, such a strange mixture of arousal and sadness. It was her constant companion these days.

Mercy's head whipped up and her glance to the open door of her bedroom when she heard the front door to the apartment open and shut, locks engaged.

"Why is this door unlocked?" Wanda bellowed from the other room.

"I'm sorry, Mother," she called out to her. "I was just heading out to do laundry but forgot something," she fibbed. She hated lying to her mother, but sometimes Wanda's obsessive controlling demands got to be too much. Carrying the laundry basket, she headed out to the living room. Her mother looked tired as she kicked off her shoes and sat on the couch. "Are you okay?" Mercy asked. "It's not quite time for lunch break—"

"I'm home early," Wanda muttered, lying back on the couch, bare feet coming up to rest upon the opposite arm from where her head lay on a throw pillow.

"Are you all right?" Mercy asked, laundry basket tucked against her stomach as she looked down at the other woman. "Need anything?"

Wanda said nothing, simply waved her off as she got settled in for a nap. Making sure she had her key, Mercy headed down just past the hotel and waited for a car to drive by before she hurried across the street to the small washateria that was available to both the tenants of the apartments and guests of the hotel when it operated as such. The building was a square and squat with four washers and four dryers, each coin operated. In her laundry basket, Mercy had a little purse filled with the coins they saved for that purpose and her laundry soap.

She chose a machine and set her basket down on the closed lid of the unused machine next to it. There was only one other machine in use, a dryer, and it was at the other end. She glanced over to see Riley sitting in one of the chairs set out for those waiting for their laundry to finish. She gave him a small smile before turning back to her task.

"No fun," he muttered.

She chuckled, slipping the coins into the machine. "No, not at all." She poured in the right amount of soap then began to load the machine. "How's it going at the mill?" she asked conversationally.

"Oh," he said with a tired sigh, running a hand through dark hair. "Good, I s'pose. Got me a new supervisor I ain't so fond of."

She smiled and met his gaze. "Sounds like me and one of my teachers this year."

"What grade you in?" he asked, sitting back in the creaky wooden chair. He pulled out a small pocketknife and began to pick at the perma-dirt underneath his fingernails, as so many of the men had who worked the hard, physical jobs at the lumber mill.

"Eleventh grade this year," she said, choosing her cycle and hitting the start button on the single load she tossed in. She set her empty laundry basket in front of the now whooshing machine and sat in a chair similar to Riley's on the opposite end, three chairs between them.

He nodded. "Getting' there." He gave her a smile, which she returned with a nod. "So, uh," he said, looking down at his nail that he was picking at with the tip of the pocketknife blade. "Your mom finally calm down?"

Feeling embarrassed all over again, she sighed. "Yeah. I'm really sorry about that, Riley. Sorry you had to hear that. She can get a little…excited, I guess, sometimes."

"She don't need to yell at you like that, Mercy," he said quietly. "Ain't right."

She nodded, looking down at her own hands, which fidgeted in her lap. "I know."

His machine buzzed to a finish. "Well," he said, pushing to his feet. "Best finish this up. See you around, Mercy."

"Have a good day, Riley." She watched him go after gathering his small laundry load into a canvas bag and flinging it over his shoulder as he headed out. She liked the young man, thinking he was a sweet person. After that time she and Bethany had helped him after his horrible spill down the stairs during his seizure, there seemed to be a bit of a bond between them. His gratitude was evident, and her heart went out to him.

She'd seen him have a few more seizures since, but nothing as violent as that one night. He was a sweet and handsome young fella, and she wondered why he wasn't married. She never saw him with a girl or anyone. He was quiet and kept to himself. She wondered if perhaps his shyness kept him single, or perhaps girls were turned off by his fits.

Sitting there, she kicked herself. She should have brought her homework.

More than two hours later, Mercy finally returned to the apartment. She'd learned the hard way to stay with the clothing, still angry as she'd lost her favorite skirt to whomever had taken their laundry right out of the dryer the first time she did laundry there.

She balanced the basket, filled with folded laundry, against her hip as she unlocked the door. Pushing it open, she was startled to hear something thud in her mother's bedroom.

"Where is it!"

"Mother?" she called out, entering fully and kicking the door closed. Starting again at another thud, Mercy dropped the laundry basket and hurried to her mother's room only to see the woman looking pale, disheveled, and frantic. "What's wrong?"

"Where is it?" Wanda demanded again, her

chest heaving and her thin frame almost trembling. Her hair was plastered to her face and neck in sweaty strands and a fine sheen of sweat covered her face. Her flesh was flushed though, looking clammy.

"Where is what?"

"My medicine. You took it, didn't you?"

Utterly baffled, Mercy shook her head until she remembered earlier. "Do you mean the bottle of laudanum? I found it under the bed earlier. It's in there." She pointed to the trash can.

Nearly shoving her daughter out of the way, Wanda hurried over to it, falling to her knees as she fished the bottle out. Her hands were shaking as she twisted the cap off and held the open bottle aloft over her mouth. With a frustrated cry, she looked at it. "It's empty!"

"Yes," Mercy said, feeling very nervous about the entire situation. "That's why I threw it away."

Wanda dropped the bottle on the floor and pushed to her feet. "Go to the pharmacy." Her words were breathy and her face screwed up in pain as she hugged herself. "Money's in my wallet," she said through gritted teeth.

"Mother," Mercy said, now scared. She placed her hand on Wanda's back. "What's wrong?"

"Please just go," her mother whimpered.

Money tucked into the pocket of her skirt, Mercy took off down the street, knowing she didn't have a ton of time left before the pharmacy closed. She was panting when she reached it, nodding her gratitude at a man who held the door open for her as she ran up to it. Stepping inside the small store, which had the pharmacy counter along the back wall but also sold medical incidentals in the other part of the store, she saw Bethany's uncle Nate, the town's pharmacist.

From what she understood, Nate wasn't actually the sibling of either Justice or Thea, but Justice had mentored the man, a few years younger than Justice, when he'd been a teen, and the two saw each other as siblings and were just as close as if they were related by blood.

She'd only seen him a couple of times, at Leo's funeral and once at the soda shop. He was a quiet man, seemed very sweet with kind, intelligent brown eyes and hair that was a mixture of light brown and gray. His wife, Tabitha, was lovely and also sweet. Their son, Franklin, apparently was a doctor in Denver.

"Well, hello there, young lady," he greeted from the other side of the counter, wearing his white pharmacist's coat.

"Hello, sir. Um, I need to pick up some medicine for my mother, Wanda Faulkner."

"Of course," he said, moving away from the counter and to the shelving behind the counter that was filled with prescriptions ready to be picked up. He grabbed what he sought and carried it to the counter near the register. "I expected your mother yesterday."

"Sir," she said, bringing up the money she'd taken from her mother's wallet. "Why is my mother taking this?"

He paused in punching buttons on the register, fresh bottle of laudanum in his hand. He looked at her over his glasses. "She didn't talk to you about this?" he asked.

She met his gaze. "Um, no, sir."

Wanda was sleeping peacefully, though even in sleep she winced in pain from time to time. Mercy sat on the floor in the corner of the small bedroom. Her legs were pulled up, thighs against her chest. She watched her mother sleep on the bed, all tucked in.

Stomach cancer. Nothing more to be done. Keep her comfortable.

She buried her face in her hands. How had she not noticed her mother's failing health? How much weight she was losing? How tired she was, pale and even meaner than usual. Nate had told her that likely she wouldn't be able to work much longer. The doctor had apparently told Wanda that she was looking at anywhere from six to eight months.

Bringing her hands down to cover the lower half of her face, she studied her mother again. She felt so lost, so completely alone. *Bethany, I need you. Even just a letter, anything!* She'd written so many letters to her, but with no address, nowhere to send them, they'd stayed in her bedroom and in her heart. She'd write her another one tonight, telling her what had happened and ask what on earth she was supposed to do.

Maybe the answer would come in her dreams.

❧❧❧❧

As the holidays approached, it was becoming clear that Wanda was going to need more help when she was home. Mercy had no idea how things were going to work, but she'd been called out of school more than once to take care of her when she'd had to leave early because she was vomiting blood.

As winter break approached, she was beginning

to suspect she was going to have to make a horrible choice. She stood at her locker, so lost in thought she had no idea how long she'd stood there. It wasn't until she felt the soft touch on her shoulder that she shook herself out of it.

Glancing to her left, she saw a concerned Sam standing there, waiting to walk home with her. Now a sophomore and pushing sixteen, he was looking more and more like the handsome man he'd be. Peach fuzz over his lip and a squared jaw and deep-set blue eyes, Sam was shaping up to be as good-looking as his older cousins. She could see the Wynter in him.

"You okay?" he asked, his voice much deeper than the boy he'd sounded like a year ago.

"Yeah," she said, forcing herself into the moment. "Yeah, I'm fine. Sorry."

He took her loaded school bag from her as she tried to juggle it while shrugging into her winter jacket. It was early December, and cold as the Dickens out. Once she had her jacket in place and locker slammed shut, he handed it back to her.

"Thanks, Sam." She shouldered the heavy bag, loaded down with all she'd need for her homework for the weekend. The two made their way out of the school and into the cold, overcast day. She looked up to see the pregnant clouds overhead, the smell of snow in the air. "Have you heard from Billy?" she finally asked after repeatedly promising herself she wouldn't. But she couldn't help it. She hoped that by asking about him, she'd hear about her.

"Yeah," he said, also looking up at the sky. "Think we're gonna get hammered," he muttered. "He's in France, I think." He glanced over at her. "Pretty darn neat that Bethany's art got her working with the Seabees."

She glanced over at him, eyebrows drawn. "Seabees?"

"Yeah," he said, meeting her gaze. "You know, the crews that build bases, air strips, things like that."

"What on earth is she doing with them?" Mercy's voice was a bit more breathless than she intended, but talking about her, out loud, made her feel that perhaps Bethany was a real person and not just a fantasy she'd created in her mind.

He shrugged. "Not sure, honestly. Don't think Billy knows, either. But, guess some bigwig general or something saw her sketching on the train on their way to San Diego before being shipped out and all that." He shrugged. "You know how good she is. Felt she'd be better used there."

"Is that safe?" Mercy asked.

He snorted. "Is anything over there?"

Sam prattled on and on about this and that, largely about the new guy he liked, but her mind was spinning. Yes, she understood that Billy and Sam were cousins, so of course he'd correspond with him, or perhaps Sam had heard it from their parents. But still, the passionate way that Billy had begged her to write to him, let alone her time spent with Bethany…and she'd heard nothing.

Why? Five months now that they'd been gone. It felt like a lifetime. She was so grateful to have Sam, whom she'd grown even closer to, but still. Finally, they reached her building, nothing special going on. She was supposed to work that night.

"Thanks for walking me home, Sam," she said, turning to the young man who had become a dear friend. She squeezed his arm before heading inside.

The drastic change in temperature from the cold outside to the warm inside sent a shiver down her body. Each step felt like a small mountain as she was so tired.

Reaching the second floor, she dug out her key and walked to her apartment door. She glanced over her shoulder, hearing the muffled sound of Riley's radio from behind his closed door. Sounded like he was listening to a radio program—she could hear the canned laughter.

She unlocked the door and let herself in. It was quiet, too quiet. But then she heard her name being called weakly, then the sound of water.

"Oh god," she whispered, panicked as she dropped her school bag at the door and hurried to the bathroom, as the kitchen was empty.

Wanda's pale, shriveled body lay in the tub, the water cloudy and tinted red. From the smell, she could tell her mother had gotten sick while trying to bathe. Sunken dark eyes looked up at Mercy. "I can't get out," she gasped.

Knowing there was no way she was strong enough to get her mother's wet, slippery body out, she turned around and dashed out through the front door, which she hadn't even closed. "Riley!" she exclaimed, banging on the closed apartment door. "Riley!"

Within moments, the door was pulled open and a concerned-looking Riley stood there, half his face covered in shaving foam, a towel slapped over his shoulder. "What's wrong?"

"I need your help," she exclaimed, saying nothing more as she turned and ran back into her own apartment shared with Wanda.

"No!" Wanda exclaimed, seeing Riley running

in after Mercy. "No! Go away!" She tried weakly to cover her nakedness.

"Mother, he's here to help," Mercy said, reaching up and grabbing the bath towel that was hanging on the towel bar. She would use it to wrap around her mother's nakedness as soon as they got her upright.

"No," Wanda whimpered, tears streaming down her cheeks.

"It's all right, Mrs. Faulkner," he said, bending down and gently gathering her in his arms. "I gotcha," he said. He stood erect and turned, Mercy immediately covering her nakedness with the towel.

Mercy led the way to Wanda's bedroom. "If you can get her on the bed, I can get her dressed."

He nodded and eased his load down, Wanda still crying. "There ya go, Mrs. Faulkner," he said quietly, instantly backing away from her once she was safely down. He looked to Mercy, a question in his eyes.

"Thank you," she said, meeting his gaze. "Truly."

He nodded, then left them alone.

❧ ❧ ❧ ❧

Later that night, after Wanda had been dried, dressed, and given her medicine to help with the pain and sleep, Mercy had left the apartment. She sat on the bottom step, down by the door to the street so nobody would hear her cry, especially her mother. Her face was buried in her hands, shoulders shaking with the power of her sobs.

She quickly tried to dry her tears and her face when she heard footfalls heading down the stairs. She used the sleeve of her sweater and scooted over on the step to let whoever it was pass by. They didn't, instead plopping down on the step next to her. Glancing over, she saw Riley looking back at her.

"How's she doin'?"

She said nothing for a moment, feeling ashamed as she knew she looked a mess. She turned away and wiped her cheeks and eyes, her face feeling heated from her upset. "Thank you so much for your help earlier."

"Sure. Glad I was home."

"Me too," she said, giving him a shy smile, grateful for his help. "There's no way she can continue working," Mercy said, surprised she'd said the words. "She's just too sick." She let out a long, heavy sigh. "I think I'm going to have to leave school, Riley." She shook her head. "She can't be alone." She covered her face again, letting out a long, frustrated growl. "I don't know what I'm going to do," she whispered, more to herself than to him.

He was quiet for a long moment before he said. "Look, I got kinda a crazy idea."

She dropped her hands and looked over at him.

Chapter Eighteen

Somewhere in the Pacific

Did you get that, Bethany?"

"Yes, sir," she said, sparing a glance up at the uniformed man. "I'm good. Please continue."

He nodded and continued his explanation to those gathered, Bethany's hand working frantically on her sketch as the projector clicked to the next slide. Part of her brain listened to what he said in case she needed to add any of that into her sketch, but the other part of her brain was focused on what was on the large screen at the front of the conference room.

Her sketch would be taken and printed up and distributed, placed wherever it needed to go, be it dealing with upcoming construction projects for the Seabees, bunker plans to be inserted into important files for the generals, or a reproduction of aerial photographs taken by the war planes, added in intentions for targets, or whatnot.

Never in a million years had she thought the talent she'd been born with would end up in national security someday during a war. She was proud of what she was doing and adding to the war effort. She was looking forward to doing her time and leaving, but she'd always be proud of what she was doing now.

A million hand strokes later, the meeting finally ended and her work was complete, the entire sketch pad immediately given to the powers that be as it was now officially classified information. She'd be given a fresh pad for her next assignment. Released, Bethany left the room and was heading down the hall, high heels clicking on the tile floor, when she stopped at the sound of her name.

Turning, she saw one of the officers jogging after her. He was a man that wasn't much younger than her own father, but she waited for him to catch up to her.

"Nice work in there," he said, hitching a thumb back toward the room they'd just left. "Your skill is incredible."

"Thank you, Commander," she said, her voice firm, professional.

"Listen, I can't even draw two stick figures, so I wondered if you'd maybe like to get drinks and can give me some tips." He gave her a charming smile. "I hear there's a wonderful singer at the USO."

She'd been waiting for this, as she'd seen him eyeing her months. She wasn't interested for a variety of reasons, not the least of which was that she had not one iota of interest in men, but she also knew he was a married man with three children. Typical, she thought. Pushing those thoughts out of her head and keeping them out of her expression, she gave him a tight smile.

"I appreciate the offer to educate, sir, but I have plans tonight. My brother, Ned, who is based here, and I will be meeting our other brother, William, who is in the area for a brief time." Her first genuine smile of the conversation touched her lips.

His eyebrows shot up. "Family reunion."

She nodded. "Yes, Commander. I'm very much looking forward to it. William is my twin, so..." She shrugged. "I haven't seen him in almost a year."

"Well then," he said, nodding, body language moving away from friendly, almost flirty to damn near at attention. "I hope you enjoy your time with your brothers." With a curt nod, he turned and walked away.

Left alone in the hallways, she mentally shook her head and continued on her way.

❧❧❧❧

In another world and another time, Bethany could absolutely see that she could have easily fallen for the person who had become a close friend on base. Never in her wildest dreams did she think she'd run into another Justice Kilkoyne, but there Danny Felts was, sitting next to her in the car. Though their stories and reasons were very different, both women had similar androgynous good looks that could fool the eye, yet both were absolutely beautiful women in their own right.

Like Bethany, Danny had lost her older brother early on in the war and had decided to leave the family dairy farm in Nebraska and do something with her life that was greater than herself. Bethany had figured it out pretty quick, to Danny's shock and upset. But, once she'd understood Bethany's own family and that Bethany could be trusted, they'd become fast friends.

Danny was an amazing human being, and Bethany felt that her lady love back home, Kate, was indeed a lucky woman. And then, as far as she knew, though she had so many questions, Bethany had her own amazing lady back home. Problem was, she hadn't heard a word from her, not one letter responded to in ten months.

It weighed heavily on her every single day. Every time she went to the post office on base, she hoped that maybe today would be the day that a letter from Mercy would be mixed in with those coming in from her family. Not so far. Her family had mentioned Mercy in passing in their letters, but she'd not asked them about her specifically. She already felt like a fool.

"You okay?"

Turning at the soft voice, she met Danny's gaze, her face lit up in an eerie green hue from the dashboard lights. Bethany nodded. "I am." She gave her friend a weak smile.

"Are you excited to see Billy?" Danny asked.

Bethany didn't respond for a moment as she considered the question. She hadn't seen him since the day Billy had left San Diego, a day ahead of Bethany, and it hadn't ended well. She'd been honest with him, had told him about her night with Mercy, feeling he deserved to know the truth about not only what had happened, but also Mercy's interests, which were not with him.

They hadn't spoken since.

Remembering there was a question on the table, she cleared her throat. "Yes, it'll be good to see he's okay, I suppose." She let out a heavy sigh, watching as the nighttime scenery passed them by. "I hope he's happy."

They pulled up to the building, which had servicemen standing outside chatting, smoking cigarettes and, no doubt, trying to pick up the swarm of young women that usually showed up at these things. Many were looking for an American GI to meet and perhaps hook up with.

Danny parked and glanced over at her. Her black hair was cut short, short bangs draping down near one of her beautiful blue eyes. "Ready?" she asked.

Bethany nodded, looking from her friend to the gathered group of young people, then back again. "Let's do this."

The room was loud, filled with chatter, laughter, and the singing of the woman who stood on the stage backed up by a small orchestra. A bar was set up at one end, young men in pretty much every branch uniform lined up to get their drinks. They spotted Ned sitting at a table with some of his fellow pilots. Initially joining the Army, he'd switched to the Navy to become a pilot and, to Bethany's surprise, had thrived.

She didn't see him often, as they worked in entirely different areas, but she did see him a couple times a week, if even for a quick wave as he trotted off toward the hangar or his plane. From her work, she knew her brother was heading out on a dangerous mission the following morning. She was grateful to get some time with him that night.

"There she is!" he exclaimed, standing from his seat with a few of his pilot buddies. Bethany smiled at him and accepted his embrace, which he growled into as he lifted her off her feet in his enthusiasm.

Chuckling, she playfully pushed him away once she was on her feet again. "Thanks for the bumpy landing."

He grinned and gave her a sloppy salute, which made her roll her eyes. "Ned, you remember my friend Danny Felts, don't you?"

"Sailor," Ned said, extending his hand to Danny.

"Sir," Danny said quietly, shaking his hand as Ned outranked her.

Ned looked from one to the other, taking in Danny's Seabees uniform then Bethany in hers, the typical WAVES blue skirt and matching uniform jacket. White blouse and appropriate neckwear and insignias finished it off. Even in her heels, she wasn't as tall as Danny, who appeared to be a slightly shorter-than-average man, or taller-than-average woman, for those in the know.

He gave Bethany a look of question with a raised eyebrow. The question was clearly about whether she and Danny were in a relationship. She smiled and shook her head. "Just friends."

Ned nodded. "Well, you look good, sis. Been meaning to tell you that." He squeezed her shoulder. "You do the uniform proud."

"I wear it better."

They both turned to see Billy walking toward them, a very cocky grin on his handsome face and a very pretty blonde on his arm. Like the others, he was in his dress uniform, looking every bit the Army man.

"Hey, little brother!" Ned extended his hand, Billy taking it and shaking it firmly before they exchanged a tight hug. "You may wear Army green well, but I'll be an admiral before you can even dream of being a general."

"Dream on," Billy said, the two laughing as they pretended to box for a moment.

Bethany watched, surprised to see the lovely young woman, also in uniform, who stood back. Her blond hair was swept up, much like Bethany's, off the collar, and her green eyes were nothing but adoration as she watched the two brothers reunite.

Finally, Billy turned and met Bethany's gaze. His eyes, which had been filled with twinkling excitement, seemed to cool a bit as he took her in. She said nothing, waiting to see what he'd do. She could feel Ned's gaze on them as well as Danny's. Ned, of course, knew nothing of what had happened back in Wynter after he'd left but no doubt was confused by the chill in the air between the twins.

"Good to see you, Bethy," Billy said, his voice a bit flat.

"You too." She accepted his hug and returned it. He did give her a squeeze, but it was nothing like what it would have been before. A year ago, it would have been a rib-cracking squeeze that probably brought tears of joy to both of them. This was the longest they'd ever been apart since sharing a womb.

"Everyone," he said, placing his hand on the blonde's back and urging her to step forward into their little group. "This is Greta."

"Lovely to meet you, Greta," Ned said, turning on the charm as he kissed her fingers.

Billy looked from Danny to Bethany, a question in his eyes and a bit of a smug look.

"Billy, this is my good friend, Danny. Danny," she said, turning to her friend, who had watched everything silently. "My twin, Billy."

"I've heard a lot about you, Billy," Danny said, extending her hand. "In our little circle of friends on base, you come up a lot." She grinned. "Even my girl back home knows about the Wynter twins."

Billy grinned and nodded. "Yeah." He looked back to Bethany, the ice melting a bit. "We've had our fun." He clapped his hands together. "Listen, gonna get me and Greta here something to drink. Anybody want anything?"

"I'll come with," Bethany offered. She looked to

Danny. "Coca-Cola?" At Danny's nod, she and Billy headed to the bar.

Standing in line, Billy turned to her. "So, he seems nice," he said conversationally.

"Danny's just a friend, Billy," she responded, noting the innuendo in his tone.

He snorted, crossing his arms over his chest. "I was gonna say, for betraying your brother, you moved on pretty damn quick."

She stared at him, stunned. "How on earth did I betray you?"

"Is that a real goddamn question?"

Noticing some people were beginning to look at them, Bethany grabbed his hand and yanked his arms out of their tight hold and tugged him behind her and out of the line. She stopped once they reached a place over by the bathrooms where they were relatively alone. She turned on him.

"She was never yours, Billy," she growled, voice low. "How dare you treat her or talk about her like a goddamn piece of meat!"

"You knew I liked her," he said, just as angry. "You even gave me advice on how to get her."

"Which you didn't bother to take."

"Didn't exactly give me time, did you?" he accused, arms once again crossing over his chest. "You seduced her before I even got the chance."

"I did not seduce her," she hissed. "I absolutely did not."

"You fucked her," he accused. "You even said so."

"I never said that." She glared at him. "And don't you dare make something that was so beautiful so ugly." The two stared each other down before she spoke again. "Mercy and I were attracted to each other, Billy. It wasn't some underhanded attempt to steal her from you. Truth was, she came to me."

"Bullshit."

She shrugged. "Believe it or don't," she said, intending to return to the line at the bar. "It doesn't matter. And besides," she snorted, nodding toward the table where Ned was talking to Greta. "You hardly seem all that devastated by it."

Jaw muscle working as he glanced to the woman he'd brought with him and back to Bethany, he said, voice flat, "You're right, it doesn't matter anymore. She got married." He brushed by her. "We both lose."

She stared after him, barely able to breathe. Could that be true? No, she thought. Absolutely no. Turning away from the room at large, she took a long, shaky breath, slowly releasing it. She stared absently at the wall, looking at nothing in particular except for the beautiful face that swept before her mind's eye.

"Hey."

Bethany's eyes closed and her head fell forward at the soft voice and even softer touch to her upper back. "She's married," she whispered.

"Did Billy tell you that?" Danny asked gently. At Bethany's nod, she asked, "And, do you think maybe that's why she hasn't been responding to your letters?"

Again, Bethany nodded. "I have to wonder." She turned and looked at her friend, concern in Danny's eyes. "I can't wrap my mind around this."

Danny nodded. "I can't even imagine, Beth. I really can't. It would kill me if Kate married somebody else."

Bethany nodded, reaching up absently to lightly touch the area where the angel pendant rested beneath her blouse. "I'm not even sure what to do, what to believe."

"Well," Danny advised, leaning back against the wall. "Maybe write your family and ask them."

Bethany nodded. "Good idea." She looked at her friend with pain-filled eyes. "Do you think she ever cared, Danny?"

Danny glanced down to where Bethany's fingers still touched the pendant, which she'd told her about. "What does your heart say?"

Bethany grasped the pendant between her thumb and forefinger through her shirt, rubbing it as if it would give her the answer. But her heart, for all its bluster and strong opinions, said absolutely nothing.

Chapter Nineteen

At four thirty in the morning, it was cold and Bethany was freezing her buns off. She stood huddled with Rhonda, Ned's girlfriend at the moment, at his request.

"This better be good," Rhonda muttered. "Tired, cold. Want coffee."

Bethany smirked, amused. "I agree." She liked the spunky brunette, mainly because she gave Ned a run for his money.

The two stood about a hundred yards away from the flight strip to stay out of the way and watched as the tarmac crew scurried around like cockroaches to get the pilots and flight crew loaded into their plane and everything ready to go for the boys to head off into the predawn darkness to complete their mission.

"There he is," Rhonda said, pointing.

Bethany saw him, dressed in his flight suit. Even from a football field's length away, Ned's swagger was evident. She shook her head. As much as it got old in regular life, as a pilot that cocky confidence had served him well. She was proud of him.

"Here we go," Rhonda said, excitement eclipsing her tired tone. She grinned at Bethany before looking back to the huge plane which had roared to life, the propellers spinning into their dizzying cycle.

Bethany had wondered why Ned had told them to go to this specific place to watch, as it seemed an odd angle. But, as they watched the huge plane race down the runway and finally go airborne, she understood. As the plane turned in the air to head in the right direction, it flew directly overhead, the two women and the ground they stood on vibrating as the deafening engines propelled the beast higher into the sky.

Bethany and Rhonda's excited screams and cheers were completely drowned out. It was magical, Bethany feeling the passing plane in her bones. The two followed the plane until it was out of sight, the lights winking in the darkness until they, too, were gone.

"Holy smokes!" Rhonda exclaimed. "Forget the coffee, I need a drink!"

Bethany laughed, the two women turning to head back to their barracks.

❧❧❧❧

It was Saturday, and Bethany was doing laundry to prepare for the next week. She'd have tons of ironing to do to make sure her uniform was perfect. She also planned to shine her high heels. She wished the ladies were able to wear the same uniforms as the guys, which looked so much more comfortable. But, of course, that wasn't about to happen any time soon.

She stood at the counter folding her first load, which consisted of her undergarments and towels. The second load, currently tumbling to a dry end, was her uniform blouses. She glanced over when the door to the on-base laundromat was pulled open, a young sailor searching the room until his gaze landed on her.

"Um, ma'am," he said, voice quiet. "Commander

needs to speak to you."

She was surprised, considering it was a weekend. "Sure. Is everything okay?"

The serviceman wouldn't meet her gaze.

❧❧❧❧

The scenery whizzed by—small towns, large cities, wide swaths of nothing—her mind going faster than the chugging vehicle beneath her. Her chin rested on an open palm, elbow balanced on the arm of the seat she'd sat in for miles and miles. Her mind was a tempest of emotions, bouncing back to what lay in the train car that was loaded with cargo, and where she was headed now.

How was she going to do this? Face them? She and Billy both had been given the choice to stay or go, considering now that two Wynter sons had been lost. Billy had chosen to stay, and at times Bethany understood his choice. He'd miss the emotional fallout of their mother burying a second child.

Had she done the right thing by taking the out, escorting Ned's body home, then staying? Was she a coward? Had she abandoned her peers, her duty? Let down her country? She wiped away more tears. They would be in Wynter soon, her father picking her up and a hearse coming to gather her brother.

The train finally eased into the tiny station at the edge of town with very limited trains coming to and fro. Most folks who wanted to take the train anywhere had to catch it in Denver. She was grateful that she was able to go directly into Wynter; she wasn't sure how well she'd do closed in a car with her father for the hour-and-change drive from Denver.

She was glad, admittedly, to see the familiar surroundings of her hometown. She'd be glad to see her parents and grandparents and friends. Her stomach was a bit in knots when she thought of Mercy. She had no clue what was happening with that and what she'd discover. It made her nauseous to think about.

The first smile in several days brushed her lips when she saw her father waiting on the platform. It widened a bit when she realized Gran was with him. The train finally came to a stop and she gathered her belongings, which consisted of her bulging duffel bag and her uniform cap, then pushed out of her seat.

Placing her cap on her head, she made her way down the aisle, along with the couple other passengers to step off the train. The man who had gotten off before her waited to help her down. He tipped his fedora at her once she was on the platform safely.

"Thanks for your service, miss."

She gave him a small smile. "Thank you, sir."

She dropped her duffel bag and said not a word, the tears already coming as she stepped into her father's open arms. He said nothing, just held her. It took several moments but finally she calmed down. He left a kiss on the top of her head before pulling away a bit.

She looked up into her father's face, able to see his devastation. "I'm sorry, Dad," she said. "So sorry."

He gave her a sad smile as he used his handkerchief to wipe gently at her tears. "Don't be sorry, sweet girl." His voice was so soft, emotion tinging it. "I'm so glad you're home and safe." He left a kiss on her forehead, Bethany's eyes closing at the affection before she was released.

Justice stepped up to her and draped a protective

arm across her shoulders. "I'll stay with her, Henry," she said quietly. "You see about your boy."

Bethany leaned into Justice, feeling so safe in her presence, so calm and loved. "Are they going to be okay?"

Justice let out a heavy sigh, resting her head against her granddaughter's. "In time." She squeezed Bethany to her tightly before releasing her. "Having you home will make all the difference in the world, sweetheart."

Bethany decided she had to know, and of anyone who would understand, it would be Gran or Grandma. "Gran?"

"Yeah?" Justice looked down at her, Bethany meeting her dark eyes.

"Is it true?" She forced herself to say the next part. "About Mercy." Her heart fell at the expression that crossed the older woman's face. "I see."

"Well, hold on a sec," Justice said, indicating that they should move on to a bench to sit as they were in the way of people moving about the platform. "Mercy's mother took sick over the winter," she explained, looking into Bethany's eyes. "Wanda had to leave work, Bethy, and Mercy had to leave both work and school to take care of her. Riley Stockton stepped up, offered to help."

"By marrying her?" Bethany was unable to keep the bitterness out of her voice. "Why didn't you help her?" she asked, fresh emotion rising in her chest and behind her eyes.

"We didn't know how bad it had gotten," Justice said gently, taking one of Bethany's hands in her larger, darker one, years and years of hard work on the farm giving her a tan twelve months out of the year. "Once we found out, your daddy and I got them out of that apartment and into a house. That's where they're at now."

"And Wanda?"

Justice shrugged, glancing farther down the train as Ned's casket was removed from the train car and carried to the hearse that was backed up onto the platform. "She's still alive, though honestly not sure how long."

Bethany nodded, absorbing all she'd been told. She wasn't sure what to think, and she knew that during these crazy times, so many did what they had to do. And, if Mercy had told no one what was happening, she had absolutely nobody but her mother. Why hadn't she asked for help?

Many questions she wanted answers for, but those would have to wait. She was eager to see her mother and needed a hug. She had the feeling she'd have a lot of consoling to do.

❧❧❧❧

Dropped off at the house so her father could take care of arrangements at the funeral home, Bethany looked around her bedroom. Her duffel bag was tossed to the bed, as was her uniform hat. Everything was as it had been the day she'd left not quite eleven months ago, yet it all looked so different. But then, she thought, nothing had changed externally, it was all inside.

She felt like such a stranger in her own home. She looked at her bed, her chair and dresser. Her gaze flicked up to her sketches on the slanted ceiling. She thought of the young woman who had last slept in this bed, the one she dropped her gaze to.

She turned when there was a knock at the door, though she didn't even need to call out permission as the door opened and Rachel burst into the room. She was already crying when she reached her daughter, though it seemed the tears were relief that her baby was home. Bethany held tight, her own relief palpable.

After several moments of strong, tearful hugs, Rachel pulled away but not out of the embrace. She looked Bethany over, touching her hair, her face, fingering the lapel of her uniform blazer. It was almost as if she were making sure her little one was in one piece and actually and truly home.

"You've never worn your hair so short," she said, fingers lightly touching the deep mahogany locks which just barely brushed Bethany's shoulders. She shook her head as she took in Bethany's face. "You're all grown," she whispered. "Soon to be nineteen." She shook her head again, disbelief in her eyes. "My baby."

"Well," Bethany said, grinning. "Technically Billy's the baby, born almost two minutes after me."

Rachel smiled, fresh tears welling in her eyes. She nodded and took Bethany into another embrace. "So glad you're home."

Bethany's eyes fell closed as she nodded. "Me too."

"You need to go visit Mercy, sweetheart," Rachel said, surprising Bethany with the non sequitur.

"Why?" she asked, feeling herself harden, hugging herself as she took a small step back from her mother.

"She needs a friend right now," Rachel said. "Things haven't been easy for her, Bethy." She let out a heavy sigh before she sat on her daughter's bed, pushing the duffel bag aside. "I wish so much she'd come to us. We could've helped her, and her mother. And," she added, looking up at Bethany, who felt herself shutting down. "Riley. He seems like a good person, but I know he's struggling mightily too."

"With what?" she asked, voice flat. She absolutely did not want to know about the man who was married to her.

"His fits. I think they've gotten worse. Honestly," she added, sadness in her tone. "I think Mercy is taking care of them both to a degree. Well, Wanda completely, but I think he's been in bad shape too."

Bethany plopped down on the bed next to her mother. She looked down at her hands resting in her skirted lap. "Gran said she had to leave school." She looked over at Rachel. "Is that true?"

Rachel nodded. "It is. She left at the end of last semester."

Bethany shook her head. "Not right."

"That's why I say, honey," the older Wynter woman said softly, resting her hand on Bethany's leg. "She needs a friend. One that perhaps she'll listen to."

"What do you mean?"

"Well, I think Mercy thinks it's all her responsibility, her mother, plus Riley getting her out of a real bind when Wanda really got sick. I think she feels obligated to take care of him as well. Not that that's a bad thing," she added. "But she doesn't have to do it all alone."

Bethany nodded, now with a better understanding of what happened. As much as she felt better, she hurt for Mercy. Now, it sounded like she was plain stuck in her situation. She took a deep, shaky breath, then nodded. "Okay. I'll go see her."

Pulling her truck into the parking lot across the street, just as she'd done a million times before she'd left, Bethany set the brake and looked across the street. The buildings looked the same, though she knew there were many changes and differences. Two of the young men she used to work with at the soda shop were now dead, buried up at Miner's Hole, where Leo was and where Ned would be in a couple days.

The apartments upstairs were now missing three of the tenants that had been there just under a year ago. She held a scrap of paper in her pockets with a new address written on it in her mother's small, neat handwriting. She was told her Grandma Thea was working in the soda shop right now, so she was going to kill two birds with one stone. She'd get to see her beloved grandmother and some of her former coworkers.

Of course her father had said she could slip right back into her job at the shop, but the truth was, Bethany had no clue what she wanted to do. Nursing had always been her dream and her goal, but she just wasn't sure anymore, not about anything. She felt very much like her life had been derailed.

Stepping inside, she smiled at the chorus of *Oh my god!* that she received. She accepted hugs and was touched by some tears and even put up with a few wolf whistles at her in her uniform. But when she saw the very blue eyes that she and Billy had inherited, her own tears almost started all over again.

Unlike her daughter, Thea was quiet and collected as she gathered Bethany into her arms. Bethany melted into the embrace, craving the wonderful soft-spoken calm that was her grandmother. Not that there was anything wrong with being emotional, but Bethany had had so much of it over the past weeks since she'd seen Billy and how ugly he'd been with her, since she'd heard the news about Mercy, and certainly since Ned had been killed on his mission that morning, along with everyone else on board.

She was rocked gently and her hair caressed. "My girl," Thea murmured into the tight, warm hug. A kiss was left on the side of her head before she was looked over by the lovely older woman. Thea smiled at her and cupped the side of her face. "I've missed you so much."

"I've missed you too, Grandma." She felt so at peace in that moment, and it felt wonderful. "What are you doing here?" she asked, indicating the shop around them. "Why aren't you at the farmhouse creating crazy amazing things out of material?"

Thea took Bethany's hand and led her to the manager's office, closing the door softly behind them. They took the two chairs that sat in front of the desk, Thea never letting go of her hand. "This past year has been so hard on your parents," she said. "Really taken a toll. Justice and I have taken on a lot of the duties here in town, to give them a break."

Bethany's head fell. "I knew I should never have gone," she murmured, more to herself than her grandmother.

"No, sweetheart," Thea said, thumb running over the back of Bethany's hand. "This has been an unimaginable situation that honestly, nobody ever thought would happen again." She let out a heavy sigh. "This town has changed a great deal since you and Billy left."

Bethany glanced up to see the tiredness in her grandmother's eyes as she seemed to stare at nothing for a moment. "Well," she said, "I'm home now, Grandma, and I'm not going anywhere ever again. I promise you and Gran, Mama, and Dad, I'll do all I can to help. Do whatever you guys need."

Thea looked confused. "I thought you were going to nursing school when you came back?"

Bethany shrugged. "And that may still happen, at some point. But right now, I feel so lost. I really need to do what I know, and what you guys need. Hell, I'll take this over as manager, if Dad needs that." She shrugged again. "He'd mentioned it before all this war nonsense happened."

"Well," Thea said, tucking some dark strands behind Bethany's ear. "That's for you and your father to discuss, but this place needs a sure, stabilizing hand." She gave her a sad smile. "The whole town does. I think everyone feels lost, uncertain."

"You have my word, Grandma. I'll do it, whatever it takes."

Chapter Twenty

Almost frustrated to tears, Mercy was on hands and knees cleaning up yet another mess. She felt like she was living with two toddlers. Her only reprieve was when Riley went to work, which he was in his bedroom getting ready for. She scrubbed some more, the red of the pasta sauce soaking into the rug.

"I'm sorry, Mercy," came an apologetic tone above and behind her.

"You know, Riley," she bit out. "If you ate in the damn kitchen as I've asked you to so many damn times, this wouldn't happen."

"I said I was sorry!" His heavy booted steps clomped across the wood floor back to his bedroom. "Ain't my fault I had a fit!"

She sighed, so irritated, so tired so… So! "No, Riley, that is absolutely not your fault." She glanced back over her shoulder toward his bedroom to see him tugging on a button-up shirt over the white tank top undershirt he wore with his trousers. "Absolutely not your fault," she said again, never wanting him to think she blamed him for his seizures. "But walking around with a plate of food is." She plopped down on her behind next to the stain. She glared down at it before looking back over to him as he combed his hair, still damp from his bath. "I have enough to clean up with my mother," she muttered.

He let out a heavy sigh as he walked over to her, looking down at the stain. "You can leave it, Mercy. I'll take care of it when I get home. "

She shook her head. "It'll be set in by then."

He walked away, headed to the kitchen. The fridge was opened. "Did you pack a lunch for me, Mercy?" he asked.

He walked to the kitchen doorway, hands bracing along the top of it in the way he often did, his lanky height allowing such a high reach. She looked up at him from where she was on all fours again. Riley literally took a step back from whatever he must have seen in her expression as he disappeared back into the kitchen.

As she continued to scrub, she heard the sound of a lunch being tossed together. He'd begun working nights at the mill, which paid a higher wage and left her alone at night. She was more than okay with it. Sleep for Mercy was a special and rare thing, as Wanda got worse at night, but at least she didn't have to clean up after a grown man as well.

She sat back on her haunches, looking at her handiwork. There would be a stain, but since she'd gotten to it as soon as it had happened, it hadn't been able to soak into the fibers of the rug. That was something, she supposed. The house, though larger than the apartment and far more suitable to a woman who could no longer navigate stairs, was still small.

The three bedrooms were small, though they'd used the largest for Wanda to accommodate her medical supplies and doctors and such in and out, giving the next in line to Riley and saving the smallest—smaller than that she'd had at the apartment—for Mercy. She was fine with that as most nights she stayed with her mother, anyway.

Wanda had reached a point where the pain was nearly twenty-four seven, so it made no sense for Mercy to be up and down all night long, back and forth. She just stayed in the room with Wanda and read or napped during Wanda's short bouts of sleep, and took care of her when she was awake.

Dropping her sauce-stained rag into the bucket of soapy water she'd used to work on the spill, she was about to get to her feet when there was a knock at the front door. It was evening and the porch light wasn't on, so she couldn't see the person standing on the small front porch.

Irritated at yet another thing to deal with, Mercy pushed to her feet, wiping her hands on the apron she always wore tied over her dress nowadays. With her mother's inability to hold down much of anything, more often than not it came back up, and often in Mercy's lap. She'd learned the hard way to protect her clothing as best she could. As it was, she didn't have a large wardrobe to begin with.

Hands dried, she walked over to the front door and pulled it open. A woman stood on the other side, dark hair pulled into an updo and tucked beneath a uniform cap that was the same blue as the blazer and skirt that fit the woman's body to perfection. Her white blouse was crisp, her military insignia polished and women's neckwear in place.

For a moment, Mercy didn't recognize the beautiful, incredibly sophisticated-looking woman standing before her. It wasn't until she met the sky-blue eyes that it occurred to her. She gasped, eyes widening in stunned shock.

"Oh my god," she whispered. Her instinct was

to throw herself at her, desperately needing to make sure she was real, but as she looked at her and then at herself—stained, exhausted and an absolute mess— she stopped. Instead, she felt incredibly unworthy.

She hadn't bathed that day—no time—and her hair was put up and out of the way in a bandana. She herself had lost weight from simple lack of time to sit and eat properly, and her dress hung on her, ill-fitted and bland. Closed up in the bubble that was a household filled with the sick and needy, Bethany's sudden appearance was a reminder of the world beyond that had continued to turn after Mercy had effectively given up her life to take care of her mother and Riley and his increasing needs.

"I'm sorry," she murmured, looking down at her hands, which fidgeted with her stained apron. "I don't want to get you dirty."

Bethany smirked, taking a step forward. "I'm washable," she said softly, gathering Mercy into an embrace.

When she realized she was going to be hugged despite her appearance, Mercy intended to just give her a small squeeze then pull away. But the moment she felt her, smelled her perfume and absorbed her warmth, that plan went out the window. She clung to Bethany in a full-body hug. For that moment, her world righted itself. For that moment, she felt maybe she could actually dream.

But only for that moment. It was interrupted by Riley's voice.

"Who's here?"

Mercy felt Bethany stiffen, then release her. She took a step back and glanced at the man walking up behind Mercy, who was surprised to feel the close proximity of the man she'd married in a quickie ceremony at the courthouse.

"Um," Mercy said, stepping a bit away from him but turning so she was effectively perpendicular to both Bethany and Riley, who faced each other. "Riley, you remember Bethany Wynter. Bethany, I'm sure you remember my old neighbor, Riley."

"Her husband," Riley said, extending a large hand in greeting.

Mercy was surprised by his sudden territorialism, which she hadn't seen from him before. Hell, they didn't share a bedroom, had never consummated the marriage, nor had she ever much referred to him as her husband. It had been an act of necessity, not love or want, on both sides, as they'd discussed it.

"Of course," Bethany said, taking his hand in a firm grip. "It's nice to see you again, Riley. Thank you for helping Mercy and her mother during a difficult time."

He nodded, dropping his hand after the quick shake. Turning to Mercy, he left a quick kiss on her cheek. "Gotta get to work. Be home later."

She flinched at the unexpected peck, looking at him with surprise. What on earth? She watched him go, her earlier irritation returning after Bethany's sudden appearance had vanquished it. She looked back to her hands, feeling ashamed as she felt Bethany's gaze on her.

"Um," she managed. "When did you get back into town?"

"Earlier this afternoon," Bethany said.

Mercy nodded, again looking down at her hands. "How long are you staying?"

"For good."

Riley appeared again, his lunch box in hand. He walked past the two women, Bethany moving out of his way so he could head out to work. He tipped his hat at both of them before he stepped out into the evening. Mercy waited until she heard him climb into his car before she cleared her throat.

"Um, would you like to come in? I can make some coffee."

"Sure."

Mercy gave her a small smile then walked to her bucket and picked it up, carrying it to the kitchen. "Riley had an accident," she explained, nodding toward the damp spot on the rug. She set the bucket on the counter in the small kitchen. "Have a seat, if you like." She indicated the kitchen table and chairs.

She quickly got the percolator started as she heard the soft squeak of one of the wood chairs as Bethany got seated. "How are you? My goodness, it's been so long." She tried to keep her voice light and friendly, even as inside she was screaming for answers. *Why didn't you write? Why didn't you let me know you were coming back? Where have you been?*

"Yes," Bethany agreed. "As wonderful as it feels to be home, it doesn't feel like home."

Mercy nodded. "I'm sure. No doubt, wherever you were was so different—"

"Mercy, why didn't you respond to my letters?" Bethany blurted. "Was it because of Riley? Because you got involved with him?"

Stunned, Mercy turned to look at the woman staring back at her. "I never got a letter from you," she said, almost a whisper, tinged with the hurt she'd been feeling for nearly a year. "Not a single one."

"What?" Bethany gasped. "I wrote you nearly

every day for the first two months I was gone." Bethany looked away, her full bottom lip tucked beneath her top teeth before it was released. "Eventually, I just stopped."

Mercy was frozen to the spot for a long moment, no idea what to say. She was shocked, relieved, and horrified all at the same time. She pushed away from the counter and walked over to Bethany, who looked so small sitting there all the sudden. "Come with me," she said quietly.

Bethany followed her through the small house, past the bedroom where Wanda slept and to the tiny one tucked at the back of the house. Mercy flicked on the lamp on the dresser to reveal a twin-sized bed tucked against the wall with barely the width of a small round rug to fit on the floor between it and the dresser.

Lowering herself to her knees, she reached under the bed and tugged out a small suitcase. She plopped it on the bed and stood. Unclasping it, she pushed the top open to reveal some of her heavier winter dresses and the couple sweaters she had. No room to have out both summer and winter clothes, they stayed in there until everything was swapped out.

She removed the clothing to reveal a stash of folded pages beneath it. She gathered them, holding them out to Bethany. "I wrote you every day, sometimes twice a day," she said shyly. "I had nowhere to send them, so I just kept them. Kept writing."

Bethany looked at them, page after page after page. "My god," she whispered, a hand coming to her mouth. She looked at Mercy. "Do you think your mother threw them out?" she asked. "My letters? Did you get Billy's? He said he wrote you too."

Mercy shook her head. "I got nothing." She

blew out a breath, hugging herself. Profound sadness and anger begin to warm her from the inside out. "I wouldn't put it past her." She met Bethany's pained gaze. "I'm so sorry. I didn't know."

Bethany set the letters aside on the dresser and clasped her hands in front of her mouth, almost as though she were praying. After a moment she asked, "If you'd gotten my letters, would you still have married him?"

It hurt Mercy so much to hear the pain in Bethany's voice, a woman she still loved. "Bethany," she whispered. "I didn't marry him because I loved him. I still don't. I married him because I had few other choices. I'd rather be up in that tiny apartment, getting ready to enjoy my last summer break before my senior year. Working at the soda shop."

"Why didn't you go to my parents?" Bethany demanded, her hands on Mercy's shoulders. "Why? Why him? Why marry him?"

"I didn't want to burden them," Mercy responded honestly. "They were already dealing with you, Billy, and Ned being away at war, in danger, and Leo killed. Plus…" Her voice faltered and she looked down. "Plus, when I didn't hear from you." She moved away from Bethany, not wanting her to see the tears that were welling in her eyes. "I thought I didn't mean anything to you, that I was just another Helen. A distraction, maybe."

Bethany moved up behind her, turning her around with gentle hands and pulling her into a hug. "No." She cupped the back of Mercy's head as she urged it to rest against her shoulder. "No," she said again softly.

Mercy allowed herself to fall into her, to be *held*

by her. Again, her world was righted, but this time, just maybe it could stay that way, and not just for the precious, fleeting moments of an embrace. Bethany kissed the side of her head before she pulled out of the hug but stayed close.

"First thing," Bethany said, brushing her fingers across Mercy's cheek. "We're going to get you some help." Her brow furrowed as she looked into Mercy's face. "You look so tired."

Mercy nodded. "I am. But this is my duty, Bethany. To take care of her. I know that. I am fine with that."

"Yes, but there is no reason in the world why you should be doing this all by yourself. And," she added, "you're going back to school. When did you leave?"

"After the holiday break," Mercy said, moving away from her to plop down on the bed. An emotional evening, she felt utterly spent. "But," she continued, glancing over at Bethany, who sat next to her. "Sam was so sweet." She smiled. "He worked with my teachers to get my homework for me every week, even though I'd already dropped out."

Bethany smiled. "Gotta love that Pops. Do you still have it? The schoolwork?" At Mercy's nod, she said, "Okay. You only missed a semester, so maybe something can be worked out, considering the circumstances. Maybe get it back to them this summer, and if you pass..." She shrugged.

For the first time in seemingly endless months, Mercy felt a bit of hope. "Do you think they would?"

"You were a really good student, Mercy. I know they'd sure as hell rather see you finish than walk away."

Mercy almost wanted to cry again, but this time

tears of happiness. "Really? You really think I may be able to finish?"

That smile that Mercy knew so well on Bethany—confident, beautiful, almost cocky—quirked those gorgeous lips. "Absolutely. We'll make it happen, one way or the other. And I'm going to send you help." She waggled a finger at her. "Tomorrow morning, you expect it. Got me?"

Mercy sat up straight and brought her hand up in a salute.

"Oh, no, no, no," Bethany teased, waving her attempt away. She stood erect, heels clicking together as she stood at attention. Her hand flew up in stiff salute proper form.

Mercy giggled, unable to help herself at the serious look on Bethany's face, which she knew was exaggerated in that moment. Also, she just felt so damn happy! She felt hope that maybe, just maybe, the sun would come back out.

⚜ ⚜ ⚜ ⚜

"Do you want some more, Mother?" Mercy asked softly, holding the glass of water up near her mother's parched lips. Wanda, near skeletal now, shook her head. She rarely talked anymore, so she looked into Mercy's eyes. She was a shell of who she'd once been, almost unrecognizable. "Okay." Mercy set the glass aside on the bedside table. "Want me to read to you again?"

At her mother's nod, Mercy reached for the Bible, which also rested on the bedside table. While she was still able to communicate, Wanda had asked her to start reading the holy book, starting at the beginning, so that's how they spent much of their time when Wanda was awake. She got more comfortable where she sat on the side of the bed and was about to open to her bookmark when there was a knock on the front door.

Glancing in that direction, Mercy turned back to Wanda. "I'll be right back, Mother."

Setting the book on the side of the bed where she'd just been siting, she smoothed her skirt down in the back as she made her way from the bedroom into the living room and front door. She was very surprised to see Thea Kilkoyne standing on the porch, several bags from the grocery store at her feet and the bright, beautiful morning behind her.

Mercy had only met the woman a handful of times but had enjoyed each meeting. A quiet, contemplative woman of unusual beauty, even still in her older years. She pulled open the door and smiled.

"Hello, Mrs. Kilkoyne. Can I help you?"

The older woman smiled as she took Mercy in a tight hug and left a kiss on her cheek. "None of this 'Mrs. Kilkoyne' nonsense," she said in her soft-spoken way. "You call me Grandma or nothing at all."

Mercy chuckled. "Yes, ma'am. I mean, Grandma. Is everything okay?"

"Everything is exquisite," Thea said, lightly touching her cheek with her fingers before she handed Mercy the bags she was carrying. "You take those and I'll grab these." She indicated the other bags at her feet. "Then, we'll discuss."

Mercy took the bags and backed away so the other woman could enter. "Um, all right," she said, confused. "Discuss what?"

Thea met her gaze, an eyebrow raised. "Discuss how I can best help my bonus granddaughter."

Chapter Twenty-one

Again, she started as the guns blasted, in perfectly synced handling and fire. Finished, the lonely sound of "Taps" began, the lone, uniformed bugler standing off by himself for the mournful song.

Mercy's gaze went to Bethany, who stood next to her mother, who was being held by Henry. She so badly wanted to go to Bethany. She could feel her sadness across the thirty feet that separated them. And, as her parents were essentially holding each other up, she was left to be strong on her own.

She could feel the distance like it was a living, breathing thing, one hand on her chest, one on Bethany's, keeping them apart. Truth was, she was keeping them apart. She felt it was the family's right to be up there, not hers. The huge funeral had taken place in the church, and this was at the cemetery for family. She was shocked when she'd been asked to join.

Chewing on her lip for just a moment, she decided she needed to act. She hated the scared, uncertain shadow she'd become in the last year, after working so hard to become strong and go for what she wanted, just like Bethany. She murmured soft "excuse mes" to those she walked past or in front of until she reached Bethany's side.

Bethany said nothing, nor did she look at her, but immediately grabbed Mercy's hand. As their fingers automatically entwined, Mercy knew she'd done the right thing. And, as Bethany leaned slightly into her, Mercy knew she was home. As she stared down at the flag-draped casket before them, she considered what to do.

She had a lot of thinking to do, as her current situation with Riley was untenable. She'd rushed into the situation out of fear and desperation, erroneously thinking she had no other options. Now, she realized she did—there was hope and there was a life for her outside of illness and impending death.

But what to do regarding Riley? Despite the parameters they'd agreed upon for their marriage, she'd still made a commitment to him, to being there for him, helping him. As it was, he was back at the house now, sitting with Wanda so she could go to the funeral. Granted, it had taken some convincing, but he'd done it.

The song ended and uniformed soldiers stepped forward to fold the flag from atop Ned's casket in their ceremonial way. It was presented to Henry and Rachel, as well as murmured condolences on behalf of President Roosevelt and a grateful nation.

Once the service was over, Bethany turned to Mercy. "Are you going back to the house with us?"

Mercy shook her head. "No," she said, regret in her tone. "I need to get back to the house. My mother can't be left alone anymore." She shrugged, apology in her eyes. "Riley is with her now."

Bethany nodded. "I understand. Come on, I'll drive you home."

The drive was silent, Mercy glancing over at her friend. She seemed to be mulling a lot around in her mind, so Mercy remained silent so as not to interrupt. The truck pulled up in front of the small house, and to her surprise, Bethany turned off the ignition. Again, the older woman remained silent.

"Um," Mercy said, glancing down at her hands in her lap. "Would you like to come in, say hello to Mother?"

Bethany finally looked over at her, meeting her gaze for several moments before she finally nodded. "Yeah." She pulled the keys from the ignition and tucked them into her palm as the two climbed out of the truck.

They entered the house, the sound of a radio program on in the kitchen. Mercy glanced that way, noting Riley sitting at the kitchen table smoking a cigarette. A bottle of beer sat on the table near his resting hand. She shook her head, hating the cigarette smoke in the house. She wasn't keen on the smell.

Saying nothing, she led the way to Wanda's bedroom. Pushing open the door, she saw that her mother was awake, her sunken gaze landing on the two women who entered the room. "Hey, Mother," Mercy said. "Look who I brought."

"Hello, Mrs. Faulkner," Bethany said softly. "It's so nice to see you." She walked over to the bed and looked down at the near-skeletal person who looked back up at her. She reached down and took a bony hand between both of hers. "If you need anything, Mrs. Faulkner, you find a way to let Mercy know and we'll move Heaven and Earth to get it for you or make sure it's done, okay?" She turned to Mercy, who stood just inside the bedroom doorway, not wanting to interrupt. "You call, no matter what time of night, okay?" she said. "You remember our number?"

Mercy immediately spit out the five-digit number, two letters and three numbers. "Yes," she smiled.

"I remember."

"Good," Bethany said, giving her a teasing smile in return. She looked back to Wanda, who was studying her. "Anything at all you need," she said gently. "Don't forget to let us know." She seemed as though she were about to release Wanda's hand and leave, but she said, "And, don't you worry. No matter what, I'll always make sure Mercy is taken care of."

To her surprise, a ghost of a smile actually touched Wanda's lips just before her eyes closed and she fell to sleep.

Bethany released Wanda's hand and turned to Mercy, nodding that they should leave the room. Closing the door behind them, Bethany shook her head. "Wow," she murmured. "I can't believe how much she's deteriorated." She met Mercy's gaze. "I don't even recognize her."

"It happened really fast," Mercy agreed. "I think she'd been sick for a while but just hadn't told me." The two moved to the living room, taking a seat on the couch, their thighs nearly touching. "She wants to be buried back in Pueblo," Mercy continued.

"With your father?"

Mercy shook her head. "No, with her parents." She shrugged. "I don't understand it. I never once met my grandparents, so I'm not sure about the situation there."

"When it happens," Bethany said, placing her hand on Mercy's knee briefly. "We'll make sure she gets her last wish. Okay?"

Mercy nodded, blowing out a breath. "Am I a horrible person," Mercy whispered, looking at Bethany with shy eyes, "if I say part of me doesn't feel she deserves her last wish?"

Bethany shook her head, her smile understanding. "No. You've been through a lot since your father died, I don't blame you for feeling that way at all." Bethany let out a heavy sigh before looking to the front window for a moment. Finally, she looked back to Mercy. "I should go. I need to help set up for visitors at the house."

Loath to see her go, she did understand. Mercy rose to her feet as Bethany did. "Okay. I'm so sorry I can't go and help."

"Don't be." At the front door, the two embraced, Bethany holding her for a long moment. Finally, she let her go, lightly brushing her cheek with the backs of her fingers. "See you later."

Mercy nodded, unable to speak as she was afraid she'd beg her not to go, or to take her with her. She stood at the front door and watched Bethany walk to her truck. Once Bethany had the driver's side door open, she stood there and looked back to the house. Their gazes met and held before Bethany climbed in and drove away.

"You know, I thought it would go away."

Closing the front door, Mercy turned to see Riley leaning against the archway that separated the living room from the kitchen. He was in baggy trousers and a white undershirt. His arms were crossed over his chest.

"You thought what would go away?"

"All that, with Bethany." He indicated just outside the house where the truck had been moments before. "I seen you two. Seen her sneak in and out of that apartment window." His gaze was fixed on her, and it was hard. "I honestly thought, her bein' older and popular, all that, that she was making you do stuff. Word is, Bethany Wynter ain't natural."

Mercy bit her tongue for a moment, as she knew that was a lie. She felt he was trying to goad her. Where was this jealousy coming from? She was about to ask when he continued.

"After the accident when I was nine years old, hit in the head and I started havin' fits, Mama and Daddy took me to that awful place. They left me there, Mercy. Awful. Shock therapy, livin' in filth with the crazies." He pounded his own chest, startling her. "I ain't crazy! I ain't never belonged there, so when I turned eighteen, I got out."

Mercy had never known his story; he'd never shared it with her and she hadn't felt it was right to ask. She cleared her throat, trying to tame her racing heart, little fingers of nervous fear walking down her spine. "I'm so sorry that happened to you, Riley," she said. "You're right, you're not crazy and you never deserved that." She remained by the door, the space of the small room between them. "Have you seen them since?"

He shook his head. "Nah. Mama was a Bible reader." He snorted derisively. "I think she thought the Devil had gotten hold of me or somethin'." He studied her for so long it began to make her uncomfortable. "I used to watch you, so darn pretty. How you were with everybody. So kind, sweet." He smiled. "Sweet to me. Ain't had a girl be sweet to me before."

She felt her nervousness grow. The look in his eyes changed from anger at talking about his parents and their horrible betrayal to an injured child to a lovesick schoolboy. "Riley," she said, hoping to cut this off at the pass. "When we talked about this, you understood why I agreed to your plan, and it was a plan. You said so, to ensure I was free to take care of my mother until she died."

"You know," he said, a little chuckle in his tone, as if she hadn't spoken. "I ain't ever kissed a girl. Twenty-two, ain't never even kissed one." He shook his head and whistled softly through his teeth. "Damn shame."

Really getting nervous now, Mercy swallowed. "Riley, you knew from the outset that this wasn't a marriage like that. You knew that," she repeated, hoping it would penetrate whatever fog he seemed to be in.

He looked away from her, jaw muscles working. "Now that she's back, you're gonna leave, ain't you? Knowing I need your help."

Now anger began to bloom inside her like a black rose. "Need my help?" she asked. "Need my help to do what?" Hands on hips, she stared him down. "Cook for you? Clean up after you? Do your laundry? In this situation, I haven't minded doing those things, because you are working hard every day, bringing in the financial help to allow me to take care of my mother here at the end. But Riley, these are all things you did for yourself, and just fine I might add, before this happened." She indicated the house around them.

"'Before this happened'?" he said, "Before we got *married*, you mean." He stared her down. "Whether Bethany Wynter is here or not, you're *my* wife, Mercy. Now, I've been patient with you, with this whole situation. My whole life, I ain't had nothin' that belonged to me or that wasn't taken away. She ain't taking you away, neither!"

"Riley," Mercy said, attempting to keep her voice calm, even as she was a tempest of nerves and anger inside. "Bethany has nothing to do with this. We don't have that kind of marriage, and you know that. Your own words were, 'married in title only.' Remember?"

"Well, I changed my mind!"

Everything in her told her to get out. She turned and grabbed the knob of the front door when she was grabbed from behind. She tried to scream, but her mouth was covered as she was lifted off her feet and part-dragged, part-carried to the back bedroom.

※ ※ ※ ※

Tears still streaming down her cheeks, she turned to her side and curled up in the fetal position, trying to protect herself. She could hardly breathe, and everything hurt. She could feel him move off the bed, a quiet sniffle escaping him.

"Oh my god," he whispered. "Oh my god." Another sniffle. "Mercy, I'm—"

Suddenly, hard, intense banging on the front door sounded, as well as Mercy's name called out in a panicked male voice. Henry Wynter. Mercy lifted her head, terrified, but a tiny kernel of hope sprouted. Riley moved to the bedroom door and pulled it open and left the small room that held Mercy's things.

Wincing, she uncurled herself and pushed to a sitting position. Her eyes widened with what happened when the front door was opened.

"Sir, I'm sorry, I—" Riley cried out along with the sound of a vicious punch and then his bulk hitting the floor. "Sir, I—"

"Get up!" Henry raged.

"Don't hurt him, Hank," another voice said. Mercy recognized it as Justice's.

She flinched when she heard someone heading to the bedrooms. Riley's bedroom door slammed open, then Wanda's, and finally, they arrived at Mercy's.

"Bethany," she whimpered.

"Oh no," Bethany gasped, tears instantly coming to her eyes as she made her way to the bed. "Dad!" she called out, sitting carefully on the bed next to Mercy.

"What?" he growled from the other room, another punch sounding.

"Call the police!" Bethany called out.

Justice appeared in the doorway, the older woman's hands shoved into the pockets of baggy trousers. Her ever-present suspenders hitched over her shoulders. "Does she need a doctor?" she asked softly.

"I don't know." Bethany looked at Mercy, brushing auburn strands out of her face, struck to tear streaks. "Sweetheart?" she asked softly.

"I...I don't know," Mercy muttered, her mind foggy, her body hurting and her soul shattered. "I don't know."

Bethany hugged Mercy's head to her chest. "Gran," she said. "Wanda...Um." She swallowed. "The handset of the phone is still in her hand."

Justice nodded. "Understood."

Left alone again, Mercy's eyes fell closed as Bethany cradled her, very gently. "It's okay," she whispered. "I've got you."

Chapter Twenty-two

Slowly coming to wakefulness, Mercy blinked several times. She didn't recognize the bedroom where she lay. It wasn't the one back at the house, certainly not the apartment, and it wasn't Bethany's. Looking to her left, she saw someone was in bed with her, sleeping on their side, back to her. She knew it was Bethany. She had vague memories of being cuddled into sleep by her the night before.

She lay there for a moment, trying to get her bearings. She took a mental inventory of her body and found that she was incredibly sore. Every single muscle was angry at her, let alone any other parts. She also realized she had to pee, and soon.

Groaning quietly, she forced herself to roll out of the warmth and safety of the bed with Bethany but tried to be quiet to not wake her. She was in a head-to-toe cotton sleeping gown that she didn't recognize but was grateful for the heavy material. Somehow it felt like a suit of armor.

She quietly left the bedroom, the door barely making a sound as she closed it behind her. Looking around, she found herself in an upstairs hallway with several doors. She had to smile when she glanced into one of the other rooms and saw a pair of suspenders draped over the trunk that was against the wall beneath the window. The four-poster bed was made to perfection, the room tidy and clean, just like the one she'd woken up in.

Armed with a better understanding of where she probably was, she hurried to another door, a bathroom. Relieved, she closed herself inside to do her morning business. Once finished, she flushed and removed her sleeping gown. She'd taken a bath before bed, she remembered now, but felt the need to clean herself again.

She felt so dirty, and it wasn't because she'd done anything wrong, as she knew with every fiber of her soul she hadn't. But she could still feel his hands on her, his touch, and it made her want to vomit.

She avoided looking at her eyes in the mounted mirror above the sink basin as she worried she wouldn't recognize the woman staring back at her. The thought of that scared the hell out of her. She quickly did her task then dressed again, feeling much safer with the nightgown covering her body.

Pulling the door open, she saw that the bedroom door was now open that she'd just closed twenty minutes before. The bed was empty and she heard voices downstairs. Heading in that direction, she was happy to see Bethany and Thea sitting at the kitchen table, a mug of coffee before each.

"Justice and I talked about it last night," Thea was saying. "We'll get the farmhouse all set up for you girls. If," she added, "that's what Mercy wants. Obviously, she'll have a say in this too."

"Hi."

Both women turned to look at the sound of her voice. Bethany instantly was on her feet and hurried over to her. The look in her eyes said, *I really want to hug you but not sure if I should touch you.* Reading it loud and clear, deciding that yes, she needed to be held in that moment, she basically moved into the other woman's personal space.

Bethany's arms were gentle, a bit tentative. As Mercy relaxed against her, head resting on her shoulder, the arms tightened and the embrace was complete. Mercy felt like she was in a cocoon of safety and warmth. She hugged her back and let out a sigh, feeling like the many months of uncertainty, confusion, and misery were over.

She knew her mother was gone but had yet to truly deal with that fact. As she understood it, Wanda had used what little life she had left to crawl to the phone, left in her bedroom to call doctors and such, and had mustered up enough voice to relay the number to the operator. Though Wanda likely passed shortly after the call was connected, Henry, who had answered, had been able to hear what was happening over the open line.

Wanda Faulkner's last act on this earth had been to finally be a mother.

Neither of them said anything, nothing really to say. She knew she had so much to process and work through, not just from the previous night or months, but from a lifetime. It would take her time, but at least now she could begin the process of healing.

After several moments, Bethany pulled away enough to look into Mercy's face. She cupped the side of her face that wasn't bruised. Riley hadn't hit her directly, but in the struggle, she'd taken an elbow to the jaw. She'd bitten her tongue and her lip in the process, so both hurt.

"How are you?" Bethany asked softly, fingers caressing Mercy's cheek before her hand fell away.

Mercy nodded, meeting Bethany's concerned

gaze. "Yeah. Sore, but stopped bleeding."

Bethany's beautiful eyes flashed with rage before she looked away. It seemed she was trying to get her emotions under control. She swallowed and took a deep breath. "Do you need to go to the hospital?" she asked softly. "I'll take you right now."

Mercy shook her head, taking the other woman into another hug, though this time to comfort her. "No. I'm okay, I think." Mercy glanced over when she felt a hand to her back and instantly a smile came to her lips. She accepted Thea's tight, motherly embrace. Since she'd been helping her over the previous week, she'd truly come to adore the older woman.

"Do you want some coffee, honey?" Thea asked, pulling out of the hug after a long moment. At Mercy's nod, she said, "You girls sit down and I'll get it. We need to talk."

⚝⚝⚝⚝

She blew out a breath, then another. "Damn it!" She turned her face away from the small house, angry at herself, her fist pounding into her skirt-clad thigh. "I thought I could."

"Hey," Bethany said, covering that fist with a warm hand. "It's okay. We'll take care of it, okay? Me and Pops."

Mercy nodded, not feeling any better. "I've got to get over this," she said, watching as a car passed Bethany's truck, parked at the curb in front of the small house that she hadn't been in in three days. They needed to clear it out as it was a rental, but she also needed an outfit for her mother's funeral.

"And you will," Bethany assured. "Give yourself

some time, Mercy." She squeezed the hand in her own until Mercy met her gaze. "This all just happened. If you think about it," Bethany continued, "Your life has been one giant roller coaster since your father died. You've barely had time to stop and catch your breath until the next drop hit. And," she said, nodding toward the house beyond Mercy's window. "That was a doozy."

"Are you sure?" Mercy asked, her voice barely above a whisper. "That you want to be stuck with me? I mean, here you are, graduated top of your class, been through war and already back, and I can't even seem to navigate my way out of high school." She gave her a small smile. "I don't want you to feel you're sharing a house with a total kid as you're getting your life going."

"Okay," Bethany drew out, taking Mercy's hand in both of hers and moving it to her own thigh. She met a shy brown gaze. "Regardless of any of this," she said, nodding to the house behind Mercy, "you'd still be in school because you're younger than me." She quirked an eyebrow in challenge.

Mercy looked down at their hands, a small smile brushing her lips. "Okay, fair."

"Listen, how about this," Bethany said, voice taking on a cheery tone. "Do you have your driver's license?"

Yet again feeling less than Bethany could ever want, she shook her head, looking down at her lap. "No. Mother wouldn't allow it,"

"All right, well now that Gran and Grandma are going to get guardianship of you until you turn eighteen in a year, you can. You have your father's car."

Bethany's words hit her. It was something she never thought she'd be able to do. A feeling of wonder washing through her. "Oh my gosh, you're right."

She glanced over at a grinning Bethany, who said, "You ready?"

"For what?"

"To get your life back."

Mercy met that grin the best she could. "Or perhaps for the first time."

⊰⊱⊰⊱

Just a few weeks later, Mercy was working with Bethany to clean the old farmhouse, which Thea and Justice were going to rent to them. Thea had sat down with the two young women the morning after the horrifying events at the house with Riley and they'd discussed the idea.

Initially Mercy's breath had caught, so many emotions rushing through her at the thought of actually living with Bethany. Thea had given them some very sage advice that morning. *Move in as friends, as roommates. You girls aren't the same young women you were as your feelings began to form. Get to know who you both have become so you can build a foundation built upon love and not circumstances.* She'd given them both a very knowing smile as she'd taken a hand of each in both of hers. *Trust me on this.*

Mercy knew, for her part, that she absolutely was not the same person, and the truth was, she was trying to figure out who she was. And Bethany…well, now there were shadows in her eyes that hadn't been there before she'd left. She was a quieter version of herself that Mercy was trying to unwrap and learn.

As she scrubbed down the walls in the kitchen area, she considered the last handful of days. The small house had been cleared out by Bethany, Sam, and some of their school friends. Mercy had been so grateful, as she just couldn't make herself return to that damn house. Now, with her mother gone, Riley still sitting in jail, and Mercy out of the situation, she'd come to understand just how miserable she had been. How every single day uncertainty and underlying fear had been her constant companion.

No, it wasn't fear of Riley and certainly not of her mother anymore. Riley's actions that last day had been completely out of character of the man she'd come to know over the past year. She'd never in a million years have guessed him capable of what he'd done. And yes, she had to live with that memory and the way it had changed her forever, but she was slowly analyzing his actions.

That was actually something she wanted to talk to Bethany about. No doubt she'd think Mercy had lost her mind, the direction her thoughts had gone, but she was firm in her growing resolve.

Dropping the large sponge she'd been using to scrub the walls into the bucket of warm, soapy water, Mercy evaluated her handiwork. She was making definite progress. Through the many years the farmhouse had been rented to this itinerate farmer then that one, it hadn't been cared for properly. Yes, repairs had been made over the years, either by Justice or whoever was living there at the time, but no real love had been shown to the house. Well, that was the problem, she thought. It had been seen as a house, not a home.

If she and Bethany were going to live there,

regardless of how long or short a time, she was determined to create a real home for not only them, but for herself. She'd never had that. She'd never felt in charge of anything, never felt it was *hers*. It certainly hadn't helped that her mother had held over her head that she was merely a guest in her home her entire life.

Now, all that was behind her. Her mother's funeral, an extremely small affair, had been held a few days before. As per her wish, she'd been buried next to her parents. A few of her father's former coworkers had shown up to the graveside service, but the number had been less than twenty, including Mercy, Bethany, her parents, and grandparents.

It was over. Mercy had truly thought it would hit her, one night or one morning, randomly out of nowhere, and she'd break down. It hadn't happened. Not to say it couldn't, but she truly believed it wouldn't. She felt like a terrible person, regardless of Bethany's assurances that she wasn't, but she felt no grief over her mother's passing. She felt only one thing: relief.

"Hello!"

Mercy glanced over her shoulder at the exuberant greeting called out by Henry Wynter from the front porch. A warm May day, the wood storm door was open, leaving only the screen door to keep out bugs. Wiping her hands on the apron tied around her waist, Mercy walked to the living room.

"Hey, Mr. Wynter," she responded with a smile. To her surprise, he stood on the porch, seemingly no intention of entering the house. After a moment of confusion, she realized he was waiting for permission to enter. "Come on in."

He did just that, carrying in a five-gallon bucket of paint that he set down on the floor at his feet. "Per

Bethany's request," he said. He removed his fedora, using a handkerchief from his pocket to wipe the sweat from his brow before replacing the hat. "Goodness, warming up out there."

"It is," she agreed. "It's been making me feel a little nauseous today, honestly."

"Sorry, kiddo," he said. "I'll bring by some fans I've got at the house. That should help."

"Thank you so much, Mr. Wynter. I truly appreciate that. I know Bethany will too."

"You call me Henry," he said, giving her a fatherly smile. "Got me?" At her nod, he asked, "When do you start back up at the soda shop?"

"Next week," Mercy said, grinning. She was excited to get back to work, to be contributing again. "I've been able to get some good work done on the house, so…"

He looked around, hands on hips. "It's looking amazing." He gave her a winning smile. "So glad you gals will be able to bring some life back into this place."

Mercy folded her arms over her chest, a sense of pride washing through her. "I think this place will be amazing when we're done," she said. "Gran told us there's some furniture she wants to bring out of storage for us to use, some things she and Grandma really want us to have."

Henry looked at her, eyebrows raised in surprise. For a moment, Mercy was confused on what the issue was, but then she surmised it was her use of Justice's true gender. He said nothing, but a small smile quirked his lips. "I think that'll be great, Mercy. Real great." He walked over to her and gave her a one-armed hug and a kiss on the forehead. "I need to get to some meetings downtown, but if you gals need anything, don't you dare hesitate to call."

She nodded, returning his smile as he moved to the door. "Will do."

❧❧❧❧

Later that night, Mercy got ready for bed. She was absolutely exhausted and sore as all get-out from her active day. She'd gotten a lot done and was proud of her progress, but damn, she was paying the price tonight! She was freshly bathed and changed into her lightweight sleeping gown.

She was in the room she and Bethany had shared during their weekend there taking care of Helen. She was sleeping in the same bed with brass head and footboards. A second bed had been brought in for Bethany's bedroom across the hall. She understood the necessity, but part of her wished they were sharing a bed nonetheless. She sat brushing out her hair, still damp from her bath.

"Come on in," she called out at the knock on the closed bedroom door. Her smile was instant when Bethany entered. She, too, looked tired. "Hi."

"Hey." Bethany walked over to the bed and plopped down, flat on her back. The entire bed shook with her action.

Mercy glanced down at her reclining form, reaching out to rest her hand on Bethany's stomach. Her hand was immediately covered by Bethany's. "You look so tired," she said softly.

Bethany nodded. "I am." Bethany met her gaze from where she lay. "Now that Dad has me completely taking over the entire business, it's a lot to learn." Her thumb absently ran over the back of Mercy's hand.

"Well," Mercy said, "I happen to know that you're brilliant and will pick it up in no time. And," she added with a sweet smile, "I'll be there soon to help in any way I can."

Bethany's smile was serene. "It'll be wonderful to have you back at the shop. Are you excited?"

Mercy changed her position, moving to lie across the bed next to Bethany, both their feet hanging off the side. She rested on her left side, head cradled in her hand. "Yes, very much." She studied Bethany's eyes. "Think you can handle that much of me? Living here with me, and then at work too?"

"Oh, I think I can handle it." Bethany grinned. "And you."

Mercy quirked an eyebrow. "Oh? I don't know, that's a whole lot of me to put up with."

"Yeah, but it's a whole lot of *me* to put up with, too." She chuckled. "I may just pull out a sketch pad and draw you again."

Mercy stared at her, brows drawing. "Again?" She nearly burst into laughter at the, "uh-oh" look that crossed Bethany's features. "Busted?"

Bethany's expression was absolutely charming, like a kid caught trying to hide the cookie she stole from the cookie jar behind her back. "Um, maybe."

Mercy playfully poked her stomach. "When?"

"When we were all at The Hole that last time," Bethany finally said, apology in her tone. "You were reading and the boys were fishing. Couldn't help myself."

"Did you make me look terrible?" Mercy asked, eyeing her.

Bethany burst into laughter. "Impossible."

"Liar," Mercy teased. She was about to say something else, enjoying the moment, but stopped as she had to focus for a moment.

"What's wrong?"

Mercy closed her eyes as she sat up, taking a few slow, deep breaths. "My stomach." She removed her hand from Bethany's and placed it over her own. "I felt nauseous earlier today, and..." Another wave washed over her. "Oh boy."

"Mercy." Bethany also sat up. "Are you okay?"

"I need to..." Mercy pushed up from the bed, a hand going to the wall to brace her as yet another wave hit her, to the point of having to swallow down the nausea that was creeping up into her throat. She thought maybe it was going to pass when she rushed through the open bedroom door and to the bathroom. She barely made it before her stomach let loose.

Chapter Twenty-three

Mercy was absolutely baffled why Thea had taken her to this place, but there they were, strolling amongst the neat rows of their closest couple hundred friends, buried with marked headstones. Neither of them said a word as Thea led them toward the oldest section of the cemetery. There, graves were marked with dates in the eighteen hundreds and early nineteen hundreds.

Finally, they stopped in front of a grave. "Buck Teedle," Mercy read. "Wow, he's been gone a long time." She looked to Thea for an explanation. "Who was this?"

"Rachel's biological father," she explained, looking down at the aged headstone before meeting Mercy's surprised gaze. "And yes, he was killed in an accident in the mine about halfway through my pregnancy. I'm sure you've noticed Bethany's uncle Nate has a slight limp to his gait? Well, he was in the same accident. A collapse."

"Wow," Mercy murmured, looking back to the stone. "I'm so sorry. So tragic."

"It was tragic for Buck, yes. But to really understand why I brought you here, what I want you to consider, I need to start from the beginning."

Mercy nodded. "Okay."

"Justice and I met back in Pennsylvania. She was just a little older than you, Mercy. I was all of twenty-one." Thea's smile was so beautiful and bright, much like Rachel and Bethany's. "Truly love at first sight. I joined Justice and her mother Ninny on their journey west. We intended to start over in California."

"Wow! How'd you end up in Colorado, then?"

"Our plans were literally derailed in a horrible train wreck here," Thea explained. "We both thought the other was dead. Horrible time."

"Oh no," Mercy whispered. She thought about how hard it had been with Bethany off somewhere in the world, no word if she was dead or alive, and how awful that had been.

"I met Buck during that time, and he helped me get through that horrible time, in some ways very much like Riley helped you. Though Buck and I had a relatively traditional marriage, if you follow."

Mercy nodded, unable to imagine Thea with anyone else. "I do."

"Imagine my shock, a year and a half later, when I found out Justice was still alive." Again, the return of that brilliant smile.

Mercy's eyebrows shot up. "And you were still married to Buck?"

Thea nodded. "And pregnant."

"Oh. Boy."

Thea chuckled. "It was a hard time."

"Did you love him? Buck?"

Thea was silent for a long time as she stared down at the headstone. Finally, she said, "I was grateful to him, Mercy. He'd been there when I needed someone. I was so devastated at losing Justice, losing my chance at happiness. But, love him? No. Not as a wife should. You see, even though Buck insisted we start a family, I was devastated when I found out I was pregnant.

Somehow, it felt like I was stuck with him forever." She hugged herself, as if lost back in that emotion.

This, of course, sent Mercy's own mind reeling to her own situation. She thought of Bethany, had thought of nothing else in the days since her worst fears had been confirmed by a doctor. Why on earth would Bethany ever want to get tangled up in this?

She tried to chase those morose thoughts away and asked, "What did Justice say? When she knew you were pregnant?" Her voice was barely more than a whisper as she was trying to swallow down the emotion that threatened to surface.

"I think she was hurt, as it brought to mind how I got pregnant. But once she understood how I'd ended up with him, I think she knew we'd both done what we had to in those days. We both had to make decisions. Understand?" she asked gently.

Mercy nodded, looking down. She pursed her lips together, trying valiantly not to cry.

"Once we were together again," Thea continued, wrapping an arm around Mercy's waist. "She was overjoyed, knowing she'd be a parent with me. She'd get to be a 'father,' as it were, to our little girl." Her smile brimmed with love. "Justice fell in love with Rachel from the moment she saw her, mere minutes after she was born." She chuckled. "Rachel had her wrapped around her little finger from day one."

Mercy smiled, able to again see the look of endless love and adoration that she'd seen in Justice's eyes whenever around her daughter. "I can believe that."

"Now," Thea said, reaching up and brushing some auburn strands out of Mercy's face from a light breeze that had sent them there. "I'm telling you all this because I want you to understand something. I know you're upset, I know you're afraid. And, whatever you decide to do—and it *is* your decision, sweetheart—we'll all support you. But I want you to think about the fact that it may be a blessing in disguise for you, as it was for me."

Mercy met her gaze, desperately searching for some hope in what the older woman was telling her.

"I got to raise my daughter with the woman I loved," Thea said softly, Bethany's eyes looking back at her through her grandmother. "If not for Buck, Justice and I would never have had our family." She smiled. "And, you wouldn't have had your Bethany."

Mercy smiled, though it was sad. "True. But I don't know that she would want this." She rested her hand on a belly that was far from showing any growth.

"Have you asked her?" Thea challenged.

Mercy shook her head. "No. You took me to the doctor, and I haven't told her what he said. And since I had the marriage annulled days after the attack, Riley isn't exactly in my life, either." She hardened. "Nor do I want him to be."

"Well," Thea said, caressing the long, soft strands of Mercy's hair. "Whatever you decide, sweetheart, you need to speak with Bethany. Be honest with her about what you want, whatever that is. Let her in."

Mercy considered her words and appreciated the motherly comfort greatly. She nodded, meeting Thea's gaze. "Okay. I will."

Thea turned Mercy to face her and took her in a warm hug. "Whatever you decide to do," she said into the hug, "As long as it's for the right reason, it's the right decision."

Mercy was only half listening as Bethany went on about her day at the soda shop and the new guy she'd hired. Mercy had yet to work with him but had heard he was a bit stubborn and hardheaded.

"…honestly not sure he'll last," Bethany was saying.

Mercy nodded absently. "Yeah," she murmured, drying the dish she'd rinsed after Bethany washed it. She set it aside on the counter with the others. Her head snapped up when she heard her name. "Huh?"

"Are you listening?" Bethany asked, brows drawn in confusion and slight irritation.

Mercy looked away, feeling terrible. "I'm sorry." She met Bethany's gaze. "I'm sorry. I was. And yes, it sounds like Joe is difficult too." She set her drying towel aside, facing the counter and resting her hands on it for a moment before she said, "I need to talk to you."

Bethany met her gaze, her expression turning to concern. "Of course. We're almost done here, so how about we finish up then go sit and talk. Okay?"

Mercy nodded, appreciating the gentle tone.

Ten minutes later, the two were seated on the brand-new couch in the living room, a gift from Henry and Rachel as the young women began the next phase of their life in the little farmhouse.

Shoes kicked off, Mercy sat sideways with her legs tucked up under her. She was scared to death, but she knew Thea was right. If she wanted any shot at having Bethany in her future, she needed to include her in the present.

She cleared her throat and began softly. "As you

know, I finally got up the nerve to go to the doctor last week. Grandma took me." At Bethany's nod and full attention, Mercy steeled herself to continue. "Um..." She looked down as her fingers fidgeted in her skirt-covered lap. "Good news, I don't have the stomach bug. Bad news," she said, blowing out a heavy breath, unable to meet Bethany's beautiful eyes. "When Riley attacked me," she murmured. "I got...He..." She looked away, running a hand through her hair. "God, why can't I just say it?" She looked up when she felt gentle hands take one of hers.

"When you got sick that night," Bethany said gently. "And had to go throw up, as you've done many times since, that's been morning sickness, as it were. Hasn't it?"

Mercy could only nod, unable to speak.

Bethany maneuvered herself so she was leaning back against the arm of the couch, one leg falling to the floor to leave her legs open. "Come here," she said. "Turn around."

Understanding, Mercy did as asked, ending up lying back against Bethany between her legs. Bethany wrapped her arms around her, her back to Bethany's chest. She felt a cheek rest against the top of her head.

"For starters," Bethany said softly, "you don't have to be afraid to tell me anything. Okay?" When Mercy nodded, she continued. "I absolutely hate that son of a bitch for what he did to you, attacking you like that." She kissed Mercy's head. "What do you want to do?" she asked gently.

"I don't know," Mercy said. "I was so afraid you'd want me to leave."

"Baby," Bethany said, her fingers stroking Mercy's where they rested against Mercy's stomach. It was the first time she'd used such an intimate term of endearment since before she'd left for Europe. "What Grandma said is true, and her advice to us is wise. We need to build a foundation to grow on, and we both have been through so much this past year. Yes, it's changed us both, forced us to grow up in ways we'd never expect. But, even so, my feelings for you haven't changed. The fact that I know I want to be with you hasn't changed."

Mercy's eyes fell closed in absolute relief, so much so, she felt she could burst into tears.

"And this," Bethany continued, unwittingly breaking into her thoughts. She gently patted Mercy's tummy. "It's not your fault. This wasn't some careless Helen situation."

"I know, but..." Mercy pulled away and turned to look at her, worried. "I don't know that I can do what Helen did."

"Then don't," Bethany said simply. "You don't have to do that, Mercy. If you decide that you want to keep this baby, keep it. You're not alone in this."

"But if I keep it, with me living here as your roommate, even as your friend, it affects you, too. Your life. The noise, or—"

"Hey," Bethany said, taking Mercy's face in gentle hands, essentially forcing Mercy to look at her, meet her gaze. "As I said, we may be essentially starting over, rebuilding after all that has happened, but I'm in this for the long haul." She caressed Mercy's cheek with soft fingers. "You're not just some classmate or friend that I moved in here to help with bills." She smiled. "You're here because I want to build something *with* you." She leaned forward and left a soft kiss on Mercy's lips.

Mercy sighed at the kiss, her emotions rising again, but this time in gratitude and relief.

Bethany kissed her again. "We're in this together, whatever you choose."

"But," Mercy said again. "Do you even want kids?"

Bethany sat back but held Mercy's hand. "Yes," she said. "I always wanted them, just wasn't entirely sure how that was going to work since I didn't want the man that would be attached to them." She gave her a small grin.

Mercy smiled shyly. "Well, then I guess I took one for the team, huh?"

Bethany looked at her with so much love in her eyes, Mercy felt a huge weight lift from her shoulders. "I think you'll make an incredible mother, Mercy. I know this isn't how either of us would ever want this to happen. But the situation is what it is now, and decisions need to be made. You say you don't think you can go through an abortion, and I respect that. So, if you ultimately decide to commit to keeping this baby and raising it, you have my complete and total support. I'm with you no matter what. Hey," she added with a little lopsided grin. "Justice managed. I think I can, too."

Mercy threw herself into Bethany's arms, holding her almost painfully tight. "Oh, Bethany," she whispered into her hair. She'd never felt so much love as she did in that moment. Finally, *finally* she knew everything was going to be okay, like, *really* okay. "Thank you."

Bethany held her tightly. "You don't need to thank me," she said. "Just be at work tomorrow, because I really need help with Joe."

Mercy burst into laughter, letting everything go. She knew there was still a lot ahead of them to deal with, and things wouldn't be easy, but she knew she wasn't alone. They just held each other for several minutes, a peace falling over Mercy that she hadn't felt since Bethany had left. She melted into it, letting it wash over and through her like warm honey.

"Can I ask for a favor?" she murmured into the hug.

"Of course."

"Will you sleep in my room tonight?" Mercy asked. "I just…I need you close tonight."

Bethany left a kiss to her neck. "Absolutely." She pulled away from her. "What do you say we get ready for bed and talk and cuddle?"

Mercy beamed. "Sounds like Heaven."

Nighttime routine complete, Mercy lay in bed waiting for Bethany to join her. She had absolutely nothing in mind except snuggling. She needed to feel Bethany against her, needed her warmth and comfort. She lay on her back, fingers laced behind her head as she stared up at the ceiling. She thought back to the very beginning, when she'd first met Bethany. Even before they'd become friends, let alone anything more, she'd always felt so safe around her, a strange peace and comfort just by who she was as a person, her energy.

She smiled when she heard the water turn off in the bathroom and the door open. Moments later Bethany arrived at her open bedroom door in her nightgown. She smiled at Mercy before flicking off the wall switch and climbing over Mercy's body in order to get to her side of the bed.

Mercy chuckled. "Sorry. Guess I should have taken the side away from the door."

"Hey, at least you're on a side and not smack dab in the middle."

Mercy glanced over at Bethany as she climbed beneath the sheet. It was a warm night, so nothing more was needed. The blanket was folded at the foot of the bed. "Well, it's the first time I've had a bed large enough to actually choose a side. Exciting stuff."

Bethany grinned. "It's the little things." She lifted her head and noticed the fan on the dresser, which wasn't turned on. "How about we turn on the fan so we can get nice and cold?" Her grin widened at Mercy's look of confusion. "Cuddle temperatures."

"Oh!' Amused, Mercy climbed out of bed and turned on the fan, aiming it right at them, then scurried back beneath the sheet. Bethany held her arm out to her, Mercy immediately cuddling up to her. Head resting on a strong shoulder, Mercy nearly moaned in contentment as she was wrapped up in Bethany's warmth.

"I cannot tell you how much I missed this," Bethany murmured, resting her cheek against Mercy's forehead.

"Me too." Mercy draped her arm over Bethany's stomach, fingers lightly wrapping around her side and tucking just under her back. "You're so warm and smell so good." She closed her eyes and took a deep breath, inhaling the scent of Bethany's skin cream and shampoo.

"You know what's really crazy?" Bethany murmured.

"Hmm?"

"Knowing that we don't have to worry about me climbing out the window, getting caught."

Mercy smiled. "Oh, no kidding." She left a small kiss on Bethany's neck before getting settled again. "I want your opinion on something," she said, voice growing serious.

"Sure." Bethany's fingers ran lightly through Mercy's hair.

"I want the police to release Riley." She felt Bethany's body stiffen, but to her credit, she said nothing. "He told me some of his story, Bethany. His seizures are from an accident when he was a kid. His mother was apparently quite religious, and said she thought they were possession by the Devil. He was thrown into an institution as a child."

"What?" Bethany said, sounding horrified.

"He was released when he turned eighteen. He's never had a girlfriend, never was given a chance to find love, *be* loved." She paused, thinking back to that day, the look in his eyes as he'd told her that.

"You believe him?" Bethany asked softly.

"I do. In all those months, he was never once violent or remotely physical or aggressive, in any way. Now," she said, fingers pressing lightly on Bethany's side to forestall anything she may say. "I'm not in any way justifying what he did, and I never will. There is no justification for that. But I think he knew he was going to lose me."

"To what?"

"To you," she said simply. "I think the moment he saw you were back, and back in my life, he knew the hourglass was almost empty. My mother was dying, literally down to days or hours. I think that very lost, abandoned little boy didn't know how to handle it and he lashed out in the most horrible way possible. But, I think it's not about a violent, predatory man but one who didn't have the emotional depth to handle losing what he'd hoped would grow to love him."

Bethany was quiet for a long time, though her combing through Mercy's hair never ceased. Finally, she said, "I don't know that I could be so generous of heart, but honestly, it tells me all I need to know about who you are, deep inside. I can't help but be biased and want to see him rot in jail, but stepping outside of myself and my love for you, I can understand your perspective."

Mercy raised her head, looking down into the beautiful face of the woman who shared her bed and her heart. "Really? You don't think I'm crazy to request for him to be released?"

Bethany held her gaze and smiled. "No, not crazy. Do you want to see him? Want him part of the baby's life?"

Mercy saw the concern in her beautiful eyes. "Oh, no," she said, shaking her head. "No. I don't want to see him ever again. I'd even ask if it's possible to request he leave the area as part of his release. I have no intention of ever letting him know about this child. In my mind, he doesn't deserve to know. Yes, I may have sympathy for his life and what he's gone through, but he still did something terribly wrong. I just don't feel he should be thrown away, yet again."

Bethany seemed relieved. She nodded. "Good." Leaning up, she kissed Mercy's lips before urging her back to rest upon her shoulder. "Good," she said again.

Chapter Twenty-four

Bethany's fingers tapped lightly on the table as she waited. She was very, very nervous but glad that she'd been trusted to do this. In truth, she had a lot to say and was grateful she was given the chance to do so. In the weeks since everything had happened, Bethany hadn't had a lot of time to truly sit down and contemplate her feelings.

What she did know was that she had a tremendous amount of rage toward the man she waited for in that moment. Until the day she died, she'd remember that image of Mercy on the bed, dress torn, mouth bloody, eyes absolutely terrified. That image, of course, led to her guilt. She'd never forgive herself for leaving that day. She should have insisted Mercy go to the Wynter house with her, and never taken her back.

That wasn't an option at the time, she knew, but she still felt that way. She wondered how long that guilt would dog her steps. So often she'd glance at Mercy and see a bit of a lost look in her eyes, or a flash of fear at an unexpected sound or if somebody came up behind her too quickly.

Overall, the younger woman was doing amazingly well, so damn strong. Some days Bethany felt Mercy was made of steel or something. Meanwhile, she was questioning her own every move the day of the attack. The day both their lives changed forever. They'd been living together at the house now for a few weeks, and though they were both trying to find their footing in a very new world of very new circumstances, Bethany had never been happier.

They were still keeping it friends, though they often blurred the line into more. A quick kiss here, cuddles there, and the longing looks that Bethany tried her best to hide. She yearned to touch Mercy, to *truly* touch her. They'd had limited time, the one and only time they'd been together. She wanted to spend the entire night making love to her, showing her how she felt, showing her what it was truly like, only to wake up in each other's arms.

She smiled at those daydreams, waking up all snuggled and naked, only to start all over again as the sun began to peek over the horizon. Her thoughts were interrupted by the sound of keys clinking against each other. Looking up, she saw the man she'd come to see being led into the visiting room by a uniformed officer, keys hanging off his utility belt.

Riley's eyes widened in surprise when he spotted his visitor, then he looked downright scared. The tall, slender man, aged twenty-three, looked all of ten years old in that moment. He wore jail-issued black-and-white offset striped pants and button shirt. His wrists were also cuffed as he was led by the officer to the table.

Bethany said nothing, simply watched him advance until he finally sat. He quietly thanked the officer, who nodded to the pair and walked over to a desk in the corner of the room, which held two wooden tables for visitation. She was relieved to know the officer would be staying.

Turning her focus to the man sitting across from

her, she cleared her throat. "Hello, Riley."

"Ma'am," he said, voice very soft, more like the man she'd gotten to know before she'd left for war.

"They told me my lawyer was comin'."

"Oh, he's waiting outside," Bethany assured, hitching her thumb to the door of the small, windowless room. "I was asked to come talk to you on the behalf of Mercy Faulkner first."

His eyes lit up. "Oh?"

Bethany pulled the page that had been sitting on her lap into view on the table, placing her hand on it as she spoke. "I'm going to be really honest with you, Riley. I personally think they should hang you by your testicles for what you did to her. But that's not up to me. So, I'm simply here to read you a statement from Mercy."

"Why did she send you?" he asked, voice tight.

"Because she never wants to see you again," she said simply and honestly. "So," she said, tapping the page. "Without further ado, here's what Mercy has to say." Clearing her throat, she began to read.

Riley, though I will never forgive you for what happened that evening, nor will I ever be able to forget, I heard you that day. I heard what you said about your childhood, the way your mother treated you after your accident and all but threw you away due to her own ignorance of your seizures.

I don't believe you're a bad person or have a bad or violent heart. That being said, you did what you did. Having the mother I had, I know the damage a parent like that can do. Because of that, and what you've gone through in your short life, I'm willing to drop the charges against you, as I don't think it's fitting for you to yet again waste away in another institution.

But with that will come some very stiff conditions. Bethany and the District Attorney will go over those with you. Believe in yourself and make this second chance count, if you choose to accept it.

Mercy

Bethany folded the letter and looked at him. "She certainly stands up to her name, doesn't she? Right or wrong."

He nodded but said nothing as he looked completely shellshocked. He took a moment, then swallowed as he looked down at his cuffed hands where they rested on the table. Finally, he said, "What are your conditions?"

"You are never to contact her in any way. Ever," Bethany said, her voice hard. "You are to leave Wynter and Wynter County and never return. Ever. Go to Denver, Colorado Springs, Los Angeles, or the moon. Whatever. If you agree yet are found in the area, trust me," she warned. "It won't go well." Her gaze bored into him. "A very important man in this town happened to be on the other end of that open line when Wanda called us that night, and he heard your attack on Mercy. I assure you," she continued. "My father will stop at nothing to make sure you pay with your life for what you did."

He nodded. "I understand." Clearing his throat, he looked up at her with shame-filled eyes. "I'll take the conditions. I agree and will disappear."

She nodded. Pushing away from the table. "I'll tell District Attorney Briggs to come in and talk to you." She stopped at her name and glanced back at him.

"Please tell her I'm sorry," he said, tears brimming in his eyes. "I'm so sorry."

She said nothing, simply nodded and turned away to leave the room.

❦ ❦ ❦ ❦

The drive home was quiet, the radio turned off in her truck as she considered what had happened at the Wynter jail. She still wasn't sure that she agreed with Mercy's decision, but it *was* her decision, and she'd support her on it. She did, however, have to admit that it felt good that it was over, that part of Mercy's life—a difficult and brutal mother and a marriage of necessity that had ended terribly. Although, she thought, there was an aspect of it that would be with them forever.

Somehow, not so long ago, she'd been a responsible yet somewhat carefree teenager with good grades, a job, and a home filled with two amazing parents and three mostly amazing brothers. Now, almost two years later, she was a high school graduate, a veteran, one of only two living siblings of the original four, and, should she accept the challenge, a life partner and soon-to-be mother.

The biggest thing she'd come to understand about herself since she'd been overseas and certainly since she'd been back, was just how much of an influence Billy had on her decisions. Well, he used to. She was strong minded, strong willed, and smart—absolutely. But so often she'd defer to him, his ideas, or what he thought was the right thing to do in whatever situation, regardless of her own wants.

Finally deciding to take her mother's advice regarding Mercy before she'd left had been a huge step for her. But now, suddenly thrust into the spotlight of adulthood with huge, life-changing decisions and roads to take, she realized she hadn't thought once about Billy. What would he do? Should she write him and ask? Maybe next time he called, run it by him?

She smiled as she realized how truly strong she felt. Here she was, turning nineteen in July, just a bit younger than Justice was when she took on marriage and motherhood. She was scared to death, honestly. She smiled when she noted an older woman in her front yard tending to a large, beautiful rose bush.

Pulling the truck to the curb, she got out and walked over to the woman. "Good morning," she said.

The older woman looked over at her and smiled. "Good morning."

"Can I steal one of your beautiful roses?" she asked.

The woman looked surprised, but without missing a beat used her clippers and clipped a pink one, the rose bud huge and fragrant. "Here are you, dear."

Bethany took it from her. "Thank you so very much." With a winning smile to the woman, Bethany took her prize and headed back to her truck.

She considered Mercy as she drove toward the farmhouse. Though just turning seventeen in a few weeks, Mercy had a maturity and depth to her that many people twice her age lacked. Sometimes Bethany looked into her eyes and saw a soul who had lived a thousand lifetimes and had brought the knowledge, wisdom, and heart of each one with her to this one.

As she navigated the gravel roads where they now lived, her grandparents' farmhouse a "country mile" away, she thought about her relationship with Mercy. Yes, she was beautiful, yes, she was crazy attracted to her and had been since almost the first time she'd seen her. And yes, she loved her.

But to decide to settle down now, decide this was her person forever, with whom she'd raise a child, was a huge step. As her truck pulled into the long dirt drive, she saw the lone figure relaxing on the porch swing her father had surprised them with.

She wore a summer dress, her hair brushed down around her shoulders to an auburn shine. Her feet were bare, one pulled up under her, the other on the small porch, pushing the swing gently to and fro.

Bethany pulled the truck to a stop next to the car Mercy had inherited from her mother. Cutting the ignition, Bethany looked at the younger woman through the windshield, just studying her. In that moment, Mercy glanced over at her.

"My god," Bethany whispered. "So beautiful." She smiled, Mercy returning the expression. Yes, she thought. *This is exactly where I belong.* Pulling the key from the ignition, she palmed her keys and grabbed the rose and climbed out of the truck. "Well, hey there, beautiful," she called out.

Mercy's smile grew. "Hey, yourself. Pot calling kettle?"

Bethany chuckled, stepping up onto the porch and leaning down to give her a kiss hello. It seemed like the most normal thing to do, as though she did it every day, which she did not. "Here."

Mercy took the beautiful bloom in her fingers, looking absolutely delighted. "This is so beautiful!" She closed her eyes as she took in the fragrance.

"I didn't have a choice of color, so," Bethany

said, glad she'd stopped to ask. Mercy looked so happy with her little surprise and token of affection.

"I love it," Mercy murmured, glancing over at her. "Thank you." She held the rose with one hand, using the other to caress Bethany's cheek. "I love you."

Bethany melted. She leaned into the touch, her eyes never leaving Mercy's. "I love you too," she murmured.

Mercy leaned over again, brushing her lips against Bethany's, though she didn't move away. They shared a few light kisses before Mercy's hand rested fully on Bethany's cheek as she allowed the kiss to deepen to a more intimate caress of lips, the softest stroke of her tongue before leaving a final kiss and backing away.

Bethany's eyes remained closed for a moment, deeply touched by the kiss. It was the first time one had been initiated by Mercy that was of a deeper, more erotic nature since everything had happened. Her heart was racing and her body was letting her know that it was awake. Very awake.

Pushing that aside as it wasn't the time or place for it, she opened her eyes and smiled at the woman who was looking at her. "I'm so grateful I got you back," she whispered, surprised the words escaped her heart.

Mercy's smile was so sweet, filled with understanding and love. She took Bethany's hand in her own. "You never lost me." She lightly squeezed Bethany's hand to emphasize her point. "How'd it go?"

Bethany laced their fingers where they sat on Mercy's leg, refocusing her thoughts. "Good," she said. "He was a bit emotional about the whole thing, but he did accept the deal."

"Did you read him my letter?"

Bethany nodded. "Despite the fact that I was honest and told him I wanted to castrate him with my bare hands, I was a good girl."

Mercy's smile was small. "I know you don't agree with what I did, Bethany, but thank you for doing that. I just couldn't face him again."

"It doesn't matter what I think, sweetheart," Bethany said, placing her other hand on her chest briefly. "None of us went through what you did, and your grace and well, mercy, just speaks to who you are. What an amazing heart you have." She gave her a reassuring smile. "He wanted me to tell you he's really sorry. I do believe him. He seemed genuine in his remorse."

Mercy didn't say anything for a long time. The rose stem she held in her fingers twisted back and forth, almost as if her fingers worked absently as a visual manifestation of the wheels in her head turning. She took a deep breath and let it out slowly.

"So," she finally said, glancing over at Bethany. "It's over, then?"

Bethany nodded. "It is. He's supposed to be escorted out of town in the morning." She absolutely loved the serene smile that spread across Mercy's lips.

"Good."

❧❧❧❧

Dressed for bed in her own bedroom, Bethany decided to do what she'd been thinking about since returning home safely more than two months ago. So much had happened in such a short amount of time, she'd forgotten about it. But now, things had quieted down and she and Mercy were settling in.

Reaching up under her hair, she unclasped the necklace that she hadn't taken off since the night Mercy had put it on her in that tiny bedroom in that slightly less tiny apartment. She palmed the angel pendant, careful to not tangle the delicate chain as she made her way to the bathroom. The door was open, Mercy already changed into her nightgown. She'd just finished brushing her teeth and was brushing her hair.

"Hey there," Mercy said to Bethany's reflected self in the mirror above the sink.

"Howdy." She grinned. "So, I have something for you. Well, I want to give something back to you, anyway."

"Oh?" Mercy raised an eyebrow. "Been going through my room again?"

Bethany snorted. "Oh yeah, baby," she drawled, noting the teasing tone of Mercy's voice. "All night long," she purred. She was surprised, and admittedly pleased, to see a little shiver run through the woman standing in front of her. "No, in all seriousness." She brought up the necklace, an end held in either hand. She waited until Mercy lowered the brush before she lifted it up and over the auburn head and lowered it into place. "It did its job well," she said softly, clasping it. "I got home safe."

Mercy looked at the angel pendant in the mirror where it rested just below the hollow of her throat. She reached up and lightly touched it. "I haven't worn this since the night Daddy put it on me."

"Well," Bethany murmured, task complete. She hugged Mercy from behind, resting her head against hers. "Now you can wear it all the time as he intended for you to. Nobody can take it or give you crap about having it." She smiled when Mercy laced their fingers which rested on her belly, yet to really start to grow. "Now your father can protect you and his grandchild."

Mercy smiled, her eyes instantly welling at those words. She turned in the circle of Bethany's arms. She looked shy and was slightly trembling. Bethany was worried for a moment, hoping she hadn't gone a little too far emotionally for Mercy. Her father was such a difficult topic for her.

"Bethany?" Mercy murmured.

"Yeah?" Bethany was doing her level best to not react to the proximity of Mercy's body to her own, only a thin layer of cotton covering them both. The summer nightgown Mercy wore was essentially spaghetti straps holding up a chemise. Her beautiful shoulders were visible, the delicate nature of her collarbones, and the teasing of her cleavage just below the V of the neckline. And, as Mercy's fingers trailed down along Bethany's sides, she was unable to hold in the small gasp.

"Will you stay with me tonight?" Mercy asked, her voice not much more than a whisper, but her eyes said everything her voice didn't.

Chapter Twenty-five

Bethany felt her heart skip a beat. She looked into Mercy's eyes, the need in them painfully evident. Even so, she wanted to make sure. Placing her hands on Mercy's hips, she gently pulled her to her, their bodies nearly flush. She wanted to give Mercy plenty of room to wiggle out of the heavy air between them if that wasn't what she meant or if she needed to change her mind.

Not seeming to, Mercy's own hands moved to run up Bethany's bare arms to her shoulders. Her eyes fell from Bethany's, downcast. "I don't know how to ask for what I want," she whispered.

Bethany's hands moved from Mercy's hips to caress her behind. "Is this part of it?" she asked, using the firm flesh to pull Mercy's hips even tighter against her own.

A small gasp escaped Mercy's lips as she nodded. "Yes."

Bethany cupped her face with a hand, her thumb running lightly over Mercy's soft cheek. Mercy's lips were even softer. The kiss began as just lips, a connection to let Mercy know it was okay, message heard loud and clear.

Mercy sighed into it, her body relaxing into Bethany's. The kiss began to deepen, Bethany's body pulsing for the woman that she so very much wanted to show how she felt. She wanted to show Mercy just exactly what she meant to her. After several moments, the kiss came to a natural end.

Without a word, Bethany took Mercy's hand and, after flicking off the bathroom light, led her to Mercy's bedroom, flicking that light on. She kissed Mercy's hand before releasing it as she turned to the bed and pulled the covers down. She glanced over to make sure Mercy was still okay. She looked a bit nervous, but that same need and desire was in her eyes.

Knowing she'd have to fully take the lead, Bethany reached down and gathered the nightgown she wore, pulling it up and over her body and head. Letting it fall to the floor, she pushed down her panties, Mercy's hungry gaze devouring her.

Naked, she walked over to Mercy, looking her in the eye as she grabbed the hem of her nightgown. She saw no fear or indecision in her eyes, so Bethany gently tugged it up and over her head, letting it fall atop her own on the floor. Her panties followed and, taking Mercy's hand again, she pulled her onto the bed with her.

Mercy lay on her back, Bethany on her side next to her. She caressed the side of Mercy's face with her fingers, tucking some auburn hair behind her ear. "I want you to tell me if I do anything you don't want or like, or if you change your mind. Anything, okay?"

Mercy nodded. "Okay."

Bethany looked at the gorgeous body before her. She ached to touch her, taste her, feel her against her own body. "You are so absolutely beautiful, Mercy," she murmured.

Mercy smiled and reached up, cupping the back of Bethany's head and pulling her down. Their kiss was easy and wonderful, passionate yet measured. Bethany allowed her free hand to wander. Her fingertips grazed over the softness of Mercy's skin, down her side, and across her belly until she made her way back up her torso and finally over to cup her breast.

Bethany was thrilled when Mercy sighed into their kiss, her back arching as she offered that breast to her touch. She slowed the kiss down a bit, wanting to get Mercy's body ready in every way. She also wanted to show her with mouth, fingers, and her entire body just exactly what physical love was all about.

They'd had their one experience together before Bethany had left, but right now, the most pivotal moment had been Riley's attack. She could never take that memory away, but she'd do her level best to replace any fear of physical touch with the understanding of what it was meant to be.

With a final kiss, Bethany left Mercy's mouth, yearning to explore every inch of her. As her fingers lightly rolled the hard nipple that her hand was on, she explored a warm, soft neck. She relished the little sighs she heard from the woman she was loving, little whimpers as her arousal built. Bethany hummed into her task in response and appreciation of Mercy's enjoyment of what she was doing to her.

When Bethany reached Mercy's other breast and heard her name whispered on full lips, she nearly came right there. She was extremely gentle with both mouth and fingers, as she knew Mercy's breasts were incredibly sensitive in her early pregnancy.

She felt fingers in her hair and the body beneath her become restless, hips rocking gently of their own accord. She truly thought Mercy Faulkner was the most naturally sensuous woman she'd ever seen. What made it even more sexy, however, was that Mercy had no idea.

"Baby?" she asked, lifting her head and looking at Mercy, a hooded gaze meeting her own. "Can I touch you?" Bethany asked, using two fingers to lightly tap between Mercy's legs. She did her best in that moment to ignore the volcanic wetness that came back on her fingertips in just that small touch. But, she had to make sure.

"Please," Mercy whispered in response.

Bethany nodded before returning her focus to the bounty before her. She slowly and carefully moved atop Mercy, who accepted her fully. They shared a slow, sensuous kiss before Bethany began to kiss her way down Mercy's body. She allowed her hair to trail along with her to add more sensation to an already sensitized body.

Bethany glanced up the length of Mercy's body to make sure she was okay. She smiled, loving how much faith and trust was being given to her. She could see it in Mercy's eyes as she looked down at her, fingers lovingly trailing through dark hair. Bethany knew in that moment that, no matter what, she'd do all that she could to never break that trust.

She moved farther down Mercy's body and the bed until she was situated between Mercy's legs. She used lips and teeth on the insides of her raised and spread thighs as her fingers lightly trailed through the velvety folds of her sex. Mercy was so wet, so incredibly ready for her. Her mouth watered to taste her.

The first slow swipe of Bethany's tongue through Mercy's wetness had them both moaning. She took her time, eased Mercy into the bliss of such an intimate kiss, and tried to prolong her own enjoyment of this first taste. Even so, she kept part of her consciousness on Mercy, on her body language, sounds she made, her fingers in Bethany's hair. She wanted to make sure there was no sign of discomfort physically or any signs of fear or uncertainty.

Mercy's hips began to roll with the gentle licks and sucking between her legs. Her eyes had fallen closed and her head rolled to the side uselessly as the most delicious little whimpers escaped her lips. She was absolutely stunning in her pleasure.

As much as she wished she could make it last forever, Bethany could tell Mercy was getting close. She focused on her mouth at the current center of Mercy's universe, holding tightly to her thighs as Mercy's hips began to move with the rhythm she was setting with her mouth.

Breasts heaving and head thrown back, Mercy cried out, long and loud. Her back arched and fingers tightened in Bethany's hair. The loud cry melted into high-pitched whimpers as her body began to come down from the intense experience. Bethany lifted her head as Mercy's thighs went limp and fell to the bed. Satisfied, Bethany moved her way back up until she gathered Mercy into her arms, holding her close.

After a moment, Mercy returned the embrace, burying her face in Bethany's neck. She let out a long, slow breath, which warmed Bethany's skin. She pulled back just enough to look into Bethany's face, Bethany moving to her side to face Mercy.

"Everything is going to be okay," Mercy whispered. "Isn't it?"

"Of course it is," Bethany said, smiling brightly at her. "Were you worried it wouldn't?"

Mercy studied her face for such a long time,

Bethany wasn't sure she was going to respond to her question. But as the seconds ticked by, something seemed to change within Mercy. Her face, always beautiful, was so often filled with the serious intensity of what her life had always been—and certainly over the past year. In that moment, her features softened and those bottomless brown eyes sparkled. Then Bethany saw it: hope.

Mercy's smile was big and bright as in so many ways, she looked like the woman she'd grown into over the past two years in Wynter, yet a playfulness, a lightheartedness entered her energy.

"I love you," she murmured against Bethany's lips as she pushed her to her back. "I have no idea what I'm doing," she said, her hand tentatively resting on Bethany's naked upper chest. "I want to touch you."

"I love you too," Bethany said, raising her head just enough to leave a quick kiss on soft lips. She said nothing more as she placed her hand atop Mercy's, using it to move that hand to her breast. She lightly squeezed Mercy's hand in silent permission before moving her hand away.

"You know," Mercy said, her voice sounding wistful as she lightly caressed Bethany's breast. She was still tentative, but Bethany felt she was exploring, taking her time, which was driving her nuts. "I always used to notice beautiful women or pretty girls, whatever." Mercy met Bethany's gaze, her hand finally fully covering the breast. "But when I saw you that first time..." Again, that brilliant smile. "I was gone."

Bethany grinned. "I never knew."

"God, no!" Mercy chuckled. "I could never tell you that. For one, I didn't understand what I was feeling and felt so strange feeling it. For two, why on earth would someone like you, so absolutely gorgeous, crazy intelligent, popular, big family name…" She leaned down and kissed her. "What would you want with me?" she murmured against them.

"Besides everything?" Bethany responded with a grin, which was returned.

"Yes, well," Mercy responded, leaving Bethany's lips and moving to that breast where her fingers still played. "Never would have believed that one," she murmured right before her tongue slowly trailed across the rigid nipple, making Bethany gasp.

Bethany began to lose herself as Mercy began to explore with her mouth. Though she'd only had one sexual partner, she and Helen had had sex many, many times. And yes, she had cared about Helen, to the extent the blonde earned it, but she now fully understood she'd never loved her.

Now, as Mercy touched her, tasted her skin, and explored her body, Bethany knew what making love truly meant. It meant building orgasms for sure, but it also meant building trust, building a bond, and building a life—together.

She parted her legs as Mercy's fingers trailed down her stomach, their destination clear. One leg draping over Mercy's legs, Bethany made it quite clear that she was open to Mercy and her touch was most welcome. Though Mercy seemed a bit more confident in her place with Bethany, her nervousness and uncertainty was still evident.

Mercy left Bethany's breast and watched intently as her fingers eased into the wetness between Bethany's legs. She seemed utterly transfixed as her fingertips explored, eliciting a gasp from Bethany when her fingers grazed over her painfully hard and sensitive clit.

Bethany groaned, long and languid as Mercy focused on her clit, learning what brought out more noises from her. Bethany didn't help her, didn't show her with her own fingers because she knew it needed to be all about Mercy finding her own way, gaining confidence in her own incredible touch.

Eyes falling closed, Bethany's legs opened wider offering more. It felt so good, her hips beginning to rock with Mercy's fingers. She responded when she felt soft lips on her own. Their kiss was passionate as Mercy stroked her. It didn't take long, however, before Bethany was breathing entirely too hard to kiss.

Mercy moved away but remained in Bethany's personal space. Her own breathing had picked up. She was clearly in the moment right along with the woman she was swiftly bringing to a loud orgasm. After the initial rush of pleasure, smaller jolts rocked Bethany's world until finally Mercy's fingers stopped with the pressure and moved away to rest on Bethany's stomach.

They shared a few kisses before Mercy sat up and grabbed the sheet from the end of the bed and pulled it up and over them as she snuggled up against Bethany. Wrapping her arms around the woman against her, Bethany smiled, completely contented. Her body hummed, her mind was pretty much mush at this point, and her soul was singing.

"Can it be like this always?" Mercy asked, her head readjusting to a more comfortable spot as her hand slid across Bethany's stomach to curve around her side.

"Absolutely," Bethany said, fingers running through auburn hair. "It is for my parents and grandparents.”

"That's what I want," Mercy said. "I want us to be snuggled up this same way in another twenty, thirty, forty years."

"And beyond?"

"And beyond," Mercy agreed, a smile in her voice. "Making love."

Bethany grinned. "Definitely." She'd never felt happier in her entire life. To know that she could go to sleep with this woman for the rest of her life and wake up to her. The thought of being able to keep her safe, love her, and do her best to bring out the best in her. It was intoxicating.

"So," Mercy said, breaking through Bethany's thoughts. "I've actually been thinking about something, even before this happened tonight."

"Okay," Bethany said, pulling Mercy closer. "What's up?"

"Well," Mercy said, raising her head to rest against her upturned palm. "I want us to share a room." She looked so shy asking Bethany just wanted to squeeze her. "What do you think?"

"I think that every night I lay there across the hall wondering what you're doing, if you're asleep yet. If you are, if you're sleeping on your side or your stomach. Are you snoring—"

"I don't snore!"

Bethany grinned. "So you think," she teased. Growing serious again, she reached up and trailed a finger along Mercy's soft cheek. "Yes, I want that too. The thought of having to get up and head across the hall right now makes me almost want to cry." She smiled at the woman looking down at her. "I just want to be with you, Mercy. I want to be able to lay here and talk about our day, or what tomorrow will bring. I want to open my eyes and see that I've wrapped myself around you in sleep."

Mercy's smile was so beautiful as she nodded. "Yes!" She left a kiss on Bethany's lips before asking, "Which room should we use? I think this one is bigger." She surveyed it before looking back to Bethany. "It has a closet. The other one doesn't."

"I agree. I think the one across the hall should be the nursery. That third bedroom is too small for a young child or teenager to be able to grow into. What?"

Mercy shyly wiped at a tear that had sprung to her eye. "Sorry. Happy tears. Just can't believe all this is real."

"Oh, it's real, baby." Bethany chuckled. "Though you might regret that."

"Never." She covered Bethany's hand with her own and placed a kiss on the palm before she held it against her chest. "I know I have a lot to learn about you, just you do about me, but I've seen your heart, Bethany. And it and your soul are so beautiful. All the other stuff we can work around. For us both. All our crazy little quirks. I want this with you. With all my heart."

"Me too. And the baby," Bethany added.

"Yes. I'm nervous about that, I won't lie, but yes, with *our* baby. But," she added. "As you know the marriage with Riley was annulled, and I don't want his name, and certainly not for the baby. I want the baby to be a Faulkner. For my father, what he never got to see." She shrugged. "And, if it's a boy, the name can continue on."

Bethany smiled, nodding. "I think that's a

wonderful idea, baby. Baby Faulkner."

Mercy grinned, moving on top of her. "I really like the sound of that," she murmured, initiating a deep kiss.

Epilogue

1947

Are you excited, sweet boy?" Mercy grinned at the huge smile and vigorous nod she got from her three-year-old. They were in his bedroom and she was on her knees in front of him, buttoning his short-sleeved shirt.

"Is Granja gonna be there too?" he asked, dark brown bangs hanging in his eyes as he looked into her face.

"I think so," she said, finished with her task. Bethany's parents had become Grampy and Grammy and Justice and Thea had become Granja and Grandma. This was a mixture of what Bethany and Mercy had decided, and what Michael himself had gotten stuck on for titles of the family elders. The two older couples had just been so enamored with the first grandchild of the family that they would have been delighted no matter what they'd been called.

It amazed Mercy how the family had completely embraced her as one of their own—daughter, granddaughter, and wife of Bethany. And, in turn, Michael had been equally embraced. Blood or not, he *was* a son and grandson. Some days she looked at her son and saw so much of Bethany in him it took her breath away.

"We need Mommy to cut your hair," she said

absently, using her fingers to brush his soft hair out of his eyes. "She's a lot straighter than I am."

"Well, there's a term never used with me before."

Mercy glanced over her shoulder to see a smirking Bethany standing in the hallway just outside the open bedroom doorway. She sent her a saucy little grin. "I should hope not."

Bethany smirked and entered the room. She knelt down and gave Mercy a kiss, then turned to their son. "Hey, big boy. Excited for your weekend at Grampy and Grammy's house?"

His brown eyes, just as soulful as his birth mother's, grew wide. "Uh-huh! We're going fishing with Granja!"

"I'm very, very, very, *very excited* for you!" Bethany grinned as Michael giggled. She kissed his head before turning to Mercy. "Got a letter from Billy today." She wiggled the envelope she held.

"Oh?" Mercy said, eyebrows raising. "Did your dad give it to you?"

"Nope." She held the envelope up, showing the addressed party. "To me."

"Wow." Mercy took it from her and looked at it, noting the return address was London. "I can't believe he stayed in the Army after the war ended," she murmured, handing it back to her wife.

"Well," Bethany blew out, the two women getting to their feet and Mercy picking up Michael, who was all ready to go. "He's coming back home for a visit." She chewed on her bottom lip for a moment and Mercy could feel the uncertainty coming off her in waves. "With his wife, Greta."

"They finally got married, huh?" She secured the boy on her hip, his legs straddling her side and her arm under his bottom to support his weight.

Bethany nodded and leaned back against Michael's dresser, arms crossing over her chest. "And they also have a son. Justice."

Though she knew how bumpy the history between the twins had become, though for reasons she didn't entirely understand, she couldn't help but smile. "After Gran?"

"I guess so." Bethany looked really unsettled. She met Mercy's gaze. "He wants to see me."

"Sweetheart," Mercy said, walking over to her and placing her free hand on the side of Bethany's neck. "I don't really know what happened between you two during the war. But you two have been close since before birth." She smiled. "I hate seeing you two so separated. I know Billy has decided the military is for him, and he's thrived, but even so, with him so far away, you two don't have to be."

The moment was interrupted by the sound of Henry's car pulling up outside. "Grampy!" Michael exclaimed, squirming to get out of Mama's arms and get to one of his many favorite people.

Mercy set him on his feet and the toddler took off like a shot. Mama and Mommy shared a smile before the two women headed out to meet Bethany's father.

"Hey, Dad," Bethany greeted as Henry stepped into the house, gathering an excited Michael in his arms as he did.

Henry, who was lit up like a July afternoon, smiled at the two moms. "Hello, girls. Look what I caught."

Bethany chuckled, accepting her father's one-armed hug and kiss to her cheek. "Yes, well, hopefully you'll be just as successful with Gran on the lake."

"Let's hope." He gave Mercy the same treatment. "How are my girls?" he asked, looking at the two as Mercy stepped back to stand by her wife. "How's it going at the mayor's office, Mercy?"

"Really well," she said, all smiles. "He said, and I quote, 'I am more than proficient at typing seventy-three words a minute, I am proficient at keeping his life in order.'"

Henry chuckled. "Well, we miss you down at the shop, but I understand why you left." He looked at his grandson, making a goofy face to make him laugh. "Can't make it seem we have favoritism, can we, Michael?"

Clearly not understanding what he was being asked, the boy vigorously shook his head anyway. "Nope."

Mercy grinned, reaching up and smoothing her hand over the back of his head. "You be a good boy for Grampy and Grammy." She kissed his cheek before turning to Henry. "He ate a good dinner already."

"Alrighty," Henry said, looking to the bundle in his arms. "Ready, pardner?"

Bethany gave their son and her father goodbye kisses before the two left. Mercy walked up to Bethany, who stood at the open front door watching as Henry loaded Michael into his car. She could tell she was bothered. Hugging her from behind, she rested her chin against her shoulder.

"Want me to call Sam and cancel tonight, baby?" she asked gently.

Bethany covered the hands that rested at her stomach and leaned back into the woman behind her. "No," she said. "I think seeing Pops will be really good for me, actually." She rested her head against Mercy's. "I miss the little bugger, honestly."

"Me too."

Bethany turned in the circle of Mercy's arms. She studied her in that special way that melted Mercy's heart. She could see so much love and devotion in those gorgeous blue eyes. "You know," she said, her voice dropping a bit. "We've got some time before Pops and this 'special friend' he wants us to meet show up."

Mercy grinned, running a fingernail along Bethany's jaw. "I'm sure we can find some way to entertain ourselves."

"Shall we start laundry?" Bethany teased, an eyebrow quirked.

Mercy smirked, bringing her hands up, deft fingers beginning to undo the buttons of her dress. "Sure."

❧❧❧❧

The feeling of satisfaction that infused her almost made her want to cry. Sitting in the house that she and Bethany had spent nearly four years turning into a home filled with love, passion, laughter, and absolute joy was almost too much to take. Now, at twenty-two years old, Bethany just turning twenty-four, her fifteen-year-old self never could have seen this for her future when she'd first arrived in Wynter.

But now, in the living room with Bethany's hand resting on her thigh as they sat on the couch across from Sam and his boyfriend Tommy, she was happy. Happier than she had any right being. Sam had left Wynter right after high school graduation and moved to Denver. His dream was still to open up a restaurant someday in Wynter, but he wanted to spread his wings and in just a couple short years had worked his way up from busboy in a Denver restaurant to head waiter.

"You guys have to tell us the story of how you met," Bethany was saying, unwittingly breaking into Mercy's musings. She smiled over at Mercy when her hand was covered and their fingers laced.

Mercy smiled back at her, easily returning the silent message: *I love you too.*

"Well." Sam glanced at the man who sat next to him. "Obviously, you can tell Tommy is older than me," he stated, looking back to the two women. "But I've come to realize," he said, hand splayed out over his own chest. "I need a more mature man."

Mercy chuckled. "Considering they've been calling you Pops since you were a kid, I'd agree with that." She eyed both men. Sam, now twenty-one, had matured into an extremely handsome young man, though he still clung to his flat cap and vests. Tommy looked to be at least ten years his senior, but the man with sandy blond hair and expressive gray eyes clearly adored Sam.

"Pops?" Tommy said, eyebrow raised.

Sam sighed and rolled his eyes. "These knuckleheads," he said, indicating the two before them and the surrounding area, "have called me Pops forever. They had the audacity to tell me I dress and act like an old man."

"You do!" Bethany laughed. "You're grumpy like one."

"Pops," Tommy said, seeming to roll the nickname around in his mouth. He met Sam's hard gaze and quirked eyebrow. "Okay! Sam it is."

Later that night, Sam had asked Mercy to join him on the front porch while he had a cigarette. They didn't allow the smoke in the house. Plus, Mercy was thrilled to have a little bit of time with him. Bethany and Tommy were still inside, Tommy offering to help clean up dessert dishes.

"It's so gorgeous out here," Sam said, looking up into the night sky filled with stars as they stood on the front porch. "You know," he continued, looking over at her. "That's one thing I do miss, living in Denver. The stars." He took a drag off his smoke, the red glowing bright in the darkness, only the light from the windows behind them.

"Tommy seems really nice, Sam," Mercy said, leaning on the rail next to him. "I'm so proud of you." She glanced over at him, a wide smile on her lips.

He grinned. "Did okay, huh?"

"You did. Very okay." She chuckled. "What about your parents?"

He let out a heavy sigh, cigarette gripped between his first two fingers of his hand as it dangled over the rail by the wrist. "That's one reason we came to town this weekend," he said, voice quiet. "I told myself I'd never tell them until I'd met the man that I felt was it. You know? No reason to let on with some guy I'm just having fun with."

"And you think you and Tommy will go the distance?"

He nodded. "I do." He smiled out into the night. "I really do."

She wrapped her hands around his bicep and rested her head against his shoulder. He kissed the top of her head and she sighed. "Billy's coming home."

She could feel his nod as his cheek rested against

her head. "I heard. I really hope they can work it out."

She was silent for a moment before she asked, "What happened with Billy? What was so serious that those two have been at odds for so long now?"

He pulled his head away from hers and looked down at her. She met his gaze. "You really don't know?" At the shake of her head, he said, "You."

She could only stare at him. "What?"

"Yup." He took another pull off his cigarette before continuing, the released smoke caressing his words as he spoke. "I guess Bethy tried to step back from the situation with you to stay out of his way." He smiled, shaking his head. "Couldn't."

Mercy stood there, running through the bit she'd just been told. "I knew Billy was interested to some degree, but he didn't seem all that serious about it."

Sam shrugged. "See, I do think Billy cared about you and was interested, but I think it was a crush. Bethy, on the other hand, was falling for you." He finished his smoke and crushed the butt against the cement porch floor then pocketed the butt to dispose of later. "I think once Billy realized how his sister felt…" He shrugged again. "Game on. Billy has always been a very competitive sod." He smiled at her as he turned to lean back against the railing. "I think for her it was truly about her heart. For him, it became about winning."

She rested her elbows on the rail, clasped hands under her chin. "I'm not worth those two being at odds over, Sam."

His eyebrows shot up. "I disagree, and clearly so did your wife."

She smiled at that. "Well, hopefully they can

work this out, Sam. I know it really hurts Bethany."

❧ ❧ ❧ ❧

"Michael! Do not put that in your mouth!" Rachel ran over to her grandson.

Mercy's head immediately whipped around to see what was happening with her son, only to burst into laughter when she saw that he'd found the hot dog that Justice had tossed out to one of the hounds before she'd started putting those for the family on the grill. Rachel just barely caught him before he put it into his mouth.

"Close call." Bethany laughed, walking up to Mercy, who was setting the tables that had been brought outside for the gathering. The family wanted to enjoy their lunch outdoors on this gorgeous end-of-summer day.

Mercy laughed and nodded. "Thank you, love," she said, taking two glasses from Bethany, who had run back into the house to grab them when she discovered they were short. The two shared a quick peck before Bethany turned to head back inside to start bringing out food dishes.

They stopped when they heard the drone of a car engine. Looking out, a dust cloud trailed behind the car that was headed down the lane. It passed the road that would lead to Mercy and Bethany's house and continued onto the Kilkoyne property.

Realizing who it was, Mercy placed her arm around Bethany's waist. The two women stood hip to hip as the car got closer. Mercy heard a gasp of excitement not far behind them, Rachel and Thea stepping up to stand with them.

"Mama?" Michael called out.

Mercy turned around and took the boy from his Grammy's arms and held him close as she turned back to watch. The car came to a stop with a dusty hello. Mercy's heart began to pound, so much rushing through her. She was nervous for Bethany, but she was so excited for the family. The final missing part after so much loss.

The driver's door opened, and where once a boy had stood, a man emerged. Though dressed in casual civilian clothing, William Wynter had every ounce of the poise and bearing of his Sergeant First Class rank. He hurried around the car, opening the passenger-side door and the lovely blonde that Mercy assumed must be his wife, Greta, climbed out. She held a baby in her arms who looked to be perhaps just under a year.

"Oh my goodness," Rachel whispered from where she still stood behind her daughter.

Mercy watched, in awe of how things had changed. She watched how Billy made sure his wife was out of the car and had a good hold on the baby before he closed her door and finally turned to those gathered.

He looked so handsome, Mercy thought. She saw so much of Henry in him. But what got her the most was the confidence he exuded. He absolutely looked to be a man in charge of his destiny, yet was so mindful of his wife—again, like his father.

Henry hurried over to him and the two men came together in a hard hug, hands slapping the other's back in masculine greeting. "Welcome home, son."

"Thanks, Dad."

To Mercy, it even seemed as though his voice were deeper somehow. She watched as introductions were made of his wife and their son, Justice. The namesake and Thea walked over to meet, greet, and hug. Tears were already flowing as Rachel hugged her last remaining son. She looked up at him with adoring eyes before moving on to her daughter-in-law and second grandson.

Mercy felt her own emotion rising as she watched the family complete. She could feel Bethany's emotional turmoil beside her but said nothing, didn't urge her to go over to him or say anything. She knew she would in her own time.

Finally, Billy turned to look at them. His expression became guarded, giving absolutely nothing away. The gregarious family greetings of moments before faded. He walked over to them, his steps slow and his gaze on Bethany. Stepping up to her, the two stared each other down. Then, with a little quirk of his lips, he brought his hand up in a perfect formation salute.

Bethany did the same. Again, the two stared at each other. With a loud growl, like a tiger, he took her in his arms and crushed her to him, lifting her off her feet as he swung her around.

"My twin!" he exclaimed.

Bethany squealed in surprise, then delight, as she held on. When finally back on her feet, he cupped her face in his hands and grinned at her before he took her into another hug. The two clung to each other.

"I'm sorry," he whispered into it, Mercy just barely able to hear. "I love you, sis."

"I love you too," she said, her voice thick with emotion.

Finally, he released her and turned to look at

Mercy, who wasn't sure what to expect. He walked over to her and kissed her cheek. "Hey, sis," he said to her, letting her know in that moment that he fully accepted her for who she had become to his sister and their family.

"Welcome home, Billy," Mercy said, her own emotion trying to enter her voice.

"And, who's this?" he said, voice loud and playful as he took in the little boy who looked up at him from his mother's arms. Billy held his arms out to him.

Michael looked up at his mother's smiling face and encouraging nod before he turned back to the uncle he'd never met. He held his arms out, allowing Billy to take him.

"Hey, fella," Billy said, ever the father as his voice had gentled. "I'm your uncle Billy. What's your name?"

"Michael."

"That's a fine name," Billy said, lowering his voice to a masculine baritone. "Wanna meet your cousin Justice?" At Michael's nod, Billy grinned at Mercy then Bethany, who had stepped up next to her wife. "He's absolutely beautiful," he said, his voice choking up. "Absolutely." He nodded back toward his wife and son. "Come on."

Mercy looked to Bethany, who was already looking at her. They shared a smile and Bethany taking Mercy's hand, they followed.

❧❧❧❧

1957

"Oh my god, why am I so nervous?" Sam blew out, standing before Bethany. "Do I look okay?"

"You look as handsome as ever, Pops," she said, meeting his gaze with a smile. She reached up and straightened his bow tie before running her hand down the smooth front of his vest. "You've been waiting your whole life for this," she said, meeting his gaze. "Now, come on. Tommy is waiting." She grinned. "As are the masses."

He nodded, blowing out a breath. "Yes. Yes, you're right." He met her gaze. "Am I doing the right thing?"

She placed her hands on his shoulders and leaned up to place a kiss on his cheek, able to smell his aftershave. "Absolutely."

The cousins turned and, with one final shared look, walked to the door together. Bethany's own heart was racing, let alone what she knew the man next to her was feeling. Ordinarily it would be ladies first, but not this time.

She indicated the glass-and-metal door before them and grinned up at him. "Gentlemen first."

He returned the grin, then nodded. Blowing out one final breath, he pulled the door open to reveal an entire town of anxious faces looking back at him. "Okay, everyone," he called out. "Welcome to *Pop's*! Let's eat!"

About the Author

Kim has spent her life in Colorado and can't imagine living anywhere else. She's been writing since she was 9 and stumbled into her first book being published in her mid-20s. She's worked in the film industry as a writer, director and producer, but now enjoys the quiet, happy life of a professional author. She can be reached on Facebook and on her website at, www. kimpritekel.com

IF YOU LIKED THIS BOOK...

Share a review with your friends or post a review on your favorite site like Amazon, Goodreads, Barnes and Noble, or anywhere you purchased the book. Or perhaps share a posting on your social media sites and help spread the word.

Join the Sapphire Newsletter and keep up with all your favorite authors.

Did we mention you get a free book for joining our team?

sign-up at - www.sapphirebooks.com

Check out Kim's other books.

Zero Ward - ISBN - 978-1-943353-19-4

Danny Felts grew up in the heart of the Midwest on a dairy farm, expected to follow in her mother's footsteps and marry a farmer and become a mother. Danny had other ideas. As World War II heats up, she makes a decision that will change her life forever as she becomes a lie, serving with the Seabees in the Navy as Daniel Felts.

Kate Adams is about to graduate high school in her prestigious and elite San Diego neighborhood when she's dragged to the USO for a dance with friends and servicemen. There, she meets the person that will catch her eye and her heart, only for jealousy and vengeance to tear her apart.

Are Danny and Kate strong enough to win the battle within and fight for their love?

After Shadow - ISBN - 978-1-939062-10-9

Clara always knew she was different, but just how different she was was to be seen. She will be forced on a journey to places that, though nightmarish to some, make perfect sense to her. While living a life in darkness and shadow, massaging the ghosts we all want to hide from beneth the covers, she will discover her own light of day. But, can she discover her heart?

Shadow Box - ISBN - 978-1-939062-07-9

Erin Riggs is an average woman with a normal life, though with decidedly un-common fears of exploring her world or her own truths. One 3 a.m. incident would change everything forever.

Tamson Robard spent a childhood with a weak mother, desperate to land a man in order to escape a horrific secret that Tamson can't even fathom. Tamson ran away as a teenager, but is now a grown woman. Other than drugs, her only friend is a guardial angel, Penny, whom she confides in, sharing feeble hopes and unending pain.

Together, the two will discover buried truths that will lead them through tears and to death's door. Can the cossision of Erin and Tamson's worlds save them both?

Connection - ISBN - 978-1-939062-24-6

Julie Wilson lives a charmed life as a beloved teacher and aunt in the small town of Woodland. Close to her brother and guardian of two adorable Yorkies, she loves her life, the only negative being ex-boyfriend, Ray who can't seem to understand the phrase, "We're done." Believing that's her only problem, Julie has no idea what hell awaits her during a normal summer afternoon.

Remmy Foster is the quirky, friendly drifter who has never found roots after a difficult childhood, as well as the difficulties her very special gift brings into her life. Though she may call it exploring, the truth is she's running from ghosts that haunt her every step.

After a chance meeting with Julie while hitchhiking, Remmy will be thrown head first into darkness she could never have foreseen, regardless of her abilities. As the clock ticks, life and death is on her shoulders to make the right connection.

Warning - Some scenes may be too intense for some readers.

1049 Club - ISBN - 978-1-939062-97-0

Almost two hundred souls, one plane, six survivors, endless heartbreak.

When flight 1049, headed from Buffalo, NY to Italy falls from the sky, a firestorm of drama, pain, angst and sorrow ensues. Can an author, a business owner, a teenager, good ol' boy, veterinarian and ruthless lawyer survive? Better yet, can those left behind?

1049 Club is a story of survival, love, deep regret and miracles. Can the living make peace with the presumed dead? Can the presumed dead make peace with the lives and loves they thought they had before?

Blinded – ISBN – 978-1-943353-53-8

After a horrible explosion sends local television news reporter, Burton Blinde reeling both physically and emotionally, she walks away from her life and the dream job she was about to start at a major news network.

For six long years she hides out in a small mountain

town, working at the local library, though is haunted by the life she had, including mysterious messages and gifts she was receiving before her life was turned upside down, a veritable bread crumb trail leading to the unknown.

Unable to resist, Burton begins to follow the clues, which will lead her into the darkest places of human nature that she may not be able to return from.

Damaged - ISBN - 978-1-939062-45-1

Family. A group of people you are related to by blood or love.

Nora Schaeffer has come home to her family after twenty years working around the world as a photographer for National Geographic. She's welcomed into the open arms of her father and siblings.

Family. A group of people who support you, lift you up when you fall.

Shannon, the youngest of the four Schaeffer siblings, has vanished, leaving her five-year-old daughter, Bella, terrified and alone. To help find Shannon, Nora has no choice but to turn to the dark-haired specter who has haunted her for twenty years. Along the way, she finds her own long-dead heart and uncovers chilling family secrets beyond imagination.

Family. A group of people who will stick together to hide the rotten soul at its core at any cost.

Who will live? Who will die? Who will be the most damaged? And who will learn to love again?

The Gift - ISBN - 978-1-948232-47-0

The dead do speak. You just have to listen. Homicide Detective Catania "Nia" d'Giovanni is the only daughter in a large Italian family of six children. The backbone—a position not applied for nor wanted—she continues to create new glue to hold the dysfunctional group together. For Nia, family time feels more like herding cats than spending time with her brothers and feisty, aging parents.

Her heart has always been in her career with the Pueblo Police Department, especially since it will never be okay with her very Catholic mother to openly give her heart to any woman, until she meets a secretive waitress who has her at, Can I take your order?

And then it begins…

Three murders that are so gruesome, so horrible, they rock the small town to its core. Nia and her partner Oscar are left to piece together a deadly puzzle to find the key to unlock the monster they hunt.

Or, are they the hunted?

As they dissect the murder scenes where not one shred of evidence is left behind, more bodies begin to show up, each cleaner than the last, the shadowy specter that is the killer vanishing without a trace, making the woman Nia loves disappear right along with it.

When there is no evidence to follow, Nia must trust her instincts…or, is she being guided?

The Plan – ISBN – 978-1-948232-43-2

As the dark days of the Dust Bowl came to an end, the midsection of the United States tried to rebuild and revitalize. In the small, dusty farming town of, Brooke View, Colorado, teenager, Eleanor Landry and her mother were dealing with her father, a self-appointment fire and brimstone preacher to his congregation of two. A plan to survive.

As the dark era of the robber baron comes to an end, giants of industry and innovation emerged with fabulous fortunes manifested in the mansions that dotted the landscape across the country. Lysette Landon, the teen daughter of the wealthiest family in Brooke View, was everything a good, proper girl of privilege should be. Only problem was, she wasn't dreaming of finding a young man to raise a family with. A plan to be free.

One look, one touch, all plans are off.

Secrets deeper and darker than the grave would bring Eleanor and Lysette together, their families connected by a web of lies and broken promises. A plan to escape.

Be careful because, life has other plans…

The Traveler Book One: The Hunted - ISBN - 978-1-948232-91-3

A story so epic one book can't contain it.BOOK ONE:

1977: In the era between flower power and the yuppie, Sonia Lucas is a young wife and mother, just starting out in life. Without warning, a strange presence and dark force enters her life, clouds building...

1917: ...and a storm brewing as the world reeled from the horrific events of World War I just before it was ravaged by a Spanish flu epidemic that would kill millions. Sephora Lloyd is a 16 year old girl lost in the responsibilities of an adult world helping to support herself and her mother. A beautiful young nun-in-training enters her life, bringing love and hope with her. That is, until a force bigger than either of them threatens everything Sephora holds dear.

Four women - three deaths - two words - one house
THE HUNTED

The Traveler Book Two: The Hunter - ISBN - 978-1-948232-93-7

A story so epic one book can't contain it. BOOK TWO:

1890: In the dying days of the Old West, Sally Little runs her booming brothel with the passion and tenacity the business of sex requires. Savvy and indulgent, there's one itch Sally can't let herself scratch. Afraid of hurting the woman she loves, she instead unleashes...

Present Day: ...her renovation crew and fixer upper TV show on a dilapidated mansion that has known nothing but death since a murder there in 1977. Samantha Leyton sees ratings gold in bringing the sagging old house to life, but instead she discovers only she has the power to unlock the mystery that hunted four women across time, leaving death and destruction in its wake. Can she release her sisters who came before her and finally be granted the gift of love that is stronger than any evil?

Four women - Three deaths - two words - one house
THE HUNTER

Finding Faith (Wynter Series) - ISBN - 978-1-952270-16-1

Faith Fitzgerald thought that if she got an education and became a high-powered attorney in Manhattan, maybe—just maybe—she'd gain the attention and respect of her absentee father. Considering he was the only parent she had left after her mother's suicide when Faith was just a child, she thought that's what it would take.

She was wrong.

What she dreamed would be glamorous and satisfying turned out to be grueling and thankless. Since she wasn't willing to play the game between the sheets, she was forced to stay in the cubicle jungle doing all the heavy lifting while the men got the credit and the rewards.

Deciding she is done, Faith packs up and, with the flip of the bird to the rearview mirror, leaves New York and heads home to Colorado. She has nothing there: no job, nowhere to live, no relationship with her father. Truth is, she barely has a relationship with herself.

On the drive home, she finds herself in Wynter, a tiny mountain town at the foot of the Rockies. Looking more like it belongs in a made-for-TV Christmas movie than on the map, Faith is utterly enchanted. When she tries her luck and buys a raffle ticket at Pop's, Wynter's charming café, her prize is far more than meets the eye—or the heart.

Enter Wyatt, a feisty, sexy southerner and waitress at Pop's, who just happens to be married to a local sheriff's deputy. All is not as it appears with the All-American boy and his Georgia peach.

A colorful cast of unforgettable and charming characters will teach the jaded attorney that sometimes to find yourself all you have to do is go back to the basics…and have a little Faith.

Taking Liberty (Wynter Series) - ISBN- 978-1-952270-24-6

A victim of a massive corporate downsize, Liberty Faulkner suddenly finds herself without a job, without a home, and without a plan. Though certainly not part of her vision, Libby decides that the familiar is the safest path back to her life goals. In this case, the devil she knows is home: the tiny mountain town of Wynter, Colorado, a close-knit place where everybody knows everybody and everybody's business. Seems like the perfect place for the twenty-five-year-old to start over and figure out who she is without being noticed…not.

Sergeant Grace Montez escaped her dead-end job and toxic relationship in New Mexico and moved to Wynter to help build their police department from scratch. Now an established figurehead in the community, she's got her professional life dialed in and even mentors new recruits on the force. After a challenging childhood and lifetime of abandonment and disappointment, Grace hasn't been interested in another relationship—especially because no one has caught her eye since a certain quirky college student who used to make her caramel macchiato at the local coffee shop moved away three years ago.

Now that quirky college student has returned as the beautiful, mature woman Libby has become. Can Grace keep her distance, or will she finally take liberties with what is being offered?

Justice Won (Wynter Series) - ISBN - 978-1-952270-36-9

In 1890, seventeen-year-old Justice Kilkoyne and her mother, Ninny, are one bad decision away from living on the streets of Azrael, Pennsylvania. Ninny's propensity for the bottle has left Justice to play the adult, her androgynous good looks helping her pass as a young man to gain employment and keep them—if just barely—above water.

Determined to find a better life for them, Justice saves every penny to get them on a train headed west to the sunshine of California. Before they can leave, the bigotry of one shopkeeper sends Justice on the run, chased by the police for a crime she didn't commit and straight into the unwitting arms of a stunning young prostitute, who, after an unexpected connection, becomes Justice's Angel.

The day arrives to leave Pennsylvania for good. As Justice and Ninny get settled, they're surprised by the appearance of Angel, also wanting to start anew. When the trip is violently interrupted in Colorado, Angel just may be lost to Justice forever.

Can Justice find a new life when she makes her way to the fledgling mining town of Wynter, Colorado? Can her heart ever be whole again?

Curtain Call - ISBN - 978-1-952270-42-0

What do you do when you come from a long line of dancers that spans the globe and generations, yet you can't tell your right foot from your left? You fall in love with a dancer, of course!

Gray Rickman is an awkward seventeen-year-old when she first sets eyes on Christian Scott at the dance studio/theater Gray's parents own and run in Denver, Colorado.

Though only a handful of years older than Gray, Christian carries herself with poise and wisdom far beyond her years. A woman of few words, she speaks volumes with her body.

Before Gray even really knows what her type is,

Christian stars in endless daydreams and even fulfills a couple of her fantasies before vanishing out of thin air, leaving Gray in an empty bed with nothing but bittersweet memories and broken dreams.

With no choice but to move on, Gray attempts love, even moving with her college girlfriend to New York City to pursue a career in journalism. But her standard has been set, the bar way too high for any other woman to reach or clear. It's an unexpected encounter in an obvious place when Gray sets eyes on her dancer again. Will the bright lights of Broadway illuminate the way back to the woman of her dreams? Or will they blind her to any other possibility of happiness?

Break a leg, Gray. The Great White Way calls.

Encore Performance - ISBN - 978-1-952270-52-9

Grey Rickman, a journalist for The New York Times, is offered the opportunity of a lifetime and a huge boost to her career—ghostwriting a memoir for one of the world's most beloved actors. She is deeply in love with her girlfriend, dancer Christian Scott, and her world couldn't be better.

Christian, though proud of Grey and all that she's accomplished, is facing her own career dilemma. All she's ever wanted to do is perform and create, her body her kinetic canvas. But, in one of the few industries where youth matters above all else, her time is coming to make decisions that no woman in her mid-thirties should have to make: is it time to retire?

As the career of one begins to explode into the stratosphere and the other's implodes after a career-ending injury that makes any retirement discussion irrelevant, Grey and Christian begin to drift apart. Changing priorities and newly built walls lead to fears and accusations, further tearing at the fabric of the love they've worked years to create.

Will cooler heads prevail to warm up the hearts of the deeply passionate couple in time to create a new dream for their second act?

Swann Song - ISBN - 978-1-952270-63-5

Christine Swann is a world-famous singer/songwriter and lesbian icon, known for her edgy style and heart-pounding songs. Gorgeous, rich and miserable. Her music has always been her life, her escape from an unimaginable childhood, and choices no thirteen-year-old should have to make.

Now, pushing thirty, she wants out. From all of it.

Willow Bowman lives in the farmhouse her beloved grandmother left her, with her husband. A pediatric nurse and small-town girl, she relishes in the safety of her marriage that keeps difficult questions at bay and keeps her life quiet and peaceful, because that makes sense to her.

Until one night when Willow is driving home and is about to cross the old, rickety Dittman Bridge not far from the farmhouse, and she sees a figure jump off into the cold waters below.

The moment she jumps in and pulls the woman dressed in leather pants out, both their lives change forever.

Keeping Hope (Wynter Series) - ISBN - 978-1-952270-78-9

Twenty-four-year-old Hope DeSilva has been released from a three-year stint in a Georgia prison. After returning to her family property in a tiny Georgia town, she decides she's had enough of the poverty, violence, and progound family dysfunction. It's time to get out on her own. She buys a $400 car and heads to find work out west.

After the car breaks down in Colorado, she's given a ride into a mountain town called Wynter where she runs into brash, aggressive police officer Samantha Gains, who has not one ounce of patience or sympathy for a felon in her black-and-white world of right or wrong, good or bad.

But, running from her own family trauma and inexplicably bewitched by the young newcomer Hope, Samantha begins to realize that maybe her strict worldview isn't as simple as it seems. When a freak accident brings the two women together, it will take both of them letting go of their pasts to truly move on.

Take another trip to Wynter and revisit old friends as they work their magic to help Hope and Samantha find their footing—and ultimately bring them home.

She Who Would be King - ISBN

Cateline is the seventeen-year-old daughter of a nobleman in fourteenth-century France. It's a time when children aren't seen as those to be loved and cherished, but instead are used as pawns and bargaining chips on the chessboard of control and privilege.

She is married off to a prince in the country of Sursha, a Gaelic-speaking island nation near Ireland. Fergus, her betrothed, is next in line to take over once beloved King Carthac dies. Or is he?

Fallon, the youngest royal child and only girl, has been raised as one of the king's sons her entire life, for reasons she has never fully understood. A natural fighter, she was raised to be a warrior and head the Crown's Elite Guard assigned to protect her boorish brother Fergus.

Forced to fill in for her brother in an unexpected way, an instant attraction between Fallon and Cateline forms. In a game of thrones filled with deception and betrayal, even the most secret love can mean death.

Other Sapphire books from Sapphire Authors

Dusty Road Home - ISBN - 978-1-952270-72-7

Melanie Crenshaw has fallen off the proverbial map. Notoriously private on a good day, the world-famous mystery author has gone dark to avoid any public blowback or scandal from her latest failed relationship. Seeking quiet and solace, she retreats to her rural hometown, hoping isolation will be just the atmosphere she needs to finish her novel. But going back home is never as easy as it sounds, especially when a nosy reporter starts sniffing around.

Pulitzer-winning investigative journalist Pilar Stein has seen people at their worst—and has the scars to prove it. After taking time off to heal from a particularly brutal assignment, she's back in the saddle and ready to reclaim her place among the elite of hard-hitting reporters. Unfortunately, her re-entry story—a profile on elusive author Melanie Crenshaw who has suddenly disappeared—seems to lack the teeth necessary to catapult her back to the top of her game.

Appearances are deceiving, of course, and Pilar soon discovers that what she deems a simple fluff piece might well lead to the scoop of a generation...just not the one she expected.

As Melanie fights to maintain her privacy while Pilar takes a backhoe to her past, the two women find themselves torn between their own professional convictions and their growing attraction to each other. And no matter which road they take, it's going to be a bumpy ride.

Out of the Ashes - ISBN - 978-1-952270-84-0

When unusual seismic activity is detected on Mount St. Helens, volcanologist Nova "Cano" Kane, along with a team from the United States Geological Survey, is sent to investigate. The year is 1980, and there hasn't been a large-scale eruption on the mountain in over one hundred years.

Dr. Allison "Allie" Albright is a prominent professor at the University of Washington where the seismic activity is being tracked. As more scientists pour into Seattle, she braces for the possible return of Cano.

Neither Allie nor Cano has fully recovered from their breakup four years earlier. Both live with the pain and regret of how their relationship ended. Maybe it's best to leave it in the past and focus on the job at hand.

They must battle the limits of predictive science, the shortsightedness of bureaucracy, and the bias of the media, while fighting their complicated feelings for each other. As Mount St. Helens continues to churn, so too does their attraction.
Which will erupt first—the volcano or their feelings for each other?

First comes Marriage: Morgan Town -Book One - ISBN - 978-1-952270-80-2

Take one CEO, one pink-haired alien, a secret marriage, vengeful aliens, unexplained deaths, and a bitter sister out for revenge, and two women's lives will never be the same.

As CEO of MartinTech, Brynn Martin is at the top of her professional game. Her personal life is another matter, but she's not in a hurry to break her single status. All that changes on a Tuesday morning when a bombshell is dropped.

At sixteen, Micah Legon fled her abusive family and home world of Vubloxia. Now, at twenty-nine, she's content and settled in her life, running a cleanup business with her siblings. Then one morning, she gets a phone call that changes everything.

A chance encounter six years ago in Las Vegas at a "Meet an Alien" convention comes back to haunt both women. While Micah remembers the day with fondness, Brynn remembers nothing. After meeting again, both women come to an agreement. However, nothing is ever that simple.

Micah makes it her mission to break through Brynn's tough exterior. Brynn makes it her mission to keep Micah at arm's length. Nothing will stop either woman from getting what she wants. The trouble is convincing the other that her plan is the right one.